ISBN: 978-1-942500-91-9

Boulevard Books
The New Face of Publishing
www.BoulevardBooks.org

THEY CAN HEAR

Martin J. Roddini

Dedication

This book is dedicated to the memory of my wife's first true love, her dad, Danny; and to a very special woman, Joan, who gave me the greatest gift of all, my three children.

This is a work of fiction. Unless otherwise indicated, all the names, characters, businesses, places, events and incidents in this book are either the product of the author's imagination or used in a fictitious manner. Any resemblance to actual persons, living or dead, or actual events is purely coincidental.

Chapter One

The Unscheduled Meeting

"Respond to 1214 Gardener Drive for a report of a domestic dispute." It's the fourth time in the last six months that police officers had to respond to Gardener Drive for family problems. The circumstances are always the same. The husband, James Whitly, has once again threatened to "punch-her-out." He towers over his 5'2" wife, Laura, and has, in the past, used physical persuasion to win the argument. Laura, however, always refuses to make a police complaint against her husband; so, the physical threats continue. This time is no different except for the fact that Laura has decided that she is going to leave the house for a while and visit with her sister. This is the first time that Laura has taken such a bold action, and one that has totally surprised James. She quickly packed her bag and, with the assistance of the police officers, left the house.

Even though Laura has made the tough decision to leave, she knows that tomorrow she will have to see her husband again. Laura Whitly is a registered nurse in the same hospital where her husband, Dr. James Whitly, is certified in general surgery, and is the chief surgeon in the Neurology Department. It was at Marine Pacific Hospital that Laura and James met. It is quite common that nurses and doctors, working in the same medical facility, get together and ultimately marry. It was no different for Laura and James. They were very happy for the first five years of their marriage, but the last three years have been filled with arguments, disagreements, fights and accusations. James' short temper and Laura's growing impatience have combined to make for a volatile relationship. However, even though their home life is riddled with constant stress, they have managed to maintain a professional attitude at work. They hide it so well that their fellow workers are totally unaware of any family problems. Nurse Laura and Dr. Whitly are the consummate professionals.

After following the police officers to her car, Laura started the engine and didn't look back. She knew that her husband must be livid over her decision to leave, but she felt that it had to be done. Things cannot just continue as they have been. She needed time to think and see what options she has. Even though things are less than acceptable at home, she really didn't want to end a relationship that was so good in the beginning. She needed to find a way to save their marriage and reactivate those feelings of love and caring that they once shared. She knew what she wanted to do, but she really didn't know what James was thinking. Did he also want to discover ways that could possibly help their relationship, or did he have enough? The more she thought about it, the more she realized that their marriage needed the guidance of a professional. They would have to employ the services of a marriage counselor, a psychologist who could steer them through the rough waters of compromise. She even knew the person she would want to enlist to help in their possible re-stabilization, but she also knew that James would reject her selection. She kept thinking about any and all options, while James' agreement to "work-things-out" was still in doubt.

The route to her sister's house was a relatively simply one – one which she had navigated many times. However, this time her mind was focused on many things other than driving. She had a couple of close calls with other vehicles but was able to react quickly enough to avoid problems. The trip usually took about thirty minutes, but since she was not totally focused on her driving or the trip, it was going much more slowly. As she approached a busy intersection, one which was infamous for accidents and injuries, a car tried to beat the red light but was forcibly stopped by another vehicle proceeding through on the green light. The two vehicles were tangled in a web of metal. Laura Whitly's vehicle was T-boned by the other vehicle where the driver, who apparently wasn't wearing a seatbelt, was thrown from the vehicle and died at the scene. Laura had to be extricated by the "jaws-of-life." She was badly bruised and unconscious, but alive.

After attending to her immediate medical needs, the ambulance technicians transported her to the nearest hospital, Marine Pacific. As Laura was brought into the emergency room, the attending doctor and the nurses immediately recognized her. They were in shock that they had to administer to one of their own. The initial concern having passed, the emergency room staff began their routine for evaluation and treatment. Laura Whitly was apparently suffering from internal bleeding and injuries still not determined. Additionally, she remained unconscious and non-responsive. Laura was in critical condition and needed the assistance of whatever specialists were on duty. If they could not offer the best for one of their own, then for whom.

As the emergency medical team attended to Laura's immediate health needs, the staff assistant attempted to contact the patient's husband, Dr. James Whitly. Although hospital policy prohibited a doctor from attending to a relative, Dr. Whitly still needed to be contacted so that he could respond to the hospital and his wife. The assistant rang Dr. Whitly's cell phone and also the hospital pager that was assigned to him. The message on the pager just read: "Please contact the hospital ASAP."

When the pager vibrated, and he read the message, Dr. Whitly was already on his way to the hospital. After Laura left the house, he just sat and thought about what transpired. He felt most comfortable, however, at the hospital, in the confines of his own office. He spent many hours in that familiar location and did most of his serious thinking there. Therefore, it was natural for him to head to the hospital to weigh his next move. Also, in a few hours he would be the on-duty doctor at the hospital. So, going there a little earlier was no big deal, and apparently, his expertise was needed to address a medical emergency.

"Good morning, Dr. Whitly. I am really sorry that you had to be wakened to the bad news." The admissions nurse welcomed Dr. Whitly and surprised him with her greeting regarding "bad news." He looked at her in a questioning manner, and she realized then that the doctor did not know about the accident nor the condition of his wife. "What bad news? What are you talking about?" At that moment, the Emergency Room Doctor appeared and approached Dr. Whitly: "Hello, James. Your wife was in a car accident and is being treated as we speak. She is in critical condition and not responsive. We are awaiting the results of tests to find out about internal injuries and the possibility of internal bleeding. Please follow me." The Emergency Room Doctor, Dr. Richard Cotton, escorted James into the emergency room where his wife lay in a coma.

James Whitly was flooded with conflicting emotions. He had just had a heavy argument with Laura that resulted in her leaving the house, for the first time ever. It was such a serious brawl that thoughts of divorce flooded into his stream of consciousness. The police responded and had to quell the situation. Now, he was standing next to a hospital bed where his unconscious wife lay in critical medical condition. He did not know if she sustained life threatening injuries or injuries that would affect her future lifestyle. He knew that he wanted her to totally recover, but what then? Would they remain together and continue to live with the stress of constant fighting and arguing, or might this be the turnaround point where they started to consider the feelings of each other? He was not sure, but now he had to concentrate on making certain that every possible medical asset was provided for her recovery.

Dr. Cotton assured James that everything possible was being done for Laura. He told James that he would contact him with all the results and that, of course, James was more than welcome to assist in any way he thought necessary. James thanked him for his help and concern, but James wanted the services of specialists to assist with the immediate care of his wife. Dr. Cotton was a good emergency room doctor, but that was what he was, an emergency room doctor. Dr. Whitly wanted specialists to attend to his wife from the onset. Although he knew that it was a bit unreasonable, he wanted specialists attending. He questioned Dr. Cotton as to what specialists were available. The doctor mentioned a couple of familiar names, including Dr. Whitly's. James had almost forgotten that he was one of the doctors on-call. He was the neurological specialist who would be called in a case like Laura's. James asked that the other specialists who might be involved with Laura's recovery be notified to maintain a "stand-by" status and to respond immediately, if needed. These requests were totally out of the norm and James Whitly was reacting more emotionally than professionally. Dr. Cotton understood. He assured his friend and colleague that everyone would be ready to assist, if the occasion arose. James settled for that. He was not sure that his concern was being driven by real feelings or by guilt. Either way, he wanted Laura back the way she was.

As Dr. James Whitly was closely monitoring his wife's condition, a call came over the hospital pager that he was needed in "emergency room two." He was the specialist on-call, and therefore, had to leave his wife and respond to the adjoining emergency room. When he entered the room, he saw a middle-aged man lying on his back with cuts and bruises over his entire body. He was told that the man was unresponsive, and that there was a possibility that he might have suffered nerve damage. The man's condition closely resembled that of James' wife. He ordered the necessary tests and tried to evaluate the more obvious injuries. The patient apparently suffered broken bones and lacerations. However, Dr. Whitly was more concerned with the possible internal damage which could result in loss of life. The similarities between Laura's condition and this patient's immediate diagnosis were eerily similar. Additionally, they were both in a comatose state. In fact, as Dr. Whitly was treating his patient, he could not help but think of his wife and her yet-to-be-determined injuries.

Dr. James Whitly soon learned that the male patient, Mr. Leonard Canella, was the victim of a hit-and-run accident that occurred not too far from the intersection that saw his wife's accident. He knew a Leonard Canella. Could it be the same guy? How many Leonard Canellas could there be? He was a mess though. In addition to other possible injuries, he sustained a broken jaw, a fractured nose, a possible fractured eye socket, and deep lacerations across his whole face. Apparently, he suffered impact damage from the hit-and-run vehicle as well as being thrown and slamming into a parked car. It was hard to tell if this was the same guy that he once knew.

The police were still looking for the driver and the vehicle that was described as a late model white, four-door, SUV. James was very concerned with Mr. Canella's condition as breathing became a labored task for the patient. The doctor would have to wait for the results of the initial tests and x-rays before he could authorize necessary treatment for internal injuries. He hoped the results would come soon because it seemed that Mr. Canella's condition was slowly worsening. This could easily be the result of those internal injuries that have not yet been determined, the same injuries that Laura may have suffered, and whose ultimate treatment was also "on-hold" waiting for test results.

James asked the assisting physician to keep a close watch on the patient while he quickly visited emergency room one where his wife still lay unresponsive to her surroundings. Again, the hodge-podge of emotions flooded his consciousness with feelings of pity, remorse, helplessness, and concern. The anger that permeated the earlier part of the day was all but gone. There was no room for anger while Laura's life could lie in the balance. Unlike Leonard Canella, Laura's breathing was strong and stable. At least, this was a good sign. It was one less thing with which James had to be concerned. Although it had only been a brief time since the tests were ordered, it seemed like an eternity. This time the doctor was also the family waiting for results.

As he stared at his wife, his thoughts were interrupted when, once again, he was called to emergency room two. Leonard Canella was losing his battle to maintain a constant flow of oxygen to his lungs. His breathing was failing. Dr. Whitly, with the assistance of the other emergency room doctor, had to perform an emergency tracheotomy to help Leonard breathe and survive.

Having completed the successful emergency procedure, Dr. Whitly headed to the waiting area to let the family know what had been done, and what the next steps would be. As he announced the patient's name, a blond female in the last row stood up and approached the doctor. Mrs. Canella stood before Dr. Whitly and patiently waited for his report. He told her that her husband was in critical condition, and that an emergency procedure had to be performed to assist Leonard's breathing. As James spoke with Mrs. Canella, a strange feeling of familiarity came over him. That feeling was confirmed when Mrs. Canella informed Dr. Whitly that her maiden name was McFarland. Andrea McFarland was the girl he almost married many years ago. She had changed though. She now had long blond hair. She apparently had a nose job and a face lift, and she also put on some weight as was evidenced by the increased size of her breasts. However, as he looked closely, he could see the same girl he once knew. He was surprised that she drastically changed the way she looked. He did not think she was that type.

James was saving the life of the man who stole Andrea from him. Conflicting emotions, once again, were front and center. However, their relationship and the circumstances of their separation occurred many years ago. Dr. Whitly was a professional, and he would act accordingly. He looked at her and acknowledged their familiarity. He told her that he regretted having to meet her again under such dire circumstances. She agreed. Little did they both know that the relationship they once enjoyed would be the driving force in forming a new partnership which could potentially produce unthinkable results.

Chapter Two

The Deceitful Plan

Attendance in college offers more than just an education. It affords one the opportunity to engage in a whole variety of considerations, one of which is the socialization process. It was through this process that James Whitly met both Andrea McFarland and Leonard Canella. However, it was not necessarily in that order. James met Leonard in their junior year. They happened to be taking the same elective courses, and they just hit it off. They attended a number of parties on campus, and at one of these social gatherings, Leonard was introduced to Andrea who then introduced herself to James. Although Leonard vied for her attention, Andrea was more interested in James. The interest was reciprocal, and much to Leonard's dismay, Andrea and James became a couple in a very short time.

Both James and Andrea were focusing their studies on the medical field while Leonard was more inclined to the technical side of things. He was an engineering student. The three of them remained friends throughout the remainder of their college years, and all three decided to do their graduate work in local institutions.

Although Leonard and Andrea were pursuing different majors, they both accepted invitations to attend a local graduate school that offered both areas of study, engineering, and nursing. James, however, opted for entrance into a medical school located in the same state but a farther distance away. The school offered him scholarship money and potential job placement following the completion of his studies and residency. Leonard could not be happier about how things worked out. He had never lost interest in Andrea, but with James always around, he could not advance his attentions and desires. However, with the upcoming mandated separation, he would have a chance to show Andrea that she chose the wrong individual. If gentle persuasion did not work, he had other options available to him, and he would use all of them to win the prize.

Long distance romances are difficult to maintain. Although James was still in-state, the distance from home was too far to travel daily, so he had to reside in an apartment on campus. This proximity to his studies allowed him to compile more lab time and gain extra credit. He missed Andrea but was comforted by the idea that the present arrangement was only a temporary barrier to their ultimate goal of making their relationship a life-long commitment. He was totally unaware of how his friend, Leonard, was plotting a different course. In fact, James was glad that Andrea had someone there who could help, if necessary. Unfortunately, it was like putting a fox in the chicken coop. James had no idea how ruthless Leonard could and would be.

In medical school, many times you are paired off with a partner, especially when it comes to lab work. James and a girl named Sharon were assigned as partners. As a result of the amount of time one spent with his or her partner, the relationship grew into a friendly association. For James and Sharon, that is all it was. James missed Andrea and wanted desperately to be with her, and Sharon had a fiancée whom she planned to marry in the upcoming year. To an outsider though, the partnership could be assumed to be more than it was. They spent long hours together and became

dependent on each other for such things as thesis work, lab solutions, quick dinners and yes, even consolation when things got really tough, and the studies bogged them down. They became a relief valve for each other. The grueling pace of medical studies takes its toll even on the strongest of souls.

Both Leonard and Andrea knew the arrangement, and took it for what it was worth, a situation that could not be avoided. Leonard, however, saw it as the perfect opportunity to plant the seeds of distrust. He was smart, and he cleverly nurtured those seeds until Andrea began to have doubts. He played on the fact that James and Sharon spent a lot of time together and even spent late nights together. Always implying, however, that he knew the situation could not be avoided. Since the medical students did not want to interrupt their study time for such mundane things as food and drink, many times they just ate together in his or her apartment. They needed to have some relief, however, and that relief, at times, came in the form of wine or alcohol. Leonard even showed Andrea a picture of Sharon, a photo that Leonard requested from his friend, to demonstrate that there was nothing to worry about. The photo, however, showed a very pretty, young lady toasting with James after completing a lab assignment. James had no idea that his friend, Leonard, was going to use the photo to further his vile plan.

James and Andrea spoke almost every other day, but as the semester winded down, there was less time for phone calls, and more time needed to complete assignments and experiments. This just complemented Leonard's vicious assault. Seeing how Andrea was becoming stressed and concerned, her supportive friend, Leonard, suggested that he and Andrea surprise James with an unannounced visit. Andrea quickly agreed in an effort to suppress the doubt and uneasiness she was feeling about the whole situation. A face-to-face would, once again, bolster the confidence that she once had and relieve some of the angst that she was experiencing. James' love for her would again support the ultimate plans that they had. She could not wait to surprise him. Leonard could not wait either!

Leonard knew that both James and Sharon were exhausted with all the work they had to complete. The early classes and the late-night study sessions were taking a toll on both of them. A number of times, both James and Sharon just fell off to sleep in the middle of a chapter. Their minds and bodies were reacting to the apparent abuse caused by the rigors associated with medical studies. Leonard was counting on such a display. He would make sure that Andrea and he would leave late in the evening so that they would arrive very late at James' apartment. James and Sharon usually studied at James' place since it was more spacious and less noisy. With a little bit of luck,

Leonard, with Andrea by his side, would use the key that James originally gave him to enter the apartment, if needed, and witness a scene that Leonard could capitalize on. This would be the culmination of a fiendish plan that he had been working on for the past few months. He knew that with a little bit of luck and clever persuasion, Andrea would be pushed over the edge and find comfort and consolation in the arms of the one who had been with her throughout the whole stressful ordeal – the arms of Leonard Canella.

Leonard knew James' schedule and on what nights his planned late-night study sessions took place. He made sure that he arranged the trip with Andrea on one of those nights. Figuring that the door-to-door trip would take about two and one-half hours, Leonard would let Andrea know that he could not leave before ten o'clock. The two and one-half hours would put them at James' apartment between twelve thirty and one o'clock in the morning. Leonard would not rush to get there. In fact, he would take as much time as he could to allow both James and Sharon to, as usual, fall asleep together. His plan had definitely come together. If lady luck shined on him, this would be the final act.

It was a chilly night, but one that Leonard hoped would heat up quickly. He and Andrea did not speak much. When they did speak, it was Leonard who took the lead, telling her how hard James had been working, and how much he and Sharon depended on each other to successfully complete the course. Andrea's answers were mostly one-word responses. He knew she was in deep thought about her future, her boyfriend, and the girl who had been spending more time with James than she. It is just what Leonard wanted. He knew that he was capable of turning the most innocent scene into one that reeked of deception and distrust. He was good at what he did.

The ride was a boring one, and the late-night cold added to the desire to close one's eyes and rest for just a bit, so it was with Andrea. In addition to the late-night influence, she was mentally exhausted from the stress that developed as she weighed the possible ramifications of the night's visit. Leonard took the opportunity to slow down even more. He wanted to be sure that the hour would be late enough to encourage a quick nap for the studious partners. Even if tonight's scheme wasn't successful, Leonard had already thought of other options that he could employ down the road. He was not going to fail. Eventually, Andrea would be his, and James would be just a bad memory.

Andrea awoke when they were just fifteen minutes from their destination. She looked better but could not hide the anxiety that was invading her thought process. As a result, she decided to explain to Leonard that her desire to surprise James no longer existed. However, before she could verbalize her thoughts, Leonard was explaining how happy James was going to be when he opened the door and Andrea was there. She had to go through with it. Leonard drove all this way for her, and she did want to see James.

They exited the car, and the cold came at them like a slap across the face. It would be good for Andrea to collapse in the warmth of her boyfriend's arms. They took the elevator to the second floor and walked to the apartment. It was so quiet that it was deafening. As they approached the door, Leonard put his finger to his lips enhancing the aura of surprise. He put the key in the lock, turned it and opened the door. He let Andrea enter first. There was a dim light shining in the living room, shining on two figures who were apparently asleep and resting in each other's arms.

Andrea just stopped and stared. The optics preyed upon her weak, overactive and vulnerable imagination. She imagined the worst. In her mind's eye, she saw more than two people asleep and in physical support of one another. She saw lust and lovemaking. She saw deceit and distrust. She saw her world collapse. She said nothing but motioned to Leonard to back up and exit the apartment quietly. She did not take the elevator but ran down the two flights of stairs. She ran to the car with Leonard in close pursuit. She cried her remarks: "Let's just leave. I have seen enough and never want to see him again." In his sly manner, Leonard tried to make excuses for James, excuses that would only bolster his own cause. He comforted Andrea by hugging her and holding her close. He opened the car door and ushered her in as the uncontrollable sobbing continued.

Leonard had won. All he had to do now was to pick up the pieces and carefully put them back together. It would not be difficult, but it would take some time. Time was an abundant commodity for him, as Andrea responded well to his continuous comforting ways. She was true to her determination that she never wanted to see James again, and she didn't, not until he was the one who destiny assigned as the emergency room specialist on the night of the hit-and-run accident.

Within a year of that fateful surprise visit to James' apartment, Leonard and Andrea got engaged. They got along well, and Leonard was a great crutch in the recovery from Andrea's devastating emotional ordeal. Six months after their engagement, Andrea McFarland and Leonard Canella were married.

Although they were happy at first, Leonard seemed to be changing. He became more demanding and possessive. He wanted things his way. His attitude got progressively worse, and after two years of marriage, Andrea felt like an abused prisoner, not the young and happy bride she once was. Leonard became obsessed with the way he wanted Andrea to look. He insisted on such things as a nose job, a face lift, breast augmentation, different colored hair, and even the type of clothes that Andrea would wear. But it even went farther than that. Andrea was only allowed to leave the house when she was with him. She was no longer allowed to work, and she had to learn to become a skilled cook. She became the typically abused woman. She was beside herself and like other abused women, she didn't know what to do. She was frightened and totally dependent on Leonard for her survival. Although he hadn't physically harmed her, he had threatened it many times. There were cameras throughout the house, and Leonard would know if she attempted to leave. He could watch her every move.

In addition to the strict rules that she had to abide by, she had to perform exceptionally well in bed. Leonard had strange desires and demanded that she do things that she only read about in those sexually explicit magazines. Though she hated every minute of sexual interaction with him, she had to outwardly demonstrate how physically and emotionally satisfying the sexual escapades were. She was living with a stranger. He was not that consoling friend, the comforting confidant, the one who was always there for her. He was a self-centered, selfish, uncaring egotist who got great satisfaction in controlling the existence of others.

He was also that way at work, of course to a lesser extent. He owned his own business but had a hard time keeping employees. The working conditions he framed were less than appealing to workers, and his business suffered from lack of personnel. He was a very demanding boss and very rarely, if at all, would he compliment a worker on a "job-well-done."

His demeanor and attitude did not afford him the luxury of having friends. He was a loner. Andrea was the only recipient of his rantings if things at work or at home weren't going his way. So, with all of these negatives facing Andrea, when she got the call that her husband, Leonard, had been the victim of a hit-and-run accident and was unconscious with apparent head trauma, she reacted with mixed emotions. She did not want to see anyone suffer or die, but life would be so different without having to live under the dictates of a man who saw himself as a king.

It was ironic that the person responsible for saving her husband now is the same man who Leonard betrayed and stabbed in the back. As Dr. Whitly was telling her about her husband's injuries, her mind wandered to thinking about how different life would have been if she had remained with James. After all this time, it was James on whom she was depending. She wanted to tell him how wrong she was, and that she regretted her decision, but circumstances would not allow it. He was a professional whose attention had to be focused on getting back to saving his patient, her warden. Although James would have liked to spend more time speaking with Andrea, his responsibilities did not offer him that luxury. He was curt and to the point and had to hurry back to saving lives.

Chapter Three

The Operation

When the x-rays and test results came back for Leonard Canella, they were worse than anticipated. Mr. Canella was in need of multiple operations, and he would have to go under the knife for one of those corrective operations immediately. Dr. Whitly had to stop the cause of the internal bleeding that showed up on the tests. If he didn't, the patient would bleed out and die. James now had to inform Mrs. Canella, Andrea, of the need to perform an emergency operation.

When James went out to speak with Andrea, she could not be found. He had mentioned to her that he was awaiting the test results to better understand what Leonard needed to start healing. She seemed very concerned and said that she would remain in the waiting area. Apparently, she changed her mind. According to the records that the hospital had, Andrea had to give the okay for any and all medical procedures performed on her husband. This was an emergency, and the longer it took to get the authorization to operate, the slimmer the chances of complete success. Dr. Whitly asked the security guard if he knew the whereabouts of Mrs. Canella. Did he see where she went? Did she leave the hospital? The guard, unfortunately, was of no help to James. He was about to ask the guard to search the parking lot to see if Andrea had just stepped out for some air or for a possible cigarette break when she came through the hospital doors looking even worse than she did before. She explained that police officers had arrived and wanted to speak with her regarding the accident. Apparently, speaking to the police was an unnerving experience for her, and her face reflected her anxiety.

James approached her and immediately advised her regarding the necessary actions that he would have to take to attempt to stabilize Leonard's condition. She seemed to be looking right through him, and James felt that she wasn't grasping the urgency of the situation: "Andrea, do you understand what I am telling you? I must perform an emergency operation to save your husband's life. I need your permission to proceed. Do you understand?" Andrea gave James a week nod and authorized the operation. James nodded back and made a mental note that he was going to speak with her as soon as he could after the operation. Something wasn't right, and he wasn't sure that it was just because of the accident. He still cared a lot about her and, if he could help, he would.

Although he was very much concerned about his patient, thoughts of his wife and her condition constantly bombarded his stream of consciousness. He hadn't been informed about any urgent situation other than the fact that she was still unconscious. He would go in and check on her as soon as he was finished stabilizing Leonard Cannella. Unfortunately, James did not know exactly what he would find when he operated on Leonard. It could take a lot longer than he anticipated, which meant that his visit to his wife might be delayed. He was conflicted between the health of his patient and the welfare of his wife. However, he knew that his patient had to come first because of the urgency of the matter. Leonard's life could depend on what James did next, and how quickly he did it.

Emergency room one saw Mrs. Whitly remaining in her unresponsive state. The doctor had read the x-rays and the test results, and fortunately, there was no definite indication of internal bleeding. The test results for the head trauma, however, had not come back yet. The tests showed that there was possible damage to such organs as the spleen, kidneys, and abdomen. She might have to undergo corrective surgery, but, at this point, it was not of an emergency nature. The procedures could wait 'till tomorrow while the medical staff addressed Laura's immediate and obvious superficial medical needs. That might all change, however, when Dr. Whitly arrived on the scene. He would want to take charge of her welfare and bark out orders that he felt were necessary to mediate some of the damage that her body sustained. They were just waiting for his arrival, and the chaos that would surely ensue.

Dr. James Whitly worked on Leonard Canella for a long time. There were a number of sources where blood was escaping. Methodically locating and repairing each breach was tedious work which took more time than James thought he would have to spend with his patient. However, he was not going to leave until Leonard was no longer in danger of bleeding internally. Finally able to close, Dr. Whitly left the finishing measures to the assisting physician. James needed to get to his wife and find out what progress the medical staff had made. Was she out of danger? Would an emergency operation have to be scheduled? What was the extent of the damage? What were the final results of all the tests?

As Dr. Whitly entered emergency room one, he saw the attending physician in conversation with another specialist. It was he, Dr. Charles Strathmore, who noticed James enter the room. Dr. Strathmore immediately turned to face James. He had a concerned look on his face, one that James had unconsciously demonstrated many times to waiting families. Laura had sustained trauma to the head. The doctor told James that one of the tests indicated a swelling of the brain. They needed to reduce this swelling before permanent damage set in. James knew what had to be done and realized that without this procedure, Laura could suffer long-lasting and reduced mental acuity. In cases like this, the patient could even be at risk of death. He reluctantly agreed with Dr. Strathmore and gave him the "go-ahead." So, Laura was now going to be the victim of intrusive entries into her skull in an effort to reduce the pressure that swelling was placing on her brain, procedures known as Burr Hole Surgery. This drilling was not a rare procedure, but it could be a dangerous one. James bent down and kissed the forehead of his unconscious wife and slowly left the room as the nurses and orderlies prepared to move Laura to the operating room. Dr. Strathmore, as all doctors do, tried to calm James, telling him that he was sure that things would turn out fine. However, he wasn't sure. One could never be sure, and James knew this.

James took the familiar route that he had followed all day. He walked to the recovery area where Leonard Canella was recuperating from the emergency operation that he had just undergone. The patient looked okay, and Dr. Whitly was reassured by the assisting physician that there were no unforeseen complications that arose. Leonard's pallor had improved, and his vital signs were good. However, in no way, was Leonard "out-of-the-woods." He still had broken bones that had to be set, and lacerations that had to be sutured. He had a long way to go before he would be medically cleared.

Thankfully, the cuts and bruises, and the broken bones would be the responsibility of other doctors. There were no other emergency room cases that needed Dr. Whitly's immediate attention, so it gave him time to wind down a little and give some thought to the other pressing concerns in his life. The most important of these was the uncertain relationship he now had with his wife. He knew she was unhappy, and he knew that the relationship was, at best, a rocky one. They could not continue to be at each other's throats and expect the relationship to flourish. Something had to change, and the operative word was "compromise." They both had to reign in their attitudes and really try to work things out. He knew that he would try, and he expected that Laura would do the same. A tragedy like the one he and Laura were now experiencing shed new light on circumstances, and many times influenced a change in behavior. The realization that one may lose something that is very dear forces one to re-evaluate a situation. That is what Dr. James Whitly was doing as he sat and tried to relax.

Intertwined with the thoughts and concerns about his wife's health and their relationship was the fact that Andrea and Leonard again entered into his life. Although he thought about the two of them periodically over the years, they were never in the forefront of his consciousness. They were now; and the whole debacle that was once a growing romantic relationship over-shadowed any fond memories. All he could think about was how his "friend" manipulated Andrea, and how little confidence she had in his loyalty to her. Even with Leonard's deceitful influence, she should have, at least, given him the opportunity to explain and talk things out. She didn't. She went to the extreme and wouldn't even answer his phone calls. She cut all communications with him and depended on her caring and loyal partner, Leonard. As James continued to think about the past, he got more and more angry. Back then, he had made a promise to himself that, one day, he would seek and get retribution. He would pay back his good friend, Leonard. How could he possibly know that the retribution he sought might come in the form of attending to the medical needs of the villain who effectively changed his life.

As he thought further, he could not forget how downtrodden, sad and confused Andrea had been when he was telling her about Leonard's condition. He still cared for the woman he once loved and wanted to help her if he could. He would make it his business to follow up with Andrea and possibly get to the bottom of her dismay. He, at least, owed her that. No, he owed her nothing! He just needed to do it.

Chapter Four

The Scheduled Talk

Dr. Strathmore found James and informed him that the procedure he performed on Laura's brain went well. The swelling had ceased, and if everything proceeded as it should, the swelling should be reduced in a short time. Then, they can further evaluate her situation and ascertain whether or not additional treatment for the head trauma is needed. James was relieved but understood that it was much too soon to think that all was well. Only time could dictate the ultimate condition. Laura was recuperating in the recovery area and was still in a comatose state. All James could do was to look at her, be by her side, and hope for the best. He was a doctor, and it was frustrating for him to just stand-by and wait for results. It was also demoralizing for him not to be able to physically participate in the future treatment that she would need. Would he ever get the chance to speak with her about their relationship? Would he ever be able to employ an agreed-upon plan to make things right between them? Would he ever get the chance to tell her how sorry he was that their relationship deteriorated into one continuous argument? He really didn't know, but he would pray that he was given the opportunity.

James wasn't sure that his regret and remorse was a result of the effects of an accident that could frame their future. He hoped that it was pure desire to re-engage with the woman he loved and married. However, as he thought about all of these related concerns, he was also focused on the talk that he wanted to have with Andrea. He was conflicted thinking about her past decision and the ultimate result of the vile plan that Leonard successfully hatched – their marriage. He had to know if Andrea was really happy. He had to capture something from her that would offer him the satisfaction of knowing that she realized that her choice of partners was the wrong one. He went from thinking about the past to focusing on the present and the condition of his wife, Laura, and he also applied the same thinking to his own marriage. Was his choice the correct one? Should he have tried harder way back when? Would he have been happier with Andrea? The conflicting choices were destroying his concentration and his train of thought. Maybe, the quickest way to resolve the doubt was to speak with Andrea as soon as he could. He needed to clear the air and focus on his wife's well-being.

James stayed in the hospital overnight and constantly checked in on his wife. She seemed to be resting comfortably. It was a good sign that her vitals remained stable, and that the swelling showed no indication of increased activity. Dr. Whitly also checked in on his patient, Leonard, who also seemed to be doing well. However, before long, his broken bones would have to be set and the open lacerations that were temporarily repaired, would need a permanent fix. Again, James compared the two cases, Laura's and Leonard's, and he came to the same conclusion on both. The road back to good health was going to be a long and arduous one. Necessarily, he would be intimately involved in both.

Dr. Whitly rose early the next morning and answered a page that he was wanted at the nurses' station on the third floor, the floor that housed the operating rooms and the recovery rooms. Both his patient and his wife were moved to rooms on that floor and were coincidently just across the hall from each other. Fortunately, this made things a lot simpler for James. He could easily look in on both his wife and Leonard by just taking a few steps across the floor. That is not discounting the fact, of course, that other patients would undoubtedly also need his attention and expertise. But anything that could make his obligatory medical responses flow more easily, he welcomed with open arms.

Answering the page at the nurses' station, Dr. James Whitly was confronted with the worn, distraught, slightly hunched-over silhouette of Andrea Canella. He couldn't describe the feelings and emotions that overwhelmed him at the pitiful sight of the person with whom he had shared so much. He came close to her and asked if she was all right. Her response was an unconvincing "yes." He wanted to hold her close and tell her that "everything was going to be all right." James really didn't know what the problem was, but he knew that there were things really bothering Andrea. For her own good, James had to convince her to let him in. That was the only way he could possibly help her. That's if she even wanted his help.

James took her into the doctors' lounge where there was much more privacy. In fact, they were the only ones in the room. He persisted in asking her again if he could help with her problems. This time she looked at him and began to cry. In James' mind, this was a breakthrough. He cautiously proceeded to ask questions that would, at least, reveal the possible nature of her concerns: "Andrea, are the seriousness of Leonard's injuries really bothering you? I can tell you that everything possible is being done for him, and that his chances were better than average that he will see positive results from his treatment." She looked up at him and thanked him for his help but did not convince him that Leonard's health was the major concern that "brought her to her knees." He continued: "Do you have any specific health problems that are alarming you?" She shook her head in a negative manner. James discovered that it was like "pulling teeth" for him to get to the specifics of her depression.

James took a pregnant pause so that his questioning wouldn't come across as an interrogation. He didn't want to turn her off; he wanted her to open up to him. He fired off two more questions: "Are you having financial problems? Are there problems with your marriage?" She quickly looked at him and said: "It is not a marriage. It is a prison sentence. He has become a cold, demanding warden who controls every aspect of my existence. It is unbearable." She burst into an uncontrollable fit of crying that almost brought James to tears. Just at that point, a nurse entered the lounge and informed Dr. Whitly that he was needed to attend to a patient. He told Andrea that she could remain in the lounge, and that he would make certain that they would continue their conversation as soon as he could get free. Andrea thanked James, but asked if they could continue talking later on in the evening away from the hospital. He took her cell phone number and said that he would contact her later on in the day. She forced a smile, and James left with the nurse.

Andrea exited the lounge shortly after James' departure. She checked on Leonard, but only stayed for a short while. She stared at him and imagined what life would be without him, but also wondered how she would survive without his "guidance." She left the hospital and went to the parking lot looking for her car that was nowhere in sight. After a quick search of the lot, she realized that she had driven Leonard's black BMW to the hospital, not her car. She found his car and drove home to gather some items that she thought she might need when she returned to the hospital. As she drove, she frightfully recalled the reason why she didn't take her car. Thinking about it scared her. She had to confide in someone, and hopefully James would contact her and arrange for a meeting away from the confines of the hospital. He wouldn't then be Dr. James Whitly, the attending physician for her husband. He would be that guy who cared so much for her at one time that he wanted to spend the rest of his life with her. He would just be James Whitly, the guy she should have married.

Dr. Whitly attended to the waiting patient the nurse informed him about. It wasn't a serious contact, but other cases also came to his attention. As he treated them all, he couldn't help but think about his wife, but more so the problems and concerns apparently haunting Andrea Canella. He also wondered what his wife would think if she knew that he was going to privately meet with his former paramour, a woman that he intended to marry. He was sure that knowledge of his planned meeting would be fodder for another extended argument. In this instance, however, he couldn't blame Laura for her stance. If it were reversed, he would object just as forcefully as she would. Although his meeting with Andrea is an effort to help her professionally, he is also meeting with her for personal reasons that he just cannot push aside. He still cared for her, and his ego wanted to be satisfied with the fact that she also still cared for him. He was certain that it would not go any further than that, but in the back of his mind, he was not one hundred percent certain.

James finished attending to his new patients and headed to the third floor to visit with his wife and Leonard. They both were scheduled for more treatment and procedures, and they both were still in a comatose-like state. One could not predict when either one would open their eyes and again start to live in the consciousness of the present. In fact, no one could even predict if either one would ever wake up and regain consciousness. As James looked at Laura, he felt guilty that he was even entertaining the idea of meeting with Andrea. Laura was fighting to recover and survive. How could he be so cold as to disregard what he knew would be Laura's feelings? He couldn't. He would tell Andrea that if she wanted his help that it would be totally professional, and the meeting would have to take place somewhere in the hospital. He actually felt really good about his decision and took it as the first step toward a better relationship at home. He was doing the right thing.

Once again, James planted a caring kiss on his wife's forehead and left to see Leonard. As he stared at his patient, the deceit and distrust that he felt so long ago came rushing into his mind. Although he was concerned about this patient's recovery, as he would be with any of his patients, he could not separate the negative emotions from what should only be his medical concerns. If he continued to focus on the past, might the application of his medical care be compromised because of hate and yes, even envy. He had to remain the professional he knew he was, and he had to remain faithful to the oath that he took. He checked the chart, spoke to the nurse, and made certain that Leonard's vitals were still constant. He left shaking his head as to what the past had dictated.

Dr. Whitly went to the lounge and decided to call Andrea to tell her about the limits of their planned meeting. He knew that she was going to return to the hospital at one point to visit with Leonard. He wanted to catch her before she came back. Unbeknownst to him, Andrea was already there. He would have to be strong and tell her in person. He was determined not to place any stumbling blocks in the way of his attempt at rejuvenating his marriage. He owed it to himself but even more to his wife. He left the doctors' lounge hoping that she had not yet returned. However, she was there and not hard to find. She sat on the third floor waiting area where an assisting doctor was attending to her husband.

Upon seeing James, Andrea looked relieved and almost happy. She immediately rose from her chair and anxiously greeted him. He, in turn, grabbed both her hands and said "hello." The mere sight of her weakened his determination, and relaying the limits of the upcoming meeting became a difficult task. He mentioned that he would be off duty in another hour, and that he could meet with her then. As he was about to tell her that he was only offering professional help, and that he preferred to meet in the hospital, she smiled and told him that she had found a small, out-of-the-way restaurant where they could have all the privacy they needed. She quickly followed with a premature "thank-you" for his taking the time to help her. She told him that she would tell him her whole sordid tale and let him be the judge of what he thought should come next. He looked at her and could not find the determination he had just a few moments ago. Her pleading, her hopeful look, and her grateful eyes shattered the firm resolve he needed to dictate certain parameters.

James agreed to meet with her in an hour. At her persuasion, he would go with her to the quiet restaurant that she had found, and hopefully help her find a solution to some of the problems that she was facing. He realized the danger of meeting with her on such a personal level, but he was sure that his professional demeanor would permeate the conversation and function as a barrier to the fueling of past desires. He mentally scoffed at this thought as he recalled how determined he was to meet in the hospital and explain to her that he was only professionally concerned about her situation. "Yeah," he said to himself, "you see how that worked out!"

Chapter Five

The Revelation

Before he knew it, James' tour came to a close. It had been a good day for him as far as the medical tests results. Laura was responding well to the brain procedure she endured and was scheduled for an exploratory operation to evaluate what damage, if any, had been done to her other internal organs. The prognosis was that any damage that was discovered would be easily repairable, and that recovery would be forthcoming. However, Laura was still in an unconscious state, and the doctors could not be sure when or if she would regain consciousness. That concern cast a grey shadow over the other positives involving her case.

Leonard Canella was also doing fairly well. However, there was a small glitch in his recovery when the doctors found that one of his lungs had collapsed. They were able to quickly inflate the collapsed lung, and Leonard's breathing returned to a normal rate. The broken bones in his arm and leg had been set and the shoulder that suffered a minor fracture was immobilized. With all of the casting and white bandaging, he could have been mistaken for a mummy. The display, however, was necessary so that the rudiments of a healthy recovery would hopefully be realized.

Like Laura, Leonard remained in an unconscious state, and, once again, doctors did not know how long it would last, or if there was a point at which the patient would regain consciousness. Fortunately, in cases like Laura's and Leonard's, the comatose state is usually temporary, but no one could dictate how long that temporary period would be. So, although both patients were non-responsive, there was strong hope that, in time, both would recover fully.

It was with this feeling of hope that James kept his appointment with Andrea. He met her in the first-floor lobby area and was once again greeted with a warm and conspicuously thankful smile. After the brief greeting, they exited the hospital and headed for the parking lot. James, of course, was parked in the reserved "Doctors' Parking" section which was a lot closer than where Andrea had to park. James suggested that they go in his car since it would have been foolish to take two cars to the same location. To safeguard his former determination, however, it would have been better to have taken the two cars, but that was not the case. Since they were going to be together in a somewhat secluded setting anyway, did it matter if they traveled together in the same car? Yes, it did! The closeness forced upon them by the distance between seats, only served to help destroy whatever barriers remained to prevent the situation from leaving the realm of "professional" to crashing into the comfortable domain of "personal."

Andrea was right. It was a small, out-of-the-way restaurant that afforded them quiet and privacy. James wondered how she had found it. The table was small, but instead of Andrea sitting opposite James, she moved so that she would be sitting next to him. She explained that she did not want anyone else to hear what she had to say, even though, at that point, there was no one else in the place except the waiter who had stationed himself at the other end of the restaurant. When the waiter brought them their drinks, they asked him to give them a little time before they ordered their meals.

Following his report on Leonard's condition, James turned the conversation over to Andrea. He prefaced his request to "tell him everything" with the encouragement that "no matter what it is, we'll work it out." With that surge of confidence, Andrea began her story. James was surprised that she started way back at the very beginning when she left his apartment and decided that it was over. She explained to him how Leonard was there for her, and how he comforted and consoled her as she went through what she described as one of the worst times in her life. She was so hurt that she did not allow for any explanation. Leonard understood and continued his support in such a troubling time. His friendship soon developed into a relationship that bordered on intimacy. She told James that she reluctantly let the relationship go further, but that he was her crutch, and soon became the pillar she relied on. The path became a predictable one, where Leonard and Andrea were always together and planned to stay together. She explained that it was not the same feeling that she had for James, but it was so comfortable that she just went with it.

At that point, James had to interrupt. He really did not want to know how she "gave-in" to Leonard, or how she felt in his company, or hear that it just wasn't the same. James was there to help with her immediate problems and did not want to rehash the past. He realized that it was her guilt that she wanted to "get-off-her-chest." However, he had enough of it. He looked at her and said: "I understand all that, but how can I help now." She had gotten her point across and went into how bad her marriage turned out. She explained the demanding, restricting, and demoralizing rules that she was forced to live under. As tears welled up in her eyes, she relayed how she was a prisoner in her own house, and how he recorded every move that she made. With certain devices he created, he would know if she left the house, and she knew that no matter where she went, he would find her, and she would suffer the consequences.

James was listening and looking at her in disbelief. He couldn't believe that the Leonard he knew could evolve into such a selfish tyrant who would bring one of the nicest, sweetest, caring individuals to her knees in despair. Leonard had brought her to the point that "reading-between-the-lines," she really didn't care if he died. In fact, in James' mind, he imagined that she thought it would be better if he didn't make it. She would be free. James also realized that the emotions involved with a car accident had truly little to do with how Andrea felt, looked, or acted. He wanted her to continue, but wanted to ask her one question before she did; however, the waiter interrupted and asked if they were ready to order. He came at such an inopportune time that James showed his displeasure by hurriedly ordering for the two of them. James was worried that Andrea, who was in a free flow of emotions mode, would take a step back and re-set. He was afraid that she would become more reserved and less open. She was already crying, embarrassed and frightened. He reluctantly told her to take some water and try to relax. She did and remained quiet for quite a while. He did not push her.

Apparently, she mustered up enough mental and emotional strength to begin again. As she started to speak, the waiter approached with their dinner. If looks could kill, James would have murdered him. However, they waited for the waiter to leave, and James asked if she wanted to continue. She took the unexpected break and suggested that they try their food. Once again, although James didn't want to, he went with the flow, and they started on their dinners. Andrea seemed better, having revealed some of the anguish that she had been feeling. Contrary to what James thought would happen, she ate her dinner with the vigor of someone who hadn't eaten in a while. They ordered another round of drinks and relaxed at the table. All during this time, only one other couple occupied a table. It was a noticeably quiet and private place.

Having gone through half of their second round, James asked if there was anything further that Andrea wanted to say. She looked at him with eyes that said: "I definitely do." She nodded as she began to speak. If James knew what Andrea was about to relate, he might have thought twice about suggesting to continue. She unabashedly described the sexual mandates to which she had to conform. The erotic and weird behavior that Leonard engaged in and, in which, she had to participate. He felt sick to his stomach but didn't want to interrupt for fear that she might not continue with other more relevant revelations. As she described her sexually forced interactions with Leonard, she once again began to sob, but she got through the descriptions of the demoralizing and demeaning events. She took some deep breaths and tried to regain her composure.

James took the opportunity to relate something that was bothering him. He mentioned to her that when he was looking for her after examining her husband, he saw her outside of the hospital entrance in conversation with two police officers. He noticed that the reaction to their conversation was one which, to him, was out of the ordinary. He was wondering what the police had told her to put her into such a state of concern and despair.

Of all the things that Andrea had told him, this was going to be the most difficult. In a most serious tone, she began: "I told you that Leonard always knew where I was and what I was doing, and because of his, one-of-a-kind engineering creations, he was able to tell when I left the house. The receiver for this device was strapped to his wrist just like a watch. He would only take it off when he was in the house. The night of the hit-and-run accident, he forgot it and left the house for his usual walk into town without it. He was definitely a creature of habit and never strayed from his calculated route." James listened attentively but could not yet see what all this had to do with her conversation with the police. However, he didn't interrupt. She continued: "I saw the device on the hallway table and saw it as my opportunity to finally be free. However, I did not want temporary freedom where, one day, he would find me and again force me into his madhouse. I took the keys to my car and drove to town. I waited at the intersection where he would cross the street and head back home. Like clockwork, he appeared at the intersection waiting for the light to turn green and proceed across the street. I was in my car on the same side as him but across the street waiting at the red light. When the light turned green for him to cross, I also crossed. I ran the red light and drove my car directly into him and just kept going. I saw him fly up into the air and land against a parked car. I smiled and realized that I was free." James looked at her in astonishment. Andrea, that kind-hearted, sweet, caring woman, tried to kill her husband. He now understood why speaking to the police brought such a concerned, frightening look to her face. He was sitting with someone who was wanted for "attempted murder" and "leaving the scene of an accident." He could not believe that she was capable of such an act, but, apparently, she was. She told him that the police relayed to her that they were looking for a late model, white SUV. They described her car. Before long, they would trace the suspect vehicle to her, and her quest for one kind of freedom would only be destroyed by the limits on freedom that the legal system would impose. She was a wanted felon. He was associating with someone that the police were looking for. How would that affect him? How could he possibly help her without incriminating himself? His initial thought was to get away, to separate himself from her. Did he have any other choice? His pager went off and read: "Two detectives are in your office wanting to speak with Mrs. Andrea Canella."

Chapter Six

The Betrayal

Dr. Whitly called the pager number and spoke with the nurse who sent the page. She reiterated that there were two detectives wanting to speak with him regarding the whereabouts of Mrs. Andrea Canella. James mentioned that he was out and having dinner with a friend. He asked the nurse to tell the detectives that he would be available in the morning, and that he couldn't speak with them now. Nurse Hopkins hesitated in answering the doctor since the detectives were standing right in front of her. Detectives David Krane and Tracy Barret motioned that they heard the Doctor's comments, and that it was most important that they speak with him as soon as possible. Nurse Hopkins relayed the information to James who said that he would return to the hospital within the next thirty minutes. The detectives heard and agreed to wait for him.

James was beside himself. He had Andrea Canella sitting right in front of him, the same Andrea Canella that the police were looking for. He had never felt so compromised – maybe one other time! He told Andrea what had transpired and asked her what she wanted to do. Her response was an expected one: "What do you think we should do?" He immediately became concerned and aware of the fact that she used "we" in her response to him. Whether he liked it or not, it seemed that he had been drawn into a situation that could only turn out one way – bad. He thought for a while and realized that he had to return to the hospital. So, he would speak with the detectives and see what they had to say. In the interim, he told Andrea that she could temporarily stay at his house. If she returned to the hospital with him, she would be risking the chance that the detectives would take her into custody for questioning. Knowing how emotional Andrea was, James knew that she would buckle under any kind of scrutiny and admit her guilt. That might have to be the ultimate scenario down the road, but for now, it was best to see how things developed.

Was Dr. James Whitly now technically aiding and abetting a fugitive? He didn't think it had come to that point yet, but he was concerned that it was very close. If the detectives ultimately informed James that Andrea was wanted for questioning in the vehicular assault of her husband, James would surely be "obstructing an official investigation" if he did not reveal Andrea's whereabouts. The outcome of the meeting remained to be seen, but for now, he told Andrea to drive to his house when they got back to the hospital, while he went to meet with the detectives. They left the restaurant and after arriving at the hospital went their separate ways. Andrea, once again, thanked him and apologized for getting him involved in her problems. He nodded and drove off to park his car.

Although the ride to the hospital had been a short one, for him, it evolved into a tedious thought process focusing on potential problems and possible solutions. Before he knew it, he was parking at the "Doctors' Parking" section of the parking lot. He was about to enter into a face-to-face meeting with detectives who were going to ask for his help in locating a possible suspect who left the scene of an accident, and who had left a victim in critical condition. He had to "face-the-music," so he entered the hospital and asked the nurse who had paged him where the detectives were situated. Nurse Hopkins had escorted the detectives to Dr. Whitly's office. He thanked her and proceeded to his office.

As Dr. James Whitly entered his office, which now seemed less comfortable than it had been only a short time ago, the two detectives rose from their chairs and introduced themselves. He learned that Detectives Krane and Barret were part of a special investigations unit and were assigned to the case involving Leonard Canella. James introduced himself and asked how he could help. They came right to the point and said that Mrs. Andrea Anella was a "person-of-interest" in the investigation. They asked if he knew where Mrs. Canella might be. For James, this was the moment of truth. He either told them everything and cooperated with the investigation, or he lied, and obstructed an official investigation. If he did not tell the truth, what would the ramifications be, and how would it affect his professional career? If he told the truth, for sure, Andrea would be arrested and ultimately be sentenced to a long term in a penal institution. The detectives were waiting for an answer, and any delay would only support the idea that the doctor was hiding something.

Dr. James Whitly couched the future of his career with the words: "I have no idea where she might be." James Whitly made a decision based on emotions rather than logic. His entire adult life, however, mandated that he make logical, practical decisions. His medical career demanded it. Now, the reflections of the past and the dictates of his emotions were the overwhelming force determining his train of thought. He couldn't be the one who would aid in sending a person for whom he apparently still had feelings, into a life of imprisonment. She had already been imprisoned by her husband. The detectives continued to ask related questions and ultimately asked if they could "look-in" on Leonard Canella. James saw no problem with the detectives visiting Leonard, and he wanted to convey an air of cooperation. The detectives were satisfied with their conversation and visit, but they informed Dr. Whitly that they may be back with additional questions. James told them that he had no problem with them returning and assured them that he would cooperate in any way possible.

When the detectives finally left, James took some deep breaths and pondered his next move. He was now committed to helping Andrea, but he had no idea what the best way forward would be. Being back in his office and at the hospital, his thoughts, once again, strayed to his wife. With all of the other concerns and problems plaguing him, he wanted his main focus to be centered on the welfare of Laura. He left his office and went to her room. As he checked her vitals and overall condition, he couldn't help but feel the ache of betrayal filtering into his consciousness. He spoke to his comatose wife, and tried to tell her why he acted the way he did. However, as he tried to explain, he realized that whatever reasons he offered, would not be sufficient to justify what he had done. He was disgusted with himself, and how he was swayed by emotions rather than by what was right. It was a step backward in his attempt to rebuild his marriage.

As James was experiencing disillusionment, Andrea was approaching his home. She wasn't totally comfortable with the arrangement, but she relied on James' guidance. When she entered the house, she was surprised how simple the surroundings were. He didn't live the ostentatious life that a head surgeon could easily create. He lived an average life, and the surroundings reflected it. His wife was also apparently comfortable with the simple things in life. She was now in Laura's domain and was not sure that this was where she should be. But again, what other alternatives did she have? She would wait for James to find out what the detectives wanted, and what she should do next. It was quite obvious to her that the right thing to do was to turn herself into the police and suffer the consequences. That would save James from further turmoil and the ramifications of what hiding someone who was "wanted by the police" would be. She did not consider herself to be a selfish person, but she didn't relish going to prison and never seeing James again. It was wrong in every way, but she deserved some happiness after what she had gone through. In her mind, the "woe-is-me" thinking justified her present decision.

After also checking on Leonard, James knew that he had to head home. He had to deal with the mess in which he found himself, and one which he now had intentionally allowed to continue. As he drove, he tried to develop a plan that would offer the least number of negative results. He could not. The situation had become so involved and convoluted that there was no easy way out. There was no solution that would benefit both him and Andrea. Additionally, no matter what the final result, Laura would also be negatively affected. His concentration had to be re-directed as he had to swerve to avoid a parked car. His focus was not on driving, but on what seemed to be insurmountable obstacles to positive results.

As he came to his driveway, he couldn't pull his car into the garage because a black BMW was blocking the way. This had to be immediately rectified for a number of reasons. Neighbors would notice a different car in the driveway, and neighbors being who they are, would want to know whose car it was. Secondly, if the police visited James' home, they would see the same black BMW, and they would soon discover that the car was registered to Mr. Leonard Canella. How do you explain that? The answer is - you don't!

James quickly exited his car and went into the house. He saw the BMW keys on the table in the hallway and took them with him to the driveway. He pressed the automatic garage door opener and pulled the car into the garage. He repressed the device and closed the garage door. He then went to his car and drove it onto the driveway. Things, once again, looked normal. That was the only thing that resembled some sort of normalcy.

During all this time, Andrea surprisingly never appeared at the door. That seemed odd to James, and as he entered the house again, he called out for her. There was no response. He started to worry and look around the house. As he entered each room, he called out her name, but again, there was no response. Going from room to room and not seeing her really began to raise his anxiety level. He searched all of the rooms on the first floor and continued upstairs to the second floor. He constantly called out her name, but to no avail. As he finished with the master bedroom, he passed the upstairs bathroom. The door to the bathroom is usually opened. Now, it was closed. He slowly pushed the door open and whispered Andrea's name. The door fully opened; he saw her sitting on the floor against the bathtub with a kitchen knife in her hand, positioned against her wrist. As soon as she saw him, she sadly uttered: "All I have done is cause major problems for you. I do not want you to get in trouble for what I have done. There is no other way out for me. I will slowly go to sleep, and my problems will all be gone." If James had problems before, they were just compounded.

"Andrea, we will work something out. Don't do anything foolish. I am here to help you. My feelings for you have never changed, and I don't want to go through life without being able to see you or talk to you. Please, give me the knife. Let's talk about some alternatives that I've been thinking about." James had thought of no alternatives, but he had to convince Andrea that options existed. Andrea held the blade against her wrist and didn't look convinced that James was telling the truth. As he spoke to her, he got closer and closer to the knife. He would have one opportunity to grab it. He sat down just across from her, and in a pleading tone, asked her not to leave him alone. He asked her to feel his heart that was beating for her. In that moment, she started to raise her knife-holding hand, and James seized the opportunity to take a firm grip on the weapon. He took it from her, and she collapsed in tears reaching out for him. However, he noticed blood on her blouse and pushed her back just a bit to see where it was coming from. It was not her blood, but his blood gushing from the cut he suffered when he grabbed the knife. He felt better that it was his, not hers, but if he had troubles before, he had even bigger ones now. For the first time in many years, he felt overwhelming despair. He wasn't going to be able to save her. He wasn't going to be able to save his career. He wasn't going to be able to save his marriage; and he wasn't going to be able to save tomorrow. Maybe, Andrea had the right idea!

Chapter Seven

Hiding in Plain Sight

Detective David Krane and Detective Tracy Barret were seasoned police officers. Between the two of them there were over twenty-two years of experience. They oversaw many types of cases in their careers, and this one was really on the same level as many of the others they had worked on. They became partners approximately 4 years ago when Detective Krane's partner was promoted to the rank of "Sergeant" and left the Detective Division. Tracy Barret, at that time, was a floater (a detective who did not have a permanent partner), so it was natural for her to be assigned as David's new partner. Tracy had only been in the Detective Division for a year or so at that time, but David had been a detective for seven years.

Tracy Barret was glad to have teamed up with David Krane because he was a detective who was well respected on the job, and who had a wealth of experience to share. She had learned a lot from David and was still in the process of absorbing certain techniques that David always used successfully. Detective Krane never had a female partner and was enthusiastic about partnering with Tracy. He mentioned, many times, how much more intuitive females were than males. This was a quality that could only help in solving cases. So, both detectives received reciprocal benefits from their association.

Presently, they were dealing with a case that didn't seem to be that difficult to solve. They already had a description of the hit-and-run vehicle, and they knew that the details matched the description of the car that Andrea Canella drove. To prove, however, that Andrea intentionally drove into her husband would be a little more difficult. If they could prove that or if she confessed to it, they would then change the charge to attempted murder. They also were less than convinced of James' veracity when they spoke with him. He wasn't telling them everything and what he did tell them was questionable. There had to be more to the relationship between Andrea and Dr. James Whitly than they knew. They were looking into any previous connection between the two. After all, why would a well-known doctor risk his reputation and career over someone he hardly knew? It didn't make sense, and they were almost certain that Dr. Whitly knew the whereabouts of Mrs. Andrea Canella.

The process of background checks and history reviews is not a difficult one, but it is time-consuming and tedious. Detective Barret was focusing on that aspect of the case while Detective Krane started questioning employees at the hospital about the accident, and the possible relationship between Mrs. Andrea Canella and Dr. James Whitly. He was also interested in the relationship that James had with his wife. The detective wanted to cover all bases, as he should. Detective Krane decided that tomorrow he would show up again at the hospital, on an unannounced visit. Dr. Whitly would not have time to organize his thoughts into a possible scenario of untruths. Krane would be more direct and, in some ways, more accusatory. He needed to shake the doctor into understanding more clearly the ramifications of the reality he had chosen to adopt.

It took a while, but James was able to calm Andrea. He explained to her that there was no turning back for him, and that he was committed to helping her in any way that he could. Although grateful and relieved, she knew that he was jeopardizing his professional career and possibly his marriage. James mentioned to Andrea that he would have to return to the hospital in the morning, and that she was welcome to stay at the house. They both knew that if Andrea returned to the hospital and was recognized that she would more than likely be arrested by the police. However, after what had just occurred with Andrea on the bathroom floor, he was very reluctant to leave her alone. The detectives had not called for another appointment with him, so his thinking was that the hospital would be a relatively safe place. He decided on a plan where Andrea could return to the hospital and remain hidden in plain sight.

James went into his clothes closet and fished for scrubs that might fit his former girlfriend. Luckily, he came upon a set of hospital clothes that Andrea could put on and masquerade as an attending nurse. He would have her in hospital attire and wearing a face mask. He explained to her that she would be able to stay at the hospital and not be alone in the house. He also explained that he would be able to attend to his patients and not have to worry about her. It seemed like a good enough plan as long as the investigating detectives did not want to schedule another appointment. She agreed to the idea and looked forward to not staying alone.

It had been an unnerving and stressful day, and they both were suffering from physical and mental fatigue. James suggested that they "turn-in" for the night, so that they would be well rested for what tomorrow might bring. Andrea agreed, and they both went upstairs to the bedrooms. James showed Andrea to the guest room and made sure that she would be comfortable for the night. She again thanked him for everything and kissed him on the check wishing him a "good night." He left as she closed the door and headed for bed. He went across the hall to the master bedroom and just sat on the bed thinking about what had transpired and what might yet come.

Although he was extremely exhausted, sleep did not come easily. Maybe, he was over-tired or too stressed for his mind to relax. Probably the later. He laid there as his mind continued to replay the scenes of the day's activities. He had his wife in a comatose state in the hospital, his "friend" in a similar condition, and his former girlfriend sleeping in the guest room of the house he shared with his wife. He had two detectives hounding him for answers that he didn't want to give them, and he was helping a "person-of interest" evade the police. Otherwise, it was just another day. The time had come for him to make a decision that most probably would be very tough but was, above all, the right thing to do. He couldn't continue juggling his career, his marriage, and a relationship with his former girlfriend without one or all of those things suffering. The time had come to "man-up." He would still go through with the plan that he developed for tomorrow, but he was going to tell Andrea that he could no longer be involved with her problems. He was going to tell her that her visit to the hospital would be the final one, and that he did not want to know where she went afterward. This being the case, he could truthfully tell the detectives that: "I have no idea where she is."

He began to feel more comfortable and relaxed. He closed his eyes and drifted off to a well-needed state of deep sleep. At approximately three o'clock in the morning, however, he awakened to shrill screams emanating from the guest room across the hall. Still in the throes of deep sleep, he staggered to the guest room to find Andrea sitting up in bed now staring into space. She seemed to be in some kind of a trance. Apparently, she was experiencing a psychotic episode brought on by the stresses of the day and her seemingly unresolvable situation. James was a doctor but not a psychiatrist, however, he knew the rudiments of psychotic behavior and how to commence the initial response. He slowly brought her back to the present, but she was definitely suffering from the aftereffects of the episode.

His exhaustion getting the better of him, and his concern for leaving her alone weighing heavy on his mind, he laid down next to her. She reacted in a positive way to this show of comfort and wrapped her arms around him. They stayed that way for the rest of the night, sleeping in the comfort of each other's arms. The comfort and familiar position did not add to James' determination regarding his decision to sever all ties. It served to cause more doubt in taking the right path forward. He felt the strain of fractures in the support structure he had just used a few hours ago to bolster his resolve. He could not let his wavering affect his final position. Andrea would understand. Wouldn't she?

Chapter Eight

The Disguise

Morning brought stark reality into focus. James Whitly had to be forcefully direct with Andrea. He could no longer support her evading the police. He would not actively notify the police regarding Andrea's activities, but he would totally cooperate with the detectives if they required further information to which he was privy. He woke Andrea and explained that they had to soon leave for the hospital. She rose and quickly dressed in the hospital scrubs that James had provided. He further explained to her that as long as she wore the scrubs and kept the face mask in place that she would most likely escape any recognition. She would be able to visit Leonard without bringing unnecessary attention to her stay.

James had a lot on his mind but decided that he would tell Andrea about his decision to "separate" right after her planned visit to Leonard's room. He poured coffee for the two of them, but emphasized they did not have time to waste. Andrea thanked him for helping her through the night and commented on how comfortable and safe she felt in his arms. He just nodded and did not want to encourage any repetition of the compromising position in which he found himself. He just wanted to leave and get the recent events behind him. They exited the house and went to their cars. Andrea followed James out of the driveway and began the trip back to the hospital.

Both James and Andrea were comfortable with the plan, and with Andrea's past experience in nursing courses, James was pretty sure that she could easily fade into the busy humdrum of the hospital. As they parked their cars, James saw Dr. Strathmore, who more than anyone else, was intimately involved in Laura's recovery and on-going treatment. James engaged Dr. Strathmore in conversation and found out that the damage to Laura's internal organs was minimal and that the operation to repair them went well. James was relieved but still had to deal with the fact that his wife remained unconscious. He knew that regaining consciousness in a case like hers could take time, but the waiting was difficult. James thanked Charles Strathmore for his efforts and turned to see where Andrea had gone. To his surprise, she was still in her car waiting for him to give the "okay" to exit. She used her head. Things were looking up.

James nodded to her, and she exited her car and walked beside him. They entered the hospital and went directly to the third floor where both Leonard and Laura remained. With the "good morning" greetings directed toward Dr. Whitly, it was easy for Andrea to just slip by and head for Leonard's room. The plan was working. James went to Laura's room as "Nurse" Andrea entered Leonard's room. Thankfully, no one was in her husband's room attending to some of his medical needs. Doctors' rounds were over, and the assigned nurse had just left him. It was just the two of them, Leonard and Andrea.

Across the hall, James was checking his wife's chart and examining her overall appearance, which was better than he anticipated. Even though his wife couldn't respond, there were studies that indicated that patients experiencing unconsciousness could still hear what people were saying. So, James spoke to her as if she were present and alert. He explained how sorry he was for not being more understanding, and how he wanted to rejuvenate their marriage. He expressed his love for her and his determination to make sure she fully recovered. He, once again, kissed her on the forehead and moved across the floor to Leonard's room.

Andrea was deep in her talk to Leonard; so, James remained very quiet not wanting to disturb her. However, he was shocked when he heard her say: "I will not rest until you are dead. I will make sure that you never leave this hospital, and I will find a way to make you suffer the way you made me suffer. The devil awaits you, Leonard." She looked up and saw James standing there, but she offered no excuse or explanation for what she said. James was about to discuss what he heard when a voice from the corridor surprised him: "There you are, Dr. Whitly. I would like to ask you a few more questions as soon as you are through with your patient." Detective Krane's unannounced visit had the desired results. He saw a surprised and very concerned and shaky doctor. James nodded to him. He motioned to the detective to wait in his office, but Krane remained.

Both Andrea and James were stressed that the detective showed up again, and, this time, with Andrea well within his reach. James indicated to "Nurse" Andrea to take the portable drip stand down the hall. The saline bag was empty, and the stand was needed elsewhere. She immediately understood and passed right by Detective Krane who was still standing outside of Leonard's room. Apparently, the scrubs and the face mask were the perfect prescription for hiding-in-plain-sight. The detective didn't give her a second look. For an even better disguise, she had added a nurse's operation cap to her ensemble, so her hair was also covered.

Following a brief and superficial exam of his patient, Dr. Whitly escorted Detective Krane to his office. James prefaced his comments with the fact that he was very busy and, in the future, if the detective needed to speak with him that he should call James' office and make an appointment. He explained further that their conversations were taking valuable time away from the care he needed to give to his patients. Detective Krane confirmed that he understood and began his questioning. His first question centered on whether or not James previously knew either Leonard or Andrea. James was an intelligent man; so, he figured that the Detective knew the correct answer but just wanted to see if James would lie about it. James indignantly answered: "I am sure you already know that I had a former relationship with both Andrea and Leonard. So, why don't you just be direct with me, and I will be truthful with you." James had laid down the parameters.

Detective Krane looked squarely at James and said: "You haven't been truthful with me before. Why would I believe that you would be truthful now?" James answered: "Because I have nothing more to hide. You have my full cooperation." Krane followed up: "You knew where Mrs. Canella was when we originally asked you, and you probably helped her hide. I am asking you now where Mrs. Andrea Canella is?" James answered: "A short time ago, she was in the hospital, but I have no idea where she might be now." The detective looked surprised and asked: "Did she speak to you about her husband's accident?" James didn't hesitate and answered in the affirmative. "Did she admit to you that she was the one who was driving the late model, white SUV that struck her husband?"

James looked at the detective and answered by relating the story that Andrea had told him about her life with Leonard. James took a deep breath and spoke: "Andrea has been the victim of cruel and almost inhuman behavior by her husband, Leonard. She explained to me that she was a prisoner in her own home. She couldn't leave the house without his approval or his company, and she had to perform humiliating and demeaning sexual acts. He monitored her every move and even developed a gadget that continually recorded her whereabouts. She saw the accident as a way to break free from his tortuous control. She had the opportunity, and she took it."

Detective Krane nodded his head and said: "Doctor Whitly, I appreciate your cooperation, but understand that you obstructed our investigation. Where that goes from here is up to the District Attorney." James told him that he understood, and that he would contact the detective if Andrea reached out to him again. Detective Krane was satisfied and left with the warning that if James afforded any more help to Andrea, that he could be charged with "aiding and abetting" a felon. James nodded again that he understood and showed the detective to the door.

Dr. James Whitly sat behind his desk and reviewed the last fifteen minutes. He also realized that he didn't get the chance to tell Andrea that he could no longer help her. He wanted to sit down with her and explain why he had to make that choice. Unfortunately, when Detective Krane surprisingly arrived on the scene, Andrea made a quick getaway. In truth, he had no idea where she went or where she was heading. He hoped that she wouldn't consider taking refuge again in his house. He couldn't and wouldn't allow that. She probably left the hospital wearing the same scrubs that James had provided. He was sure that she was not about to stop and change clothes.

Even though he knew that it was the right thing to do, he felt that he was abandoning her, and she didn't even know it. She was scared that the detective would recognize her and petrified at the idea of having to spend possibly the rest of her life behind bars; so, there was a good chance that James would never see her again. He was certain that she would not take a risk that could lead to her capture.

James was sad and glad at the same time. Sad that he would never interact with the women he, apparently still had feelings for, and glad that he wouldn't have a clear and present danger as an obstacle to the reparation of his marriage. He was relieved that the situation was now out of his hands. He still had to worry, however, about whether or not the District Attorney was going to press charges; and he still didn't know how his involvement with Andrea would affect his professional career. In the interim, however, he would continue to treat his patients and offer his expertise whenever it was needed.

In the middle of reviewing his medical reports, Andrea's threat, which was imbedded in his mind, entered his conscious thought: "I will not rest until you are dead. I will make sure that you never leave this hospital, and I will find a way to make you suffer the way you made me suffer. The devil awaits you, Leonard." With the seriousness of that threat, James wondered if his judgement that Andrea would not risk coming back to the hospital was prejudiced thinking. If Andrea was so determined, as one would think upon hearing her threat, then the possibility of Andrea returning was real. As he continued to think about Andrea's determination, he realized that she already had the apparel to present herself as a hospital nurse. Again, he had unknowingly helped make it easy for her to carry out what amounted to the potential threat of murder.

James was faced with another situation that mandated calculated decision making. Even though he visited Leonard quite often when he was on duty, what happens when he is not there? Andrea could come at any time to carry out her plan. James had to do something to help protect Leonard from Andrea's wrath. Did that mean that the police would have to be notified and an officer assigned to his room? Could he just let the hospital security department know that a threat existed and have them assign a hospital security officer to perform "directed patrol" on the floor where Leonard's room was located? No matter what, he had to do something. He couldn't keep it to himself and risk the fact that Andrea may very well carry out her focused and unrelenting threat to kill her husband. It seemed to James that Andrea would let nothing get in the way of her completing a murderous crusade.

Here he was again, involved in the on-going situation. Whether it was the police or the hospital security, it was his obligation to make sure that Leonard Canella was protected. Ironic how he was so worried about the guy who didn't give a damn, way back when, about James' health, whether it be physical or emotional. However, Dr. James Whitly was better than that. Wasn't he?

Chapter Nine

The Choking Child

Andrea Canella walked as quickly as possible without bringing attention to herself. The nurse's uniform had apparently worked. She passed Detective Krane without incident. Now, however, she was rushing down the two flights of stairs to make a hasty exit and not push her luck. She didn't like the idea that she was forced to leave without speaking with James and saying "good-bye." She had no idea that James was going to tell her that he could no longer help with her problems. The surprise visit by Detective Krane really shook her up, and she could only imagine that James was also experiencing a rush of anxiety.

Andrea hurried to her car, her husband's car, and couldn't get in quickly enough. She started the car and drove out of the parking lot, not knowing exactly where she was heading. She just drove. She wanted to change out of the nurse's uniform so that she would more easily blend in with others. As she drove, she came upon a large department store parking lot. The perfect place where she could park the car which, she was sure, was already on the search list for every police officer on patrol. Her plan was to take her change of clothes with her into the store and utilize the public bathroom to transform her appearance.

With clothes in hand, she headed for the entrance. As she approached, she heard the screams of a woman yelling for help: "Help my baby isn't breathing. Somebody help!" Andrea, still in her nurse's uniform and closest to the woman and her child, was the obvious first responder. Apparently, the child was gasping for air and turning blue. To Andrea, these were signs that the child's airway was blocked by something the child had attempted to swallow. Andrea took the child from its mother's arms and placed the child's back firmly against her chest. She then performed the first aid procedure known as the Heimlich Maneuver. After three concentrated thrusts to the child's chest, a large hard candy projectized from the child's mouth. Her color came back, and she began to cry, both good signs. The child's mother, who also had been crying, took the child and hugged her to the point that Andrea thought the child would turn blue again.

Regaining her composure, the mother faced Andrea and began to profusely thank her for saving her child's life. She introduced herself as Sandra Harding. Andrea, not wanting to reveal her true identity for obvious reasons, introduced herself as Marie Church, a friend from her childhood days. Marie had an exceptionally long and unpronounceable German surname, and her father was the pastor for the local Protestant congregation; therefore, "Church" became Marie's easily pronounceable last name for her friends. Andrea's quick thinking resulted in her introduction as Marie Church, registered nurse.

Sandra couldn't be more thankful and asked if there was anything that she could do for Marie. This might be the perfect opportunity for Andrea to ditch the very recognizable black BMW and catch a ride away from the area. Andrea asked if Sandra could do her a favor and give her a ride to the nearest car-rental location since her car was being repaired. She explained that a friend had dropped her off at the store, and she was without a ride. Sandra didn't hesitate in granting the favor and even went further in inviting Andrea to her home. Since Andrea really had no other place to go, and displaying an air of false reluctance, she ultimately accepted the invitation. Her nurse's uniform, once again, served its purpose. It naturally provided an air of security and confidence to those who observed it.

Sandra Harding explained that she lived just fifteen minutes down the road, in the adjoining town, with her partner, her wife. This was fine with Andrea. She would change into her street clothes once she got there. This unexpected respite from the stress of escape was more than welcomed. It would give Andrea some time to think about what she would do next. Following her brief stay at the Harding residence, she would ask Sandra to drive her to the car-rental location, and hopefully, once again, become invisible.

Sandra was correct. The ride was only about fifteen minutes, and during the entire trip, her daughter, Sarah, played and entertained herself as if nothing had happened. This was the resilience of kids, while her mother, more than likely, suffered a traumatic event that would remain always as a stressful memory. It wasn't easy raising a family, but Andrea envied those who had the chance to experience it. As her life was progressing, she didn't see any way that parenting could become a viable option. She felt that she would be lucky just to maintain her freedom and be able to take care of herself, let alone a child. She was, however, getting along well with Sarah.

As Andrea roamed around the house, Sandra prepared some afternoon snacks and refreshments. It gave Andrea a chance to really look around. She came upon a picture of Sandra and presumably her partner. As Andrea looked more closely, Sandra's wife looked somewhat familiar. Of course, it was most probable that Andrea didn't know her, and that she just had one of those familiar faces. When Sandra came out of the kitchen and into the dining room area, Andrea inquired about her partner. Sandra mentioned that they had been together for quite a while, even before Tracy went into the Police Department.

They had met in college and were inseparable from that point on. After the words "Police Department" and "Tracy," Andrea didn't hear another thing. Could it be possible that she was sitting and relaxing in the house of one of the detectives who was actively looking for her? It was too much of a coincidence. Andrea had used the computer in James' house to look at photos of both David Krane and Tracy Barret. She wanted to know what her pursuers looked like. The photo that she was now viewing, and the one she saw on the computer were very similar. Furthermore, it was too much of a coincidence that the name attached to the photo was the same as one of the detectives. Andrea felt trapped. She couldn't stay at the house any longer for fear that Detective Barret would, at any moment, walk through the door. What would follow then would be the arrest and capture of the suspect who was wanted in the potential "attempted murder" case of one, Leonard Canella. What kind of bad luck could she possibly have to have been in a department store parking lot where she responded to a choking child who just happened to be the daughter of the detective who was searching for her? She couldn't win the lottery, but she successfully secured a one in a million chance of meeting Tracy's partner and daughter. It was one for the books!

Andrea started to sweat as she began to think of ways that she could politely leave without causing suspicion or concern. She couldn't delay any longer because she didn't know when Detective Barret would arrive home. She had changed her clothes and neatly packed away her nurse's uniform in a bag that Sandra had supplied. Sarah was playing in the den, and Sandra went back into the kitchen to prepare some additional snacks. It was Andrea's opportunity to flee the scene. She grabbed her bag and quietly went to the front door. She didn't want Sarah to catch her leaving. She slowly closed the front door and began to walk quickly away from the house. Her quick steps began to develop into a lazy jog. She wanted to run, but that would bring too much attention to her flight. As she turned the corner, she saw what, to her, looked like an unmarked police car coming up the block. From a distance, she couldn't tell who was driving.

Andrea needed to know if Tracy was driving the possible unmarked police vehicle. As the car got closer, Andrea intentionally let the package she was carrying fall onto the sidewalk. While she bent down to pick it up, she hesitated long enough for the car to pass and used a parked car to block her from being seen. As the car passed, she was able to see that a female was driving the car. Andrea was almost certain that Tracy Barret was on her way home. The police suspect peeked around the corner and saw the car stop in front of the house from which she had just fled. Detective Barret was home. Andrea wasted no time in quickly leaving the area.

When Detective Tracy Barret opened the front door, she was confronted with a confused and alarmed individual. Sandra explained that she thought it was Marie Church coming back into the house. Tracy's questioning response was: "Who the heck is Marie Church?" Tracy ushered her partner into the house and tried to explain the events of the day. Since she was excited and in-a-rush to get the whole story out as quickly as possible, there were expected gaps in Sandra's narrative, but Tracy got the gist of it. Tracy asked: "Why do you think she left?" Shrugging her shoulders, Sandra said: "I really don't know. She seemed comfortable and relaxed. After she changed into her regular clothes, she played a little with Sarah, and then sat down at the table. We talked a little bit about you and what you did, but it all just seemed like a way to break an uncomfortable silence." Tracy responded: "You said that she was a nurse. Did she say what hospital she worked in?" "No," was the quick response.

Tracy Barret then asked her wife what Marie Church looked like. Tracy responded with a description that sent Tracy's investigative antennae upward. The description closely matched that of Mrs. Andrea Canella. Tracy did not let Sandra know what she was thinking but told Sandra that she had to leave for just a little while to see if she could find Marie Church. Tracy told Sandra that she just wanted to make sure that Marie was okay. Tracy left in search of the suspect who was probably guilty of attempted murder.

When Tracy got back into her police ride, she put the description that Sandra had given her over the police radio. All of the police patrols in the area were now looking for Andrea Canella. The net was getting tighter, and Andrea knew that she had to go into hiding. Maybe, this was a good time to call James. He might have a good suggestion. Little did she know!

Chapter Ten

A Talk in the Park

Andrea knew that she had to get out of sight, and she wanted to get in contact with James. She came to a small cluster of stores that included a pharmacy. She hurried into the drug store and began looking for a burner cell phone. The phone would give her the ability to reach out to James and ask for his advice. Additionally, a burner phone is untraceable back to the originator. She looked around and finally saw the display promoting cell phones. She took one to the cashier and went around to the back of the store near the loading dock to keep hidden from public view. She missed James and couldn't wait to speak with him.

"Hello, this is Dr. Whitly speaking." Andrea was so happy to hear his voice that her response was delayed: "Hello James, it's Andrea. I can't tell you what I've been through over the last couple of hours. I'm sorry I left without letting you know, but I panicked when I saw that detective and heard that he had more questions for you. I am so sorry that you have to deal with all this. I never wanted to make things difficult for you. I am so tired, and I don't know what to do next." Andrea paused and finally gave James a chance to speak: "Andrea, first of all, where are you? And secondly, where have you been?" Andrea told

James that she wasn't sure what town she was in, and that she had spent the last couple of hours with Detective Barret's wife. There was an obvious pregnant pause in the conversation until James blurted out: "What did you say?"

Andrea Canella relayed the entire unbelievable event to James. After hearing the entire scenario, it even seemed more unbelievable to him. In her story, she emphasized the fact that she was almost positive that her description was transmitted to every police officer in the surrounding area. She told him that she felt like a fugitive, a wanted person, and she didn't know where to turn. In the middle of her implied plea for help, she started crying and couldn't continue the conversation. Once again, his determination began wavering as he tried to calm her down. He told her to look around to see if she could determine exactly where she was. Andrea went to the front of the parking area and looked for signs that might indicate a particular town. She was in luck. About fifty yards away from her, she saw a sign that read: "Wellsford Dry Cleaners."

Andrea told James what she saw, and he mentioned that the town of Wellsford was only about twenty-five minutes away from Mountain Pacific Hospital. Against his better judgement, he told her to wait by the Pharmacy, and that he would come to pick her up as soon as possible. She thanked him and headed toward the pharmacy. She was able to stay in the store and browse without bringing attention to herself. Also, from her vantage point in the store, she could easily see out of the window to the parking area where James would ultimately appear.

He did it again. He thought with his heart instead of his head. But how could he tell her that she was on her own in the middle of a stressfully, tear-filled story. Andrea was in deep trouble, and she knew it. He also knew it, but he couldn't just abandon her when it seemed that she needed him most. He was disgusted with himself because of his lack of real determination. Before he left, he would go into his wife's room, and although she was in a coma, he would explain to her that he was only going to make sure Andrea was able to go safely on her way. Maybe, he would help her rent another car and give her some cash to get by with, but it wouldn't be much more than that.

James went into his wife's room. Apologetically, he began to tell her what he was about to do. He explained that this would be the last time he would contact or help Andrea, and that he hoped she would understand. He continued, at length, to describe what had occurred, and why he had to meet with her this one last time. He promised Laura that he would no longer help her, and that he was going to tell Andrea, for the last time, that any contact or relationship between them was over.

I may not be able to respond to you, but I understand what is going on. For the most part, I've heard a number of your conversations whether on the phone or face-to-face with another. So, you are going again to "bail her out." Yet, you relay to me how you want our marriage to re-activate, to go back to the way it was when we weren't always fighting and at each other's throat. How can that happen when you continue to allow this woman to dictate your actions. I'm so

sick and tired of hearing the reasons why you just have to do it, "one more time." This woman is from your past, and that's where she should have remained; yet you allow her to manipulate your present.

I was happy when you told me how sorry you were about how our marriage deteriorated. I really thought that you were determined to make things right; but you continue to tumble over a main obstacle, Andrea Canella. Yes, that's right. I heard her name when the detective asked you about her. So, you are going to meet with her again. If I were conscious and aware, would you still entertain the idea of saving her? I think you would. The only difference would be that you would keep it a secret from me. Well, surprise! I know! One day soon, I hope that I will again appear in the world of the conscious, and then we will talk.

James finished his apology, and, as usual, kissed his wife on her forehead. As he left, he turned to her and vowed that he would not betray her again. He mentioned to his secretary that he needed to address some important matters and asked her to reschedule whatever appointments were still on the calendar. She acknowledged his request and asked if she could help in any way. He thanked her but told her that these were things he had to do himself. He turned to leave when the office phone rang. He stopped to see if he needed to speak with the caller. His secretary told the caller to hold on while she let Dr. Whitly know who was calling. She mentioned to James that a Detective Krane was on the line. James could not waste time speaking with the detective; so, he told the secretary to tell him that he was gone for the day. James did not wait for any response and left. It was already twenty minutes since he spoke to Andrea, and he didn't want her to be waiting for any length of time. As it was, he still had a twenty-five-minute ride to Wellsford, and that was without traffic.

James couldn't get there fast enough, but he finally arrived. As soon as he parked in front of the pharmacy, Andrea came running out and jumped into the car. She told him how relieved she was to see him, and how she knew that he would have answers to the problems that were plaguing her. James remained stoic and told her that he was going to drive to a nearby park that he passed along the way. He mentioned that it seemed like a quiet place, and one which was not well populated. They would have the time and privacy to settle matters. Andrea saw how serious James was. She braced herself for whatever James was going to say. However, it seemed like it would be bad news.

James pulled into a parking spot at the end of an area that only had two other parked cars. There was no one else around. He couldn't face her, so he started his comments looking straight ahead. She understood everything he was saying and listened carefully to everything he said about his feelings and his desire to mend and repair his marriage. It hurt to hear those words, but Andrea realized how time can change many things. He also told her that he promised the detectives that he would fully cooperate with them, hoping that they would function as his advocate to the District Attorney. He emphasized how culpable he was, and how his professional life could be damaged forever.

His final suggestion was the knife through her heart: "I will give you some money so that you can temporarily take care of your day-to-day needs, and I suggest that you find a hotel or motel in which you can stay until you make a final decision as to what you are going to do. I do not want to know where you are staying, and I prefer that you no longer call me for help."

Andrea sat in the car and couldn't feel any more disappointed and disillusioned as she did. Her knight in shining armor threw down his sword and was riding in the opposite direction. For a long while, there was total silence in the car. Andrea did not want to cry again, but she felt the tears welling up in her eyes. She was at a total loss for words, and he was fighting to make his comments stick. It was one of the hardest things he had to do, but it was done, and now he had to stand by it. Andrea was able to remain strong. She told him how much she appreciated his help, and that she would honor his wishes.

James saw a cab stand at the entrance to the park. Without saying a word, he started the car and drove to the taxi stand. He got out of the car and went over to the waiting cab driver. James took out a fifty-dollar bill and told the driver to "take her wherever she wants to go." Andrea exited the car and went to the taxi. James opened the door and helped her in. She turned to him, but the words wouldn't come out. Her look was not one of sadness, but one of disbelief. She never thought that James would abandon her like this. She was surprised and shocked, but more so, she was angry. She was angry with him but also herself. She let herself believe that no matter what, the strong bond, love, would conquer all. It was a fairytale that she allowed herself to believe. She only had herself to blame. She agreed not to contact him again, but she was sure he would see her again because she had unfinished business at the hospital!

Chapter Eleven

Another Failure

Andrea got in the taxi, and James closed the door. He nodded to the driver and the cab pulled away. James got into his car but didn't head back toward his home or the hospital. He stayed a good distance behind the taxi that Andrea had taken. He just wanted to make sure that she got settled and safely arrived at a decent location. He had done the right thing, and this was the final step. In addition to his feelings of guilt, he realized that he also cared strongly for Andrea. By following her and knowing where she was, he would be able to respond to her in case of any emergency. That was his justification, anyway.

After what seemed to be a ride that lasted forever, the cab pulled into, in James' opinion, a less than desirable motel parking lot. It was sandwiched between two bars and a club that featured exotic dancers. Time had passed, and it was getting on toward late afternoon. The sun was going down, and what seemed like unsavory creatures were on the rise. They were beginning to loiter in the area of the motel. James looked carefully at the surroundings, and the men who were just "hanging out" near the motel.

As the cab driver stopped the taxi and exited the vehicle, James could swear that he saw the driver nod to two of the "lowlifes" that were there. He thought he saw a confirmation nod in return. James began to feel that this was not the right place for Andrea, but he waited because he wanted her to understand that she should only depend on herself now. As she got out of the cab to go to the registration lobby of the motel, James noticed the two men watching her every move. With the room key in hand, she walked to her designated temporary lodging. She passed the "on-lookers" who apparently had some remarks to direct her way. She ignored their indignant comments and proceeded to her room. When she unlocked the door, she felt immediate pressure on her back and shoulders. She was being forcibly pushed into the room by her two "admirers."

James witnessed the whole thing, and he reached for the police-like baton that he kept in his car for just such occasions. Without thinking and fueled by rage, he ran to the room and burst through the door. Andrea already had her blouse torn and her bra showing. Dr. James Whitly now became James Whitly, the enforcer. He wielded the baton with reckless abandon and made contact with the two cretins. Following yelps and yells, the two men scrambled to the door with James in close pursuit. He got a few more good shots in and was sure that he broke some bones. He stayed at the door and stared at the cab driver who hurriedly entered his car to escape the potential wrath of the enforcer. James was satisfied and turned to Andrea. She was crying, shaking, and hurting from where the men had grabbed her.

James carefully laid her on the bed and superficially examined her for any obvious physical wounds. However, it wasn't those injuries that he was worried about, but the emotional scars that would most likely remain. He held her close to comfort her, and she melted into his arms. Comforting thoughts entered her mind. He didn't abandon her after all, he cared enough for her that he wanted to make sure that she was safe. Thank God, he loved her. Even though she was an emotional wreck, she was uplifted by the mere fact that he was there. In her mind, the relationship would continue, and she would, once again, be able to rely on his good judgement and consoling warmth.

In all good conscience now, how could he leave her to fend for herself? He tried that, and it almost resulted in a major catastrophe. No, he had to rely on an alternate plan, one which he had not yet developed. It was obvious, however, that he could not leave her there. The only other place that could be utilized as a temporary safe haven for her would be his home, and that violated every parameter that he intended to follow. Additionally, he would have to explain to his still unconscious wife that he failed again. Worse than that, he was compounding his failure by offering their home as a sanctuary. He was the perfect candidate to whom one would apply the axion: "Damned if I do, and damned if I don't." His position was not an enviable one.

Putting aside the quagmire involving his wife, he had to worry about the ramifications, when and if, the detectives found out that he was harboring a fugitive. It was more like "when." If that occurred, not only would his professional career be terminated, but his personal freedom could very well be at stake. That notwithstanding, his immediate concern was getting Andrea to safety and not encouraging another “melt-down.” He gently lifted her from her prone position and waited until she no longer was sobbing to inform her that he was taking her to his house. She shook her head and said that she did not want him to get further involved and risk everything. She said it, but she really didn’t mean it. She had no other place to go, and she needed his moral support. He emphasized, however, that she must stay secluded in the house until he could discover another solution. They got in his car and headed to James’ home.

Even the thought of getting her into the house was a scary one for James. His neighbors were always either watching or rather peeking to see what was going on. God forbid if they missed something. The question: “How was he going to get Andrea into the house without anyone noticing?” plagued him. He had to find a way to clandestinely move her from his car to the house. Then it came to him. He had a toolbox, work coveralls and a baseball hat in the trunk. The toolbox and the coveralls were there in case he needed to do some emergency repairs or change a tire. The baseball cap was a remnant from his attendance at a charity softball game. The nurse’s uniform worked, and hopefully, the “repairman” disguise will also be successful. He had no other choice, so it had to work.

Before they got to the house, James drove his car to an isolated area in the neighborhood so that he could retrieve the garments and toolbox from the trunk of the car. That would also be the time that Andrea changed her appearance to reflect a working repairperson. He was at a loss for options. With a little luck, this would work. He quickly removed the props and gave Andrea what she needed. The stage was set for the "repairperson saga," and Andrea looked the part. If they quickly went from the car to the front door, there would be no problems. However, if there were neighbors outside who wanted to say "hello," the plan could collapse like a paper house.

They were there. James drove into the driveway, but, of course, couldn't remotely raise the garage door without the remote that he left on the hallway table. It was just another little obstacle that raised the stress level. James looked around and saw no one outside. Dusk was settling in, making it even more difficult for anyone to clearly see and make any kind of identification. This somewhat counter-balanced the "no remote" disadvantage. He gave the okay for Andrea to exit the car and quickly proceeded to the front door. It went well. He unlocked the door and entered with a sigh of relief when he heard: "Dr. Whitly, is everything all right?" James turned and there was his next-door neighbor, Mr. Fixit, inquiring if he could be of assistance. Andrea had not yet entered the house, so her back was facing the neighbor. James slid to the side so that the "repairperson" could enter.

James' neighbor, Steve, seemed offended that the good doctor, who had on other occasions asked for his help, was now depending on someone else. Steve was not going away so easily. He inquired as to the nature of the problem that the doctor was experiencing. James explained that his buddy, the repairperson, insisted on looking at the network system that was connected to the hospital. James further explained that he had been having difficulty in filing some of his "after-treatment" reports, and because of the confidentiality of patient privacy, the repair had to be done by someone employed at the hospital. James was even surprised at how he produced a good story in so short a time. Steve was satisfied and left, still offering his assistance, if needed.

Finally, James closed and locked the door. He collapsed in the living room recliner and held his head in his hands. This time, Andrea came over to him to offer comfort and consolation. He had temporarily solved one problem, but there were so many others that were just looming. In addition, he would have to go to the hospital and face his wife again. How could he tell her that he failed again? If she were awake and alert, she probably would have told him that "it was over." He couldn't blame her if she did. He failed miserably, but did he have a choice? Did she expect him to just leave Andrea there and possibly get attacked again? He did keep his promise, though. He told Andrea that she could not rely on his help anymore. He told her that he preferred that she didn't contact him again. He even wasn't going to let Andrea know that he knew where she was staying. He really tried this time. Laura had to understand that circumstances had arisen that were out of his control. Would she understand that he put his life's vocation in jeopardy? Would she understand that he violated the agreement that he made with the detectives? Would she understand that he brought about the possibility that he would be arrested and imprisoned? Would she understand? Probably not!

Chapter Twelve

The Patients Listen

James slowly got his thoughts together. He told Andrea that he would have to go back to the hospital for just a little while. The guilt was killing him! He warned Andrea about staying away from the windows and what lights to keep on. He emphasized how vulnerable they were now. Any mistakes could mean the end of life as they know it. It was that serious. Andrea understood and promised that she would be extra careful. Although James saw that she was earnest in her cooperation, his mind wandered back to the other time he left her alone. He couldn't deal with a repetition of that event. He left not really knowing what he would come back to, or if she would actually be there when he returned. He had no choice. He had to get to his wife and explain. He needed to rip off the blanket of guilt that was crushing his chest making it even more difficult to breathe.

On the way to the hospital, his mind was working overtime. He was trying to figure out the best way to approach the subject of his failure again. The more he thought about it, the more he knew that there was no easy way to approach the subject. He would just come right out and tell her that he had no choice, and if it were reversed that she might have done the same thing. Yes, that was the best approach, and while he was at the hospital, he would also stop in and check on Leonard. He decided that he would talk to Leonard also and let him know what had been going on. Although Leonard evolved into a task master, according to Andrea, he deserved to know what was taking place. His talk would be brief and to the point, and if comatose patients can really hear what is going on, Leonard would at least be up to date if and when he regained consciousness. James was giving Leonard more than Leonard gave him, but that is who he was.

It was after hours when Dr. Whitly arrived at the hospital, and although this was to his advantage, he still used the back stairway to reach the third floor. His arrival was undetected by the nurses on the floor as he entered his wife's room. For what seemed like an eternity, he just stared at her and said nothing. He knew what he had to say and how he was going to say it, but admitting failure again was not such an easy task.

He walked closer to the bed and, almost in a whisper, started speaking to her. He began by apologizing for coming in so late to see her. It really was just a delaying tactic to the beginning of his sad commentary. However, once he got into the meat of the story, he couldn't stop. He went on-and-on about how stern he was with Andrea. He emphasized that he told Andrea, in no uncertain terms, that she no longer could depend on him for any help. He also mentioned how close Andrea came to getting caught by Detective Barret, and how Andrea had saved Barret's daughter. He rambled on 'till he exhausted every last fact of what went on in the past few hours. It was a catharsis for him, and he actually felt relieved. Unfortunately, he didn't know how Laura felt or even if she heard his entire story.

So, you failed again. I knew you would. No matter what you tell me or how determined you think you are, that woman has an emotional influence over you that I probably never had. I understand that you tried and are trying, but that's not good enough to save what we once had. Unfortunately, I can do nothing to support you, but only act as the sounding board for your continuous apologies. Frankly, I'm sick and tired of hearing how you tried, but circumstances prevented you from completing the task. As I continue to ponder the situation, I really don't think you want your relationship with her to end. I believe that when she entered your life again, she revitalized feelings that you pushed to the back of your mind, but were always there. And although you would like to deny it, those feelings are even stronger now than they once were. In my mind, you see it as a second chance to follow through on the plans that you and her once shared. James, I hate you for what you are doing, and hopefully soon, I will be able to tell you to your face. Lastly James, please leave me with some dignity and get her the hell out of my house! Oh, by the way, you are also now a criminal. I hope you enjoy your stay in your new digs subsidized by the state, Dr. Whitly.

James just stayed and stared at his wife for a while before he went across the hall to Leonard's room. He stared at Leonard, recalling the betrayal, and now the suffering he imposed on Andrea. James was still a doctor, at least for now anyway, so he checked the patient's vitals and his overall condition. Leonard was recovering well, but still remained, like Laura, in a comatose state.

Before he knew it, James was talking to Leonard the same way he spoke to Laura. The content of his remarks, however, were in stark contrast to what he relayed to his wife. He chastised Leonard for his cowardly betrayal, and how his actions changed his life forever. James expressed his love for Andrea and how, in some small way, he got some satisfaction from the situation in which Leonard found himself. Leonard was a selfish, uncaring, disloyal, narcissist who in James' mind and contrary to the way a doctor should be thinking, truly deserved what he got. James' closing remarks struck a chord with Leonard: "I feel no pity for you. As a doctor, I want you to recover and regain consciousness so that I can tell you to your face what I think of you. If, as studies indicate, you can actually hear me, then you know how I feel. By the way, if you didn't hear Andrea's remarks to you, she wants you dead. She even mentioned that she would like to be the one to send you to hell."

I heard every word you said, James. I even heard what Andrea had said. It doesn't mean a thing to me. I am who I am, and if and when I recover, I will remain that person. I might even attempt to re-claim what is mine. I don't worry about Andrea's threats because I know you will not allow that to happen. You're too much of an upstanding guy to let that happen. You wouldn't be able to handle the guilt if you didn't prevent it. You really don't know how compromised you are. You had better hope that I don't regain consciousness because I know that you are protecting someone for whom the police are searching. I heard the detectives, and they wouldn't be happy about your decision to help a fugitive. By your own actions, you

are leading yourself into a hole that you will not be able to crawl out of. I might not have to do anything.

And yes, do you think your wife would be happy with what you are doing? So, your happy home life will also be destroyed. Well, Dr. Whitly, come and speak to me any time you like. It can only add to my already oversized ego, one that will only grow as things become worse and worse for you and your paramour, Andrea. By the way, you should know that I underestimated how strong a person Andrea could be. Can you imagine her getting up enough nerve to drive a car into me and trying to kill me? You'd better be careful James. To quote a hackneyed axiom: "Be careful what you wish for, you just might get it." Come back soon!

James looked at his watch and realized that he had spent more time than he wanted at the hospital. Andrea was on his mind. She wasn't exactly in a stable frame of mind, and that could lead to a number of things that might need fixing. As he turned to leave Leonard's room, the on-duty nurse entered and was startled to see someone in the room. She immediately recognized the doctor and exclaimed that she wasn't expecting anyone to be in the room. She asked if everything was okay, and if she could be of help. James thanked her and said that he was just checking in on his patients. The nurse was amazed that a doctor would come back on his own time, just to check on the welfare of his charges. She admired his dedication and thought that if more individuals cared as much as he, medical care, in general, would be in a much better place. James smiled and wished her a “good night.” With trepidation, he went on his way to face the unknown. What would he find when he got home?

His mind entertained various scenarios on what would greet him when he arrived at the house. He drove slowly, giving himself time to prepare for whatever awaited him. It was also an opportunity to think about how he could help Andrea but not further compromise his future. He laughed to himself when he thought about saving the future. There were so many negatives that overshadowed a positive outcome, that to seriously think about a satisfactory solution or solutions would be a waste of brain cell use.

He was involved in rush hour traffic, and, to boot, he was approaching the scene of an accident. The flashing police lights sent a chill through his entire body. Would they be flashing when they took him away? It was hard to imagine that he went from a well-respected doctor with an impeccable record to someone who most likely would be looked at as someone who chose to defy good judgement and violate the law, but ironically someone who would still have a record, a criminal one. He passed the police scene and continued on his way home. “Home,” however, no longer meant the same thing.

Chapter Thirteen

Another Escape

James finally completed the last leg of his journey home. As he turned onto his street, he saw what he believed to be the non-descript vehicle that Detectives Krane and Barret used for their transportation. As he got closer, he was sure that the detectives were parked in front of his house. What now?

James pulled his car into the driveway and hesitantly exited. He turned to the detectives' vehicle and saw them exiting at the same time. No matter what, he had to keep them out of the house. "Hello Dr. Whitly, glad we caught you. Just wanted to bring you up to date on our progress and see if you have anything new for us." Detective Krane finished his opening statement and waited for James to respond. James looked doubtful as to the real intent of their visit and answered: "Hello detectives, just came back from a visit to the hospital to check on my patients. I'm surprised to see you here." Barret responded: "We didn't mean to surprise you, but we have some interesting news. Can we go inside and talk for a little bit?" That was the last thing that James wanted to do. He did not feel like talking, and he was hiding their suspect. James could not think of a good reason for not allowing them inside. He was going to have to face the music at some time. This might be that time.

James answered Detective Barret's question with a reluctant "yes," but added that he was tired from a long day at work. He hesitated at the front door as much as possible to give his "stowaway" some extra time to find a place to hide. Hopefully, she was fully aware of the visitors' arrival. He unlocked the door and pushed it open only to see what looked like the aftermath of a tornado. His exclamation of: "What the hell is this?" surprised the detectives as they entered the residence. They scanned the scene and told James to wait outside while they searched the house. This was a typical routine procedure for police arriving at the scene of a possible burglary. James stayed at the entryway as he was told, but from the corner of his eye, he saw a figure sliding alongside the house and making its way to the sidewalk. James turned and saw Andrea walking quickly down the block and eventually out of sight.

Detectives Krane and Barret, with guns drawn, searched every nook and cranny of the house. Their supposed intent was to make sure that there was no "bad guy" still in the house. In fact, however, it was a great opportunity for them to search for anything that would further incriminate Dr. Whitly in the Andrea Canella "attempted murder" case. They returned to the front door and assured James that the house was safe. They told James to look around and see what was taken, if anything. James' superficial search, of course, determined that nothing was missing. The detectives also asked if the doctor had something specific in the house that the thief might have been looking for, and if the doctor knew of anyone who might have been responsible for the mess that lay before them. James' negative replies to all the questions caused the detectives to believe that, once again, Dr. Whitly was keeping pertinent information from them. They took some brief notes and then called for a uniformed patrol officer to respond to the residence to take a burglary report.

As a result of the confusion caused by the burglary, the detectives did not get a chance to talk with James about the progress or lack of progress in the case. They asked that James come to their office the following morning so that they could share information. James agreed but told them that because of his previous appointments, he would have to come in the afternoon. The detectives agreed.

The uniformed officer came shortly after the detectives left and took the report. He informed Dr. Whitly that he would leave the report open for at least forty-eight hours so that the doctor could more thoroughly determine if anything was missing. James thanked the officer who gave him a card with his name and number. He told Dr. Whitly to call the number directly if anything else developed. James thanked the officer and told him that he would call if he discovered anything missing.

As soon as the officer drove away, James turned to face the mess that his guest had created. The diversion was a good one, but did it have to be so destructive? In addition to cleaning up the place, he had to search for Andrea. He saw her reach the end of the block, but lost sight of her as soon as she turned the corner. Knowing Andrea, she could be anywhere. He hoped that she would choose a vantage point where, although hidden out of sight, she would be able to see when it was safe to return.

The problem, however, with her safe return, was obvious. With the detectives at the house and a marked police car in front of the residence, there wasn't a neighbor that was still inside their home. They were nosy as it was, and now they had something to be nosy about.

James was right about the neighbors. It seemed that everyone on the block turned out to visit the doctor and offer any assistance that was needed. They really just wanted to see what was done and find out why it was done. Their quest for knowledge was not lost on James. He called them together in front of his home and addressed the enthusiastically curious crowd. He explained that nothing of value was taken, and that there was no obvious suspect. He further stated that he had no idea why someone would target him or his home. James closed his comments with a warning that they always lock their doors, and a request that they respect his privacy as he attempted to begin the clean-up. Mostly disappointed with the doctor's brief summation, the neighbors slowly dispersed exchanging whispered murmurs about what they thought. Slowly but surely, the street was quiet and devoid of gawking neighbors. It did not mean, though, that they were not still peeking out from behind their curtained windows.

James was hopeful that Andrea was still in the neighborhood just waiting for the right time to re-appear. She had to use careful judgement so that the gawkers would not see her enter Dr. Whitly's home. It was getting darker as the threat of rain became very real. This would be an additional advantage for Andrea's return. The thought passed James' mind as to whether Andrea would return at all. She has had so many "close calls" that she might reconsider returning to a location that has continually put her in danger. But James also knew that if she thought about it, she would realize that she really had nowhere else to go. Although not a hundred percent sure, he was confident that she would try to return.

Andrea, who was cold and who had now started feeling the effects of raindrops, sequestered herself behind a huge traffic sign that was anchored to a hill at the end of his complex. She had seen the detectives, who almost saw her, and the arrival of the uniformed police officer. From her vantage point, she also saw all the neighbors congregate in front of James' home. Finally, after what seemed like an eternity, the street seemed clear. There was no one outside, and the weather was helping her cause. Although Andrea wanted to just run right up to James' front door, she couldn't let her guard down. A careless mistake could lead to disastrous results. She had to wait even longer to ensure invisibility. It was for both their sakes.

James was getting anxious. He continued to put the place in order, but wondered when Andrea would return. It was getting cold and damp, and Andrea was not really dressed for that type of weather. All he needed now, with everything else compounding, was for Andrea to get sick. What does he do then? He did not want to think about it. If she comes back soon, the chances of her catching a harmful chill will be diminished. Where is she? Is she okay? Is she gone for good this time? He needed answers to those nagging questions.

The wait was weighing heavy on James' mind. He could wait no longer for the answer to his questions. He decided to get in his car and drive around the area to see if he could find her. This time, however, he remembered to take the remote garage door opener. If he found her, he would get her into the car, drive to the house, and pull into the garage. This would be the best way for her to return to the house and remain undetected.

James slowly navigated the surrounding area. It was difficult to see through the raindrops as he strained to search for her. He hoped that she would see his car and get his attention. He didn't know what kind of shape she was in, or if she was even able to scan passing vehicles. He could only hope. He circled the area many times with no luck. As time passed, he was becoming less hopeful that he would find her. He was more and more worried that she was not doing well. He had to find her. He pulled up to a red light waiting for it to turn green. Suddenly, the car next to him began to blare its horn. The sound explosion caught his attention, and then he saw it. The reason for the continuous honking was the figure of a person staggering out into the street in the direct path of traffic. He recognized the slim figure as that of Andrea Canella.

James put his car into "park" and ran to get Andrea to safety. She was mumbling incoherently and shivering from her extended stay in the elements. He got her into his car and turned the heat on to "full power." It was a quick ride to the house, and before he knew it, they were in the garage with the garage door shut. James had to carry her into the house. He helped her undress and put on some clean and dry clothes. Her shivering slowed down, and she was more "in the moment." He got her hot tea and stayed with her 'till she drifted off to sleep.

They had, once again, escaped a potential disaster, but still had no solution to the other pressing problems that loomed over their heads. Looking at her laying there so helpless and vulnerable brought his caring feelings right to the surface. He really cared for this woman, but how many times could he save her? He was plagued with many thoughts concerning her and her safety, but the one that was most paramount in his mind was the one that solidified their major concern: "Could Andrea Canella be eventually saved from what seemed like her assigned fate, her ultimate arrest and imprisonment?"

Chapter Fourteen

The Tornado

On the way back to the precinct house, the two detectives discussed a number of items relative to the Canella case. It was Tracy's opportunity to further describe the events of the other day which led her to put out an on-air description of Andrea. Tracy explained that Andrea's being at the same place and at the same time as Sandra and her daughter was a merciful gift from God. Detective Barret passionately explained that if it was not for Andrea's ability and quick response, Sarah might be dead. Tears welled up in Tracy's eyes, and she continued to praise the unselfish and life-saving efforts of Andrea Canella.

David looked at her in a confused way and said: "What are you saying, Tracy? That just because she was able to help out with Sarah that we should look at her in a different way. Let me remind you that she tried to kill her husband who is lying unconscious and wounded in the recovery room at Mountain Pacific Hospital. She is guilty of attempting to take someone's life even though she may have saved another. Unfortunately, one does not cancel out the other. I am sure you know that. Do not let your emotions control your investigative logical thinking."

Tracy was not happy with the "you're a cop first" lecture. She also did not care for the implication that a woman can't separate her emotions from what has to be done. David wasn't usually that way, but today he was obnoxious. She wasn't disregarding any facts about Andrea or the case. She wanted to emphasize that Mrs. Andrea Canella wasn't just a cold-hearted killer. She might have had reasons for doing what she did. That doesn't make her actions right, but it might explain why she resorted to that type of behavior. Tracy put it into her mind that when they caught Andrea, and they would, she would find out what drove their "attempted murder" suspect to such opposing out-of-character actions.

Having spoken to Dr. Whitly for a length of time, the detectives both felt that, once again, he was holding back information. Apparently, the good doctor didn't realize that he might be jeopardizing any chance for leniency either by the district attorney or a hearing judge. James wanted to help, but each time he decided that it was the way to go, his determination wavered because of circumstances that were "out-of-his-control." Both Detective Krane and Detective Barret believed that, at some point, Andrea Canella would return to James' home for comfort and consolation, but more so for advice. That being the case, the detectives arranged for around-the-clock surveillance at Dr. Whitly's house. It was an expensive proposition, but one they were sure would pay off. They went back to their office and advised the boss that surveillance was needed. After giving all the reasons why they felt so strongly about the request, around-the-clock surveillance for the Whitly residence was granted. It started immediately.

While surveillance was being arranged at the police precinct, James was racking his brain for any workable solutions to the predicament that, now, both he and Andrea were facing. However, as he thought about possible solutions, he also thought about what he would tell his wife. She heard, if she could hear, the same hackneyed explanation over and over again. Now, he would have to tell her again. It was easier expressing his feelings to someone who could not offer argument or discussion. He did not know if he could do it face-to-face. If he were to save his marriage, even if Laura had not heard his diatribe a thousand times, he would tell her everything, the whole story when she recovered. She deserved to know, and it would show just how much he wanted everything to be out-in-the-open, even if it delayed any rekindling of past affections. Hopefully, it would not totally kill the possibility of starting over.

James took care of a few things around the house and looked in on Andrea to make sure she was okay. Apparently, fatigue and the damp cold worked to send her into a deep sleep, which she needed. He felt fairly sure that Andrea would be asleep for the night; so, he saw the opportunity to relieve some of the nagging stress that he had been carrying around. He decided to visit the hospital again. Just like the last time, it would be after-hours, and the on-duty staff would be greatly reduced. He also felt more comfortable speaking to his wife when there was no light to shine on his apologetic face. How was he going to couch the fact that, once again, Andrea Canella was in their home and sleeping there. He decided that he would not beat around the bush. He would come right out and tell her. What could she do? What a stupid question that was. In her present condition, she could do nothing. That is why it is better to get it off his chest now. Hopefully, she can hear, and thankfully, she will not be able to do anything about it. As Dr. James Whitly drove, he looked at himself in the rear-view mirror and yelled: "Coward!"

Arriving after hours afforded him the advantage of avoiding the greetings of the working staff. Because the staff was reduced at night, sometimes he could enter the hospital and never be acknowledged. Fortunately, tonight was one of those nights. He took the empty elevator to the third floor and quickly turned into the corridor that led to his wife's room. So far, so good – no recognition or acknowledgement. He made it unscathed. That was the easy part, now he had to speak to his wife. "Hi Laura. Hope you are feeling better. You look good and your vital signs are right where they should be. If things remain as they are, I am sure that, before long, we will be speaking face-to-face. I can hardly wait."

Well, here he is again, my knight in shining armor. What sad story are going to tell me this time. You sound a little nervous. Did you fail again? Probably! Yeah, I'm sure you want to speak to me face-to-face! Would you have the nerve to tell me these events if I was standing right in front of you? I don't think so, even though you say differently. Believe me, I too can hardly wait to regain consciousness. Wow, I cannot hear anything. Why, the pregnant pause? It must be really bad. I am not going anywhere. I will wait 'till you want to start again.

After collecting his thoughts, James began again: "I have some news that you probably will not be so happy hearing. The two detectives, Detective Krane and Detective Barret, paid a surprise visit to the house. It was more of a shock than a surprise because Andrea was in the house when they arrived. They were waiting for me when I arrived home. They asked me to come into the house so that we could talk, and I couldn't think of an excuse not to let them in. I tried to delay, but they were persistent. I opened the door thinking that the game was over, and I would have to face whatever consequences came my way. But low-and-behold when I opened the door, I saw the results of what looked like a tornado landing. The detectives immediately reacted to what they surmised was a burglary."

Get to the point, James. What was the final outcome? You're not relating a mystery novel, just tell me what happened and how it ended.

"Both detectives, with guns drawn, went into their 'search and destroy' mode and told me to wait at the door. In a short while, they had searched the entire house and told me to look around and determine what, if anything, was missing. I did a superficial search and told them that I really would have to do a more careful examination before I could know for sure if anything was taken. They asked a few questions and then called for a uniformed officer to come to the house and take a burglary report."

James, I am half asleep already. Get to the point. What do you want to tell me? Apparently, it wasn't a burglary since your guest had been in the house. Are you going to tell me how

smart she was to create such a diversion? I know; I know. She is a wonderful, smart and cunning female. Cunning in a number of ways. James, get on with it!

"When they left the house, the detectives said that the conversation they wanted to have with me could wait 'till the next morning. I agreed to meet with them in the afternoon, since I had appointments in the morning. Just as they were leaving, the patrol officer arrived at the house. He only stayed for a brief time and told me to call him if I discovered anything missing. When he left, I tried to clean up a bit, but I was disturbed not knowing where Andrea was."

Well, it's about time. We are finally getting to the point where you have to rescue poor little Andrea, again. I am sure you were beside yourself wondering where she could be. Is she okay? Where did she go? Will I find her? And the most unnerving question of all: Will I ever see her again? Keep going, James, it is finally getting to the "good" part. I cannot wait to hear your excuses this time.

"After a brief 'once-over' in the house, I decided to get in my car and look for Andrea. It was dark, cold, and starting to rain. I did not want to compound the problems I already had by having to care for a sick individual."

Of course not. Your unconscious wife is lying in a hospital bed, but you are worried that someone who is dragging you into a bottomless pit might catch a cold. Typical you!

"I looked for quite a while but was unable to find her. I was about to go back home when I heard a loud blast of a horn coming from the car next to mine. That's when I saw the hunched-over figure of Andrea. I took her to my car and drove back home. She was shivering and really out-of-it. I did what I could for her, and finally she calmed down and fell into a deep sleep. I just felt terrible that I had to take her back to the house, but there was nowhere else to go. I did not want you to think that I thought it was okay. That's why, as soon as I could, I came to tell you about it. I feel better that you know. I do not want to keep anything from you."

I am glad one of us feels better. So, I guess she will be sleeping over. That's just great. I wonder what your plan for the morning is. Maybe magically when you return from your meeting with the detectives, she will have disappeared leaving a note that says: "Thanks for everything, asshole!"

After remaining for a while longer and looking longingly at her, James decided that he was going to visit Leonard. However, the more that James interacted with Andrea, the more he loathed Leonard, and what Leonard did to his wife. Andrea may have recovered from the physical abuse that she suffered, but, in James' opinion, the emotional hurt that Andrea experienced may very well last for a lifetime. As James thought on, he recalled the past and began chastising Leonard for a whole lot of transgressions that Leonard aimed at him. And As James continued pondering the horrendous events of the past that negatively impacted his life, Leonard was reeling with satisfaction.

<u>*Hey James, feeling bad for yourself? Get over it. I'm impressed with how much you still care for the woman who*</u>

turned her back on you. You are a fool. She is who she is and will never be anyone else. If she does not get what she wants, watch out! You are taking her under your wing and feeling bad for the situation that she alone created. You are so far in the hole that you will never get out. You are thinking with your heart or your dick, but not with your head. She will ultimately take you down.

Maybe I'm a bit demented with my possessiveness. I will admit that, and I'm sure she told you about it. Oh, and I'm sure she has told you about the deviant sexual abuse that I forced on her. Take a deep breath and smell the roses. She was the one who introduced me to sexual behavior that I didn't even know existed. She is slowly but surely hooking you in if you're not hooked already. She knows what she wants, and she will try to get it in any way that she can. I could care less what ultimately happens to you or her, but in the end, I hate to see a grown man cry.

Hey, by the way, how's Laura? By this time, you might have forgotten that she's here and is still your wife. If she still exists in your conscious thinking, just give Andrea a little more time and she will take care of that. Dr. Whitly, be careful what you wish for.

"You know, Leonard, for a long time I thought about how you stabbed me in the back. But time does heal all, and I had pushed the thoughts of revenge and hate on to a back burner in my mind. Having, unfortunately, been forced to see you again has brought those negative memories to the surface again. Ironically, not only am I ushering you to recovery, someone I once wished "dead," but I must protect you from your wife who wants to kill you. Irony at its best! Take care, Leonard. I am going to comfort your wife, you know, the one who wants to kill you."

Poor Dr. Whitly, if you could only hear me, I am laughing out loud!

Chapter Fifteen

The Sleeping Pills

James left and felt better that he had told his wife everything. He was also satisfied that he let Leonard know how he felt, and that without James' medical treatment, and now, his protection, Leonard might very well be dead. He also thought about other things. He wondered if he might get another surprise waiting for him when he arrived home. If past events served as a predictor of present happenings, he could very well experience another shocking scene or even a disappearance. Although when he left Andrea, she was "dead-to-the-world" in a deep, deep sleep. Maybe, he will escape without another "what-do-I-do-now" incident.

His mind was preoccupied with so many thoughts that time passed quickly, and before he knew it, he was in his driveway. The detective, who was assigned to the surveillance of James' home, did not follow him to the hospital. The instructions were to surveil the house and report if Andrea re-appeared at the residence. If the suspect was spotted, the detective was to notify the main office where an arrest warrant would be sought from a local judge. Thus far, no one but the good doctor entered or left the home, but all the detectives working on the case, especially Detectives Krane and Barret, thought it was just a matter of time before they would have Mrs. Andrea Canella in custody.

James entered the house, and was happily surprised that everything seemed normal, as normal as it could get. After going through the downstairs area, James ventured to the upstairs bedroom where he hoped he would find Andrea fast asleep. He approached the bedroom very quietly not wanting to wake her. He entered and found her in the same relative position she was in when he left. He was elated. There was no new problem that he had to deal with. He gazed at her and felt pity, no not pity, but sorrow because of all the pain and anguish she had gone through. He got closer and sat on the bed next to her. He had left the night table lamp dimly lit when he went back to the hospital but decided now to turn it off completely and let Andrea sleep peacefully and undisturbed. She seemed to be in that "REM" sleep that the body needs to combat stress.

No, this could not be happening! As he turned to the night table to shut off the light, he saw what looked like a prescription bottle lying on top of it. He didn't recall it being there before he left for the hospital. He looked more closely and read the label description. It was a prescription for sleeping pills that he had prescribed for his wife. If he recalled correctly, the bottle was half-filled. But now, he held an empty prescription bottle in his hand. Yeah, Andrea was definitely in a deep sleep, one that was artificially induced by the use of pills. The elation that he first felt on his arrival home quickly dissipated into feelings of urgency and terror. He had no choice. He had to get her to the emergency room so that her stomach could be pumped in an effort to save her life. He knew that once in the emergency room, Andrea Canella would no longer be on-the-run. Her identity would become known, and the police would be notified. James knew, however, that he had no choice. It was truly a matter of life and death.

Wasting no time, James wrapped Andrea in a blanket and carried her to his car in the garage. He placed her in the passenger seat, fastened her seat belt and got in the car. As the garage door opened, the light in the garage remained lit, and the detective assigned to surveillance saw what he believed to be another person in the vehicle. As James pulled away from the house, the detective was sure that he saw someone else in the car. He notified the office about what he saw but told them that he wasn't sure if the passenger was Andrea.

James sped through town and arrived at the hospital in record-breaking time. He parked in the emergency room lot and ran into the hospital for a gurney. He quickly told the emergency room staff that he had an unconscious female in his car, and that she might have taken something to induce sleep. He didn't want to give any specifics yet because that would definitely rule out any chance of evading potential arrest – hers and his. He wanted to leave the "freedom" window open, even if it was just a slight crack.

James, leading the emergency room staff, ran to his car to help place Andrea on the gurney. He quickly opened the door and saw an unbuckled seatbelt and no Andrea. The car was empty. He couldn't believe his eyes, and the staff looked at him in a "what's-going-on" stare. Many questions quickly rushed into his mind. Where the hell is Andrea? Is she okay? Had she duped him into believing that she had taken sleeping pills? Why would she do that? Then, like a bolt of lightning, the answer came to him. She wanted to get to the hospital to do one thing. She wanted to kill her husband.

When James left the car, Andrea followed suit and ran to the rear entrance of the hospital. On the way up to the third floor where her husband lay in his room, she went into the supply room that she had hid in once before, and hurriedly donned nurse's scrubs. She was now in his room staring angrily at his unconscious body. She did not have much time; so, she grabbed a pillow and decided to place it over his nose and mouth, effectively causing him to suffocate. Since he was unconscious, there should actually be very little resistance, and his death should come quickly.

As soon as James realized what was happening, he broke away from the questioning staff and, without saying a word, ran into the hospital and proceeded to the stairway that led to the third floor. She didn't have too much of a head start on him; so, he was somewhat confident that he would get to Leonard before she could do much damage. Hopefully, she didn't have a gun or a knife. If that were the case, his efforts would probably be in vain. He could not let that happen. He did not owe anything to Leonard as a friend, but he was a doctor, and he did take an oath to help and "do no harm." He could not allow harm to come to one of his patients, even if that patient deserved it. James now knew how determined Andrea was to end Leonard's life. Throwing all caution to the wind regarding arrest and imprisonment, Andrea was going to cause her husband's demise.

James was moving so quickly that his feet were running out from under him, and he had all to do to keep from stumbling. He barged through the hallway door and ran into the corridor, stopping at Leonard's room. He looked into the room and saw only his patient. His initial thought was that he judged the situation incorrectly. He moved to the bed and checked on his patient. Leonard set off a "high blood pressure" indicator as well as an increased pulse rating. These symptoms were a sign of stress to the body. He did not notice anything that might have caused the change in vitals until he observed the pillow lying on Leonard's legs at the foot of the bed.

A nurse who heard the commotion came into the room. James asked if anyone had re-arranged the bed, and if there was a reason why a pillow had been placed on Leonard's legs. The nurse was surprised to see the pillow and said that it had been placed on a chair in the room since the patient had no use for it. Maybe, James wasn't wrong. Andrea may have heard him coming and couldn't finish the job. Apparently, she left through the adjoining bathroom door into the next room.

Thanks for coming, James! Did you stop for a coffee and Danish on the way? She almost got me, Doc. Whatever happened to the security officer who is supposed to be ensuring my safety. Oh, that's right, everyone assumed that the threat was over. Well, surprise! I can only say that her determination is only second to the satisfaction she would receive upon my death. Hey, I decided that I do not want to die. I want to be there when you have to say "good-bye" to each other as you head to your own separate cells in your designated penal institutions. Save me, doc, from potential death; so that I can witness your professional demise as well as the incarceration of your loving friend who will, most probably, never see the light of day again.

Because of all the commotion, James figured that the police would soon arrive on the scene. He did not want to face the barrage of questions that he was sure would come his way. He asked the nurse to check on the other rooms to see if everything was okay. It was just an effort to free himself from the nurse's attention so that he could exit without being subjected to her inquiry. He was sure that Andrea had been there, and once again, he had no idea where she went. The whole thing was wearing on him. He had had enough. How many more times would he have to resort to clandestine meetings and harrowing escapes. He had done nothing but try to help someone who, in his opinion, had been subjected to what amounted to inhuman behavior. His thinking was clouded by emotions that surely influenced his actions. However, even those strong emotions weaken when they are constantly bombarded by other negative concerns.

Because he had to make such a swift exit from the hospital, he didn't have time to look in on his wife. He would make it up to her, if he could. But for now, it was necessary to get out as soon as possible. As he exited the rear entrance of the hospital, he saw the police cars parked at the main entrance, and he witnessed an unmarked car pull up to the emergency room entrance. Detectives Krane and Barret exited their vehicle and were approached by another detective who was apparently waiting for their arrival. James had to stay put until the detectives went inside. He would then get into his car and drive. He wasn't sure where he would go, but he just wanted to get away. As he stayed hidden behind the shrubbery, he listened carefully to the conversation among the three detectives.

Detective Krane started the conversation: "Hello Jim, what do you got?" Jim Savarese was the detective who was on the surveillance detail at James' house. Detective Savarese answered: "The night was relatively quiet with Dr. Whitly leaving the house for a while and returning shortly thereafter. Approximately twenty minutes after his return, Whitly went into the garage and, from my vantage point, I believe I saw him help another person into the passenger side of the car. As the garage door opened, he got into the driver's seat and proceeded to drive out of the garage. However, as the car turned to leave, I am sure I saw someone in the passenger seat. Unfortunately, I could not identify who it was." "Thanks, Jim. Did you follow him to the hospital?" Detective Savarese reluctantly answered: "Yeah. I tried to. However, he drove like a bat-out-of-hell, and I lost him in traffic. By the time I got here, Whitly and whoever was in the car with him were gone."

As James listened to the conversation, he realized, for the first time, that the detectives had set up a surveillance on his house. He should have known that the detectives did not take his story as totally truthful. Even though James had agreed to cooperate with the detectives, they didn't believe that he was sincere in his contract with them. So, unbeknownst to James, his compromised involvement had been duly noted. The detectives would definitely want to speak with him, and now he would be "wanted" as much as the suspect in the "attempted murder" case. For the first time in his life, he was thoroughly "out-of-sorts." He didn't know where to go or what he wanted to do. He knew, however, what he should do!

Hey, James. Is that you? I thought I heard your voice across the hall. There seems to be a lot of commotion in Leonard's room. I guess you are so busy that you don't have the time just to stop by and see me. That's just great. Take care of the other things in your life while I remain a sidebar. Without really knowing exactly what is going on, I am sure the commotion and excitement has something to do with the one who apparently is running you ragged. I hope she is worth it because the way things are going, our marriage is slowly escaping our grasp. There has to be more than just words to save a partnership, and unfortunately, you are attempting to rebuild our life on a foundation of words. Without actions, words are just empty promises. You cannot build hope on promises alone!

Chapter Sixteen

The Lion's Den

When Andrea heard the approaching footsteps in the corridor, she made her escape through the connecting bathroom door to the adjoining room. She waited until she heard the person enter Leonard's room before she exited the room that she was in. She hurried to the staircase leading down to the lobby but stopped at the entrance to the second floor. The nurse's scrubs and the uncomfortable nurse's shoes that she was able to "borrow" from the supply room now had to be discarded. When she originally visited Dr. James Whitly's office on the second floor, she remembered seeing a room marked "Lockers." She hastily headed for that room where she hoped she could find other clothes that she could "borrow."

The room was unlocked, and Andrea entered with no one being the wiser. Now, she had to hope that one of the workers forgot to lock the locker. Andrea tried each locker but, so far, none was unlocked. There were only about eight lockers left. All eight were locked, but one of them, even though locked, apparently was damaged and didn't close tightly at the bottom. This was Andrea's only choice.

She looked around for something to stick into the space between the locker door and the frame of the locker. There was a piece of an old locker metal bar lying on top of what looked like some sort of painter's tarp in the corner of the room. She was in luck. She would use that bar to pry open the already damaged locker and hope that it contained clothes that she could use.

As Andrea was about to start her handiwork, she heard approaching footsteps in the hallway. There was no place to hide. She had one option-the tarp. She crawled under the tarp and remained perfectly still. The door opened, and she heard two people enter. They were discussing some of the recent events that had occurred in the hospital, and Dr. James Whitly's name was mentioned. Much to Andrea's dismay, they didn't seem to be in any rush to leave the locker room. The tarp was dirty, musty, and hot, but Andrea was glad that it was there. After what seemed like an eternity, the two intruders left the locker room. Andrea crawled out from under the tarp and took a deep breath. It never occurred to her that this could have been the "men's" locker room. She only realized that she was in the right locker room when she heard the two females talking. Thank God for little favors.

Andrea waited until she was sure the two females were out of earshot. She took the metal bar and began forcing it into the damaged area of the locker. It gave a little, but not enough for her to force open the locker. She didn't give up and kept applying force until the upper hinge locking device bent and finally split. She was in! Things were going her way. She hit the jackpot. Not only were there street clothes available, but she noticed a pair of shoes on the bottom shelf of the locker.

Anything was an improvement over what she presently had on her feet. She dressed quickly in shoes that couldn't fit any better, and carefully exited the locker room. However, there were police officers all over the hospital and getting out unnoticed was not going to be an easy task.

As Andrea entered the corridor, she heard people coming down the corridor behind her. They had apparently received some bad news, and two of the eight people were crying and being comforted by the rest of the group. This was her chance. She procrastinated and waited for the group to catch up to her. She nonchalantly joined the rear of the group. They were so involved with each other that no one even noticed Andrea's inclusion in the group. Since there were so many of them together, they opted to take the stairs instead of the elevator. This afforded Andrea another advantage. The stairway exit was off to the side of the main entrance. She walked with the group, rubbing her eyes as she proceeded. The officer at the front entrance gave them only a cursory glance, not wanting to intrude on the family's grief. She stayed with the group for a short distance and then went her own way through the parking lot. Where to now?

While Andrea was executing her escape, James was waiting for the opportunity to get to his car which was parked in front of the emergency room entrance. A uniformed police officer was also "parked" right at the emergency room entrance. He was apparently standing guard at the door. James could not get to his vehicle with the officer standing at the entrance. He would need a diversion. He called the nurse's station in the emergency room and identified himself as Detective David Krane: "Hello, this is Detective Krane. Could you please tell the officer at the entrance to come to the third-floor nurse's station as soon as possible?" The nurse took the message and relayed it to the officer who quickly left the entrance to meet Detective Krane at the third-floor nurse's station. It worked. James walked quickly to his car and drove out of the parking lot.

Like Andrea, James was also in a quandary as to where he should be going. No place was safe. For sure, the police would be looking for him at his home. He couldn't go there. He definitely wasn't going back to his office. That would be absurd. He didn't want to hang out in a dingy motel room for the entire night, but he might not have a choice. James knew that ultimately, he was going to turn himself in to the police, but he needed some time just to gather his thoughts and put together an explanation for his actions. He also knew that whatever explanation he offered would not be good enough to justify his behavior.

As he thought about his present dilemma, he also couldn't help but wonder what happened to Andrea. He, at least, had a car; she had nothing. His present thinking, however, was tainted by the deceit that Andrea had employed against him. She had made him a pawn in her plan to eliminate her husband. She had played him and put him in immediate danger of losing everything. As long as she could succeed, she didn't care about the sacrifices of others. Still, even with all the negatives permeating his consciousness, he still wondered where she was, and if she was all right. He realized that he was "into her" more than he cared to admit. One way or the other, he had to find her. He couldn't settle his affairs until he was certain that Andrea was safe wherever she was and with whatever she was doing. He cared for her that much.

Andrea knew that both Detectives Krane and Barret were at the hospital investigating the most recent event. They were not actively looking for her; so, she made a decision to appeal to that someone who felt that Andrea had been a "Godsent," and who didn't look at her as a horrible person and a criminal. She remembered the address to which Sandra Harding, Detective Tracy Barret's wife, had driven. She remembered how thankful and appreciative Sandra was regarding Andrea's actions in saving Sarah's life. It was a calculated risk to return to Sandra's home, but Andrea didn't have too many choices, and there weren't too many places where she could go with no money in her pockets. It was either all or nothing. Sandra could turn on her and immediately call the police or listen to Andrea explain everything to her and beg for Sandra's understanding. Additionally, she would have to ask Sandra for money to pay for the taxi Andrea would hire. Talk about moxie!

Finally hailing a cab, Andrea was on her way to explore her fate, whether good or bad. When she arrived at the Harding and Barret home, she asked the cab driver to wait for a moment, and she exited the taxi. When she came face-to-face with front door, her trepidation almost got the best of her, and she fought against just leaving. Instead, she rang the bell and waited.

Sandra opened the door and shock masked her entire face: "You! What are you doing here? You'd better leave, whoever you are." Sandra wasn't giving Andrea a chance to explain; so, she raised her hands in a prayer-like plea and just started talking: "I know that Tracy has told you all about me, and I can't tell you that what she said is wrong. But if I were all bad, would I have stopped to help save Sarah?" Andrea hit a nerve. Sandra just stood there staring at Andrea. Andrea continued: "I didn't know who could be trusted, so I lied about who I was. Sandra, I have no place else to go, and I need to explain to someone what is going on, and what I face. Please let me come in, even if it is just for a few minutes. Please!" Recalling what Andrea had done to help, Sandra stepped aside to let her in. Before Andrea entered, she begged: "Sandra, I have no money to pay for the taxi." Sandra, seeing how dreadful things were, grabbed her bag and gave ten dollars to Andrea.

Feeling a rush of relief, Andrea moved to a better spot inside, and started to tell her tale of woe. Sandra, at one point, interrupted and motioned to a chair for Andrea to sit in. Telling her story became a lot easier as the tension in the room slowly ebbed. Sandra listened carefully to everything that Andrea said and reserved her questions and remarks for when Andrea finished. Sandra's questions having been answered satisfactorily, Andrea asked her for one more favor: "Is it possible for me to use your phone for one quick call?" Without hesitation, Sandra handed Andrea the phone. It would seem that Andrea had moved Sandra slightly over to understanding her side of the situation. Even if Sandra didn't allow her to stay in the house for any length of time, Andrea was sure that Sandra was not going to notify the police or her wife.

His phone rang with an unidentified number, and he answered: "Hello." "Hello James, it's Andrea." James could not believe that it was actually Andrea calling. "Are you okay? Where are you?" There were so many questions that James wanted answered, but he needed to know some specifics first. Andrea hesitated and said: "I am at Detective Barret's home with her wife, Sandra." There was a long pause, then James spoke: "Are you crazy, or have you decided to surrender to the police." She answered quickly: "Neither one. I depended on Sandra's compassion to understand my problem, and she was willing to let me use the phone to get some help. Could you please come by to pick me up? I need your advice, and some place to go. I promise I will never deceive you again." Andrea gave the address to James who said that he would be there in about twenty minutes.

After he hung up with Andrea, the realization of what he was doing hit him like a brick. He was going into the lion's den; the lion was hungry, and he was the red meat. That notwithstanding, Andrea's pull was stronger than the potential for self-destruction. He pressed harder on the gas pedal. He could not get there fast enough!

Chapter Seventeen

Any Port in a Storm

After being notified by the office that Dr. Whitly left his home with apparently another individual in the car, Detectives Krane and Barret responded to the Mountain Pacific Hospital. They conferred with the detective who had the surveillance detail on the Whitly home, and then went to the third floor of the hospital. Although not identified, it was their joint belief that the other individual in Dr. Whitly's car was Andrea Canella. The emergency room staff had informed the detectives that when they went out to the car to place the unidentified female onto the gurney, the person was gone. There was no one in the car. It was then that Dr. Whitly hurriedly left them and ran into the hospital.

Connecting all the dots, David and Tracy assumed that Dr. Whitly was rushing to the third floor to check on his patient, Leonard Canella. The detectives were now in Leonard's room looking for any indications of what might have occurred or what might have been interrupted. Everything seemed to be in order, and according to the attending physician, the patient seemed to be okay.

Well, thanks for coming. Any later, you might have been examining a corpse. I hate to admit it, but the guy you are looking for just saved my life, no thanks to you two. Maybe, you should think about re-establishing a guard at my door. Although you may not see anything that indicates that I was a stone's throw from death, it might be a good idea to be "over-cautious" and have someone watching my room. Apparently, you came to the hospital because you thought that there was a possibility that something might be going down. Well, for your information, it did. Use your head and make sure nothing happens again. Do what you are paid to do, protect and serve. Boy, I wish I could give you a piece of my mind!

While the detectives were there, they decided to visit Mrs. Whitly's room. Again, there was no indication that anyone was even there. However, while they discussed what they believed might be occurring, the night head nurse came to Laura's room to inform them that someone had broken into one of the lockers in the female locker room. They went with the nurse and examined the area. They also interviewed the owner of the locker who told them that all her clothes, including her shoes, had been taken. At least, they now had a description of what Andrea was wearing, if in fact, the thief was Andrea.

So now, Andrea was in the hospital, right across the hall. That means that my loving husband cannot be far behind. The leash only stretches so far. In addition to everything else that is going on, Andrea is now a thief. Breaking into a locker is a desperate measure, and, apparently, she has become a desperate woman. These two detectives, however, seem to be relentless in their pursuit. Sooner or later, she will be caught

and probably in the company of Dr. James Whitly. I would bet the house on it!

The detectives had done all they could at the scene; so, they decided to go back home and meet early in the morning to get their thoughts together. Sleeping on a case sometimes helps. They wondered if Dr. Whitly would still come to meet with them tomorrow afternoon. If he had nothing to hide, he would. However, at this point in the investigation, the detectives both felt that James had an enormous amount of information that he was hiding. They doubted that he would keep the appointment. They left the hospital and headed home.

As the detectives were leaving Mountain Pacific, James was arriving at the home of Detective Tracy Barret. As he stepped out of the car, he just shook his head in disbelief that he was actually standing in front of the detective's house. That same detective who, with her partner, might soon place both Andrea and him under arrest. Apparently, Andrea had been looking out of the front window because, even before he started up the walkway, the front door opened. There was Andrea standing beside Tracy Barret's wife, Sandra. He hesitantly approached as Sandra waved him into the house.

James didn't know where to begin. Should he start by directing his comments to Sandra or commence with the thousand questions he had for Andrea? That decision was not for him to make, however, as Sandra began speaking: "Dr. Whitly, I am Sandra Harding, the wife of Detective Tracy Barret. Andrea has told me an awful lot about her situation and your involvement. I am not condoning anything that you or Andrea have done, but I feel that I owe a great deal to Andrea after she saved my daughter's life. That having been said, I cannot continue to make things more difficult for Tracy." James quickly and apologetically answered: "Ms. Harding, I cannot thank you enough for what you have already done. I apologize for putting you in such a compromising position. I don't know how this whole situation will turn out, but I am sure, it will end soon." Sandra nodded her head: "I am not passing judgement on you or Andrea, but you have to understand that, at this point, I too can be found guilty of assisting you. It is getting late, and I don't know when Tracy will come home; so, I have to ask you to leave." James and Andrea both thanked Sandra again, and they quickly left the house.

When they got in the car, Andrea started to thank James, once again, for coming to her rescue. He abruptly interrupted her and began a tirade describing how he felt about being used and deceived. He also questioned the sanity of her attempts at killing her husband. At the conclusion of his angered remarks, James recommended that they both turn themselves into the police and, as the saying goes, "throw themselves on the mercy of the court." This is not what Andrea wanted or hoped to hear. She remained totally quiet, and the silence in the car was deafening. This was not how it was supposed to be. James broke the silence: "Well, what do you think?" In a calm but focused tone, Andrea answered: "You can do what you want, but I am not going to spend the rest of my life in prison." She turned to him: "I will not rest until I kill that man, and if I have to eliminate obstacles in my way, I will." James took that statement to mean even him. It was a cold and calculated threat, and one which he could not ignore. He couldn't just let it stay out there unclarified: "Are you implying that I may be one of those obstacles that would have to be removed? If it is, then I totally misplaced my concerns, and yes, even my love. You should also know that I do not react well to threats, whether they be direct or veiled." Andrea realized that she may have shown her cards too soon; so, she took a step back: "James, absolutely not. I would never think of intentionally hurting you. I care too much for you." He retorted: "Andrea, you said 'never,' and yet, a long time ago, you already did."

He got his point across, and, once again, there was only silence. He broke the silence and told her that he would give her some time to think about his recommendation. He also told her that he was open to any other alternative suggestions. He emphasized that they were in this "thing" together, and that they would both be negatively affected by whatever they decided upon.

Andrea's wheels started turning. She knew that she had to keep him on her side because, with his help, it would be much easier to complete her vendetta. She told him that she would think about everything he said, and emphasized again how sorry she was for deceiving him. He took her apology and regret with a "grain-of-salt." He had heard it all before. His immediate concern was centered around where they would go tonight. He didn't want to go to another dingy motel where you could sign in as "John Hancock" and get a room, but, unfortunately, they didn't have much of a choice. He did not like living as a criminal on the run, but, in reality, that's exactly what he was. He was no longer that renowned surgeon who chaired the Neurology Department at Mountain Pacific Hospital. Hell, for all intents and purposes, he wasn't even a practicing doctor. What had he done?

James drove for a distance until he found what he thought was the best of the worst motels in the area. He told Andrea to wait in the car while he registered for a room. He left the car, and, because of her previous actions, he didn't really know if she would be there when he returned. At this point, he was unconcerned if she did disappear. If that was the case, then a decision would have been made for him. It might have even been the best thing. Using a fictitious name, he signed the register log and took the key for the assigned room. He went back to the car and with Andrea, drove down the row to the numbered room. They got out and went into their "luxury accommodations." They had no choice; so, they would make do.

James and Andrea were both very tired; so, they agreed to retire as quickly as they could. James had taken a small bottle of sparkling wine from the glove compartment of his car. It was a miniature bottle that James was saving for an impromptu celebration with his wife when she awakened. But now it was going to serve another purpose. He showed Andrea the bottle and suggested that they toast to making the right decision in the morning. She thought that it was a great idea, and it relaxed some of the obvious tension in the room.

James opened the "twist-off" top and went into the bathroom to get two cups. He poured the wine into the cups but added a little something extra to Andrea's. James had taken some powerful sleeping pills with him when he was at the hospital. He intended to take them for himself because, with all the problems on his mind, he was having problems getting to sleep and remaining asleep. However, tonight, he was going to make sure that when he awoke in the morning, that Andrea was still there and not creating more problems for him. He brought the drinks into the main room and toasted with Andrea to "better days and good solutions." They emptied their cups and got into bed. There was only one bed; so, they had to share it with the understanding that they would just sleep in it. Before long, they both drifted off to sleep. James was relaxed with the thought that Andrea couldn't cause any more chaos. Andrea "fell off" in the deep throes of a pill-induced sleep.

Tomorrow would be a big day, and James went to sleep entertaining the idea that it would probably be better if tomorrow never came.

Chapter Eighteen

Sandra's Mistake

Detective Tracy Barret drove home with the developing details of the Andrea Canella case heavy on her mind. Maybe, sleeping on it might be a good thing. Not that waking up in the morning would serve up a miraculous outcome to closing the case, but it would allow for more clear thinking. Fatigue, many times, just adds to confusing the facts with theory, and it produces a fog of ideas rather than a clear picture of events. Tracy tried to put the case out of her mind, and before she knew it, she pulled into her driveway. It could not come soon enough.

Usually, as long as Sandra was still awake, she would greet Tracy at the front door. This time, however, the door remained closed. Tracy just assumed that her wife was asleep. Tracy opened the door, and, to her surprise, she saw Sandra wide-awake sitting on the couch. By the look on Sandra's face, Tracy immediately knew that something was bothering her. Tracy really didn't need this right now, but she couldn't ignore it. She had just wanted to take a warm bath and retire for the night. Apparently, that wasn't to be. Detective Barret closed the door and moved over to their couch to sit next to her wife: "What's bothering you? You look concerned about something. Tell me what it is." Sandra looked at Tracy and clutched her hand: "I know you are not going to be happy with what I'm about to tell you but try to understand why I did what I did." Tracy's face began to show worry: "Sandra, just get to the point. What happened or what did you do?"

Sandra felt better standing up, so she released Tracy's hand and started pacing around the living room: "I had an unexpected visitor tonight. When I answered the bell at the front door, I found Andrea Canella staring at me and asking to speak with me." Tracy, both shocked and surprised by the revelation could only say: "What!" Sandra quickly continued: "My initial response was a stunned 'what are you doing here, whatever your name is?' But Andrea quickly asked if she could just come in for a moment because she really had no place else to go. She apologized for lying to me and pleaded for me to just listen to her side of the story. She admitted her guilt and looked sincere and pitiful as she spoke. I let her in the house."

Tracy Barret could not believe what she was hearing. Her partner, her wife, offered the main suspect in an attempted murder case sanctuary in the investigating detective's home. Could it be any worse? Tracy controlled her angst and asked: "How long did she stay? What did she have to say? How long ago did she leave? Did she tell you where she was going? Do you realize what you have done?" With each rocketed question, Tracy's voice got louder and louder. Her emotions were getting the best of her. She realized what was happening and took a step back. She took a deep breath and asked Sandra, whose eyes were filling with tears, to "please continue."

Sandra Harding dabbed her eyes and, after taking in three or four deep breaths, continued: "Tracy, you have to realize that we both owe her an awful lot. She saved our daughter's life, and that was paramount in my mind when I let her in. After explaining what led up to her actions regarding the hit-and-run, she asked to use the phone. Andrea called Dr. Whitly and asked him to come to the house to pick her up. He arrived in about twenty minutes, and then they both left. They did not say where they were going. I have been sitting here trying to figure out how I was going to tell you what I did. I know I should not have helped them, but I did. I know that I have made things more difficult for you, and I'm sorry. I just could not turn my back on someone who potentially risked her future to help me, our daughter and, yes even you."

Tracy just sat there stunned. It was difficult to take everything in. Not only had Sandra aided a fugitive, but she also helped her flee with another person who was a "person-of-interest" to the police. Not only had Sandra obstructed an investigation, but she put one of the investigating detectives in a hopelessly compromising position. Tracy, who was usually a decisive, goal-oriented law enforcement officer, found herself groping for possible solutions that would not incriminate Sandra. She also needed solutions that would not directly connect her to this puzzling, misleading, risky chain of events. How could Sandra put her in such jeopardy? But that wasn't the real question. The more focused question was: "How do I bring this case to a successful conclusion and still remain unscathed?" She was not sure that "successful" and "unscathed" could co-exist.

After speaking with Sandra, Tracy just left the room. She needed some time to be alone and think about things. She figured that if she could quickly bring the case to a successful ending, that maybe, just maybe, much of what previously occurred could be “smoothed over” by the arrests of Andrea Canella and Dr. James Whitly. There was no time to waste. Although it was late and she was dog-tired, Tracy needed to go out and look for Dr. Whitly’s car, and ultimately effect arrests.

Tracy assumed that Andrea and James knew that the police would be looking for them at their usual haunts like the hospital and James’ house; so, the only alternative left was a local, or not so local, motel room. Tracy prepared a search grid with all of the motels in the two adjoining towns. James had to know that his car was easily recognizable, and because of that, he would want to drive outside of the town limits before he parked in a motel parking lot. She would cruise as many motels as possible tonight and continue tomorrow. It would take half the time if she had someone helping her, but she did not know how her partner would react to the present scenario, so she set out to search on her own.

Tracy came out of her seclusion in the bedroom and told Sandra what she was going to do. Sandra begged Tracy to let her help, but Tracy was not going to compound matters by including her wife in what amounted to a manhunt, or more specifically, a car hunt. The detective was still uptight about Sandra’s actions and left without even a “good-bye.” That was more than Sandra could take and the welled-up tears began to flow freely down her face. What had she done? Why was she so foolish as to put the welfare of two total strangers before the welfare of the love of her life? She almost felt that she had caused irreparable harm to their relationship. She would have to work extra hard to cement the cracks that she had allowed to develop in their rock-solid matrimonial bond.

Detective Barret visited a number of motel parking lots but came up empty-handed. She had only put a small dent in the many locations that she had to examine, but she was already dragging. She had a long day, and now, an even longer night. Although she wanted to drive to as many motels as she could, the fatigue of the day won over, and she had to curtail her search for James' car. She did not want to fall asleep at the wheel, and she felt the strong pangs of sleep grabbing at her consciousness. For her own safety, she had to call it "quits."

Tracy came home to a totally dark house. There were no lights inside or on the outside of the house. It was unusual for Sandra not to leave the exterior lights on as long as Tracy was still not home. However, the whole night had been unusual, why not this? Tracy entered the house and remained as quiet as she could. Knowing her wife, Tracy imagined that Sandra went upstairs and probably cried herself to sleep. It's a way to escape reality and the stress of bearing the guilt involved with a hurtful action. In Tracy's mind, it wasn't such a bad thing to do. Unfortunately, it is not something that Tracy could ever do. She was a realist and wanted to face things as they occurred, accepting either the praise or the blame for her actions. She entered the bedroom and quietly undressed. She slowly got into bed and let out a big silent sigh of relief. She really wanted to tell

Sandra that everything was going to be all right, but, in reality, she wasn't sure it would be. Just as Tracy started drifting off to sleep, Sandra turned to her and told her that she had something else to say about the evening's events.

Tracy looked at her and said: "I don't know if I can digest any more information about tonight. Is it important or can it wait until tomorrow?" Sandra answered: "I want to get it off my chest now." Tracy reluctantly nodded: "Okay, I am all ears. What is so important?" Sandra started: "When Andrea first came to the front door and started asking for my understanding and patience, I looked over her shoulder, and only realized, then, that she had taken a taxi to come to the house. Andrea saw me looking and interrupted her story to let me know that she had no money for the cab." Tracy looked at her in disbelief: "Tell me that you gave her money for the cab ride! You paid for her taxi fare?" The answer came swiftly: "Yes, I did."

Tracy nodded her head in a confirming gesture and in a disconcerting but caring way, propped Sandra up and said: "With everything else that is going on around us, you couldn't sleep because you failed to tell me that you paid for Andrea's cab ride? I don't believe it, but knowing you, I should. If there is nothing else earth-shattering that you must reveal to me, I am going to try and get some sleep. We can talk about everything tomorrow and see what we can possibly do to avoid bringing your involvement to the forefront. Let's hope for the best, because it can't get any worse. Good night." Unfortunately, the events of the day and night prevented either one from having a "good night."

Chapter Nineteen

The Staircase Meeting

James was sleeping with one eye open. Even though Andrea had swallowed the sleeping-pill wine, he was still uncertain about her staying asleep through the night. Also, he had a lot of things on his mind, one of which was the condition of his wife, and when he would be able to see her again. He really wanted to speak to her, and he wanted to be there when she finally woke from her coma. The way things looked, however, his visit to the hospital would probably result in his arrest. He had to work something out where he could see her and not jeopardize his freedom. That was easier said than done!

As he started to formulate a plan, he knew that he would have to get rid of his car and rent or buy a new vehicle that the police would not be looking for. He was amusingly shocked that he was actually thinking like a seasoned criminal, planning his getaway. In fact, he was a criminal, and every day he was more and more culpable for his criminal activity. He was tired of running and hiding, and he thought, again, about just going to the police and ending this stressful, chaotic course of action. He knew, however, that Andrea would strongly oppose any such suggestion. Maybe, she would accept it after she completed her vengeful task, but right now, that was paramount on her mind.

He knew that he was letting his emotional connection to Andrea control his logical thinking. He had to weigh the possible loss of Andrea and his freedom over the ability to profess to his wife how wrong he was, and how he wanted her forgiveness to pave the way for a fresh start. Did he want to lose Andrea for good? No, not really. Did he want to lose his freedom? Absolutely not!

James knew that whatever the outcome, he would probably never be able to practice medicine again. That realization stabbed like a knife through his heart. He trained his entire life to help people maintain their health. Now, he would have to stand-by and watch others do what he should have been doing. There were so many things on his mind that they combined to induce involuntary sleep. He had solved nothing and slipped into a deep, trance-like sleep.

James awoke later than he had wanted. He had a lot to do and very little time in which to do it. He rolled over to check on Andrea, but to his chagrin, he felt, saw, and touched nothing. Even with the strong dose of sleeping pills, her adrenalin must have been working overtime because she was up and gone again. He knew she could not have gone far because she had no means of transportation. She didn't, did she? He hurriedly ran to the motel room window, looked out and observed an empty parking spot where his car once stood. It was he who had no means of transportation, not her. He meant to hide his car keys, but being extremely tired, he forgot to keep them out of sight. It's not that he didn't think of the possibility that Andrea might take the car, but he couldn't fight off the clutches of sleep long enough to complete the task that now left him stranded.

As James quickly dressed and figured out a way to get a ride, he wondered if it ever occurred to Andrea that the police would be looking for his car. That every police officer in the surrounding area would have a description of his car. They would have instructions to stop the vehicle and detain the driver. She might not be thinking with her head but rather with her emotionally influenced heart, a hateful heart that would only be satisfied when the dastardly deed was done. She was risking it all because she wanted it done now. She just couldn't wait any longer. According to her, Leonard had lived long enough.

James' plan was to exchange his vehicle for one that would not be on the police "stop" list. Well, that was out of the question, now. For all he knew, she might have already been picked up by the police, and his car impounded. If that were the case, it would make his movements even more difficult. He planned to travel to the hospital and stay out of sight until he thought it safe to enter and go to Laura's room. After the last close call in Leonard's room, James figured that the hospital had a security guard stationed in or in front of his friend's room. This eased some of his concern regarding Leonard's safety, but he knew that, even though there was an obstacle, Andrea would attempt to reach Leonard. He pondered the idea of notifying the hospital that Andrea could possibly be on her way there, but that notification would also put everyone on an "alert" status and make it more difficult for him to get in to see his wife. He selfishly decided against it.

James asked the cab driver to stop the cab about fifty yards away from the hospital entrance. He exited the taxi and walked between the rows of parked cars until he reached a point where he could see everything and still remain out of sight. He waited for a long while to see how well police and security guards were patrolling the hospital. He was also looking around the lot in search of his car. He didn't see his car, but that didn't mean that Andrea was not there. Maybe, she was just smart enough to park it in an area where it wouldn't be discovered so easily, and there were a number of those hidden areas available.

Only a short distance behind James, Andrea was looking at the possibility of dashing into the hospital. Not only was law enforcement an obstacle, but now James became a problem. If she had to put James temporarily out of commission, she would do it. She was clutching a large rock in her hand that she would use to knock out James. She didn't want to hurt him, but she was not going to allow him to stop her. And she knew that if he saw her, he would attempt to do just that. She slowly approached his position, when all of a sudden, he ran from his cover to the rear doors of the hospital and disappeared inside. She was glad that she didn't have to use force against James, but now he might even present more of a challenge.

James took the rear stairway to the second floor and clandestinely entered his office. He used only the light from the corridor as he searched his office for hospital garb. Fortunately for him, he had left a white coat and a stethoscope in his closet. He grabbed both items and prepared to leave his office when a floor nurse passed slowly by the office door and took a long look inside. Apparently satisfied that the security of the office was not violated, she continued on her way. He remained quiet and still until he was sure that the nurse was gone. As he left his office, he saw the nurse leave the floor and go through the stairway door. This was the same stairway that he was going to use to get to the third floor and his wife's room. He carefully entered the stairway and proceeded up the stairs only to find the nurse he had previously seen, crouching down in an apparent effort not to be detected.

Once again, Andrea had been able to lift a nurse's outfit and quickly proceed to the third floor. As she waited in the stairway until it was safe to proceed, she heard noises behind her on the staircase. She turned and came face-to-face with the person she left in the motel room. James looked up and saw an astonished Andrea Canella. He was also shocked to see her. They both hesitated in their movements, and they knew that they had to remain quiet. They either worked together and proceeded accordingly, or their efforts would end right there on the staircase. They huddled together and decided that no one would be looking for a doctor and a nurse walking together and talking medicine. Although they would venture on to the floor together, James let Andrea know that, in no way, would he allow her to do anything to Leonard. He would stop her even if it meant that they would both be caught. She apparently understood, but James knew that her word was like pirate's gold, never found. So, he cautiously proceeded with "Nurse Andrea" down the corridor.

It was going to be a little strange for James to speak to his wife while Andrea was there in the room. However, there was no way that James was going to let Andrea get out of his sight. The guise that a doctor and nurse would easily get by the scrutiny of a security guard proved to be correct. Dr. Whitly just nodded to the security guard and kept talking to his nurse. They entered Laura's room and took a deep breath. James motioned Andrea to sit in the chair in the rear of the room. He then turned his attention to his wife: "Hello Laura. Things have really become confusing and stressful. Unfortunately, I had to spend the night again with Andrea who is here with me now. I know that you are not happy with that, but I had no choice. It is getting closer and closer to my surrendering both Andrea and myself to the police. If I do that, there is a strong possibility that I will face prison time. In Andrea's case, there is no doubt that she will be incarcerated for a number of years."

Oh, this is just great. You are here with your "girlfriend." Do you really think I give a damn whether or not she goes to prison? I could care less! And you know what, for everything you have done to protect a criminal, it might be justified that you be sentenced to jail-time. I do not wish that for you because I think it would kill you. Understand, if you are convicted and sentenced to jail, don't think for a minute that your loyal, sappy wife will be waiting for you with open arms. Our relationship will be over. Just the way you are letting Leonard's wife control your decision-making is enough for me to end whatever we had. Adding jail to the equation will put the final nail in our marriage-saving coffin. I wish I could turn my hearing "off." I don't feel like listening to any more of the

same sob story. I also wish that I was conscious and could tell you these things face-to-face. I am not there yet, but I really feel that it will come soon. Hey, you'd better leave now before you and your friend don't have that choice. Your leaving will also help reduce my level of stress that you always seem to raise.

"I will think seriously about our surrender, so that the present chaos can be controlled, and maybe re-direct my attentions to you and me. I love you."

Please leave before I drown in your pathetic attempt at regret and wishful thinking; and "love," you probably don't even know what it means as it relates to marriage.

Much to the chagrin of Andrea Canella, James, as usual, bent down and kissed his wife's forehead. He then told Andrea to get up so that they could leave. Before she left the room, she asked if they could briefly stop in Leonard's room. James' initial reaction was to say "no." However, she pleaded with him and finally convinced him that a brief stop into Leonard's room would not hurt their successful exit. He cautiously escorted Andrea past the security guard and into Leonard's room. Again, their presence did not raise any suspicion with the guard.

As she briefly stared at her husband and motioned to James that they could leave, she crimped the oxygen line that was out of James' sight. They left together, and as they progressed down the corridor toward the staircase, they heard the squeal of an alarm emanating from Leonard's room. Nurses were running past them toward the alarm. James looked at Andrea and had no doubt that she had done something that initiated an alarm signal. He roughly grabbed her arm and directed her to the stairway. When they were through the door, James demanded: "Andrea, what did you do? You just can't help yourself, can you? I really think that you should be stopped, and I will make sure you do not have the opportunity to act again." Andrea, realizing that James was serious about his threat, looked at him and said: "James, I'm sorry," and she shoved James down the flight of stairs. He was still conscious and breathing as she left him lying at the bottom of the staircase. He was groggy and hurting, but he was able to get up and continue to exit the hospital. Although she was well ahead of him, he vowed that he would find her and stop her.

This is just great. With a guard at the door and you, James, probably standing right beside Andrea, allowed her to apparently cut off my supply of oxygen. I'm beginning to wonder how sacred life is to you. You are so immersed in emotions that you are unwittingly allowing Andrea to get away with numerous attempts at my life. You know, James, you are just as guilty as she is. Wake up! If you do not stop her right now, she will succeed; and by the way, you have to realize that no matter how much she professes to love you, she will toss you aside like a dirty old rag to reach her goal. I feel sorry for you. You will wind up being a victim of her abuse if you do not take her down, now! I cannot wait to recover!

Chapter Twenty

A Gentle Shove

Just a short time ago, while James had been sleeping and before she left, Andrea took some cash and a credit card from James' wallet. She had no other source of funds; so, she had to "borrow" from James. It was good she did because the way things worked out, she didn't have James' support or financial help. She had to find a place where she could rest and think about her next move. Her only option was another sleezy motel room. She didn't want to use James' car anymore because she was sure that the police would be searching for it; so, she opted for another taxi ride. The problem was that she didn't know where to tell the cab driver to go. She remembered last time that the driver was working with two undesirables who attempted to rob and attack her; so, she had to be really careful where she directed the driver to go.

James staggered from the stairway landing and disappeared into the parking lot. He was hurting from his fall but was more wounded by the fact that Andrea could resort to such a dangerous attack on him. Apparently, her determination to kill was stronger than her will to love. He'll have to remember that for the future, if there is a future. He had no car and really no place to go. He would take a cab to a car rental place and get some wheels. He would then decide where he was going to set up shop. He had to plan his next move and try to figure out what Andrea would do next. He knew she wouldn't stop until she succeeded or was caught in the attempt. However, she was getting better and better with her planning. He also noticed that one of his credit cards was gone, and the cash in his wallet had been reduced. Certainly, the result of Andrea's handiwork.

In her travels, Andrea remembered seeing a modern, newly renovated Bed and Breakfast lodge. She asked the driver if he was familiar with the location, and he was. She felt relatively safe in choosing this location since it was not the usual place for just an overnight stay. James would not think about this place, and she didn't have to worry about funds. She had his credit card. She was quite happy about her choice. It was clean, up-to-date, and the proprietors were more than helpful. It was the perfect place to relax and plan the next move. It was getting harder and harder to penetrate the hospital security; so, the next attempt might have to be the last. Therefore, it had to be good enough to succeed, and hopefully afford her the opportunity to execute an unhindered escape. She had a lot to think about, but for now, she would de-stress in a nice hot bath. She wondered how James was, and what he was thinking. She regretted having to resort to such a drastic measure, but he was seriously thinking about going to the police. She could not let him do that, at least, not now. He left her no choice but to react in a way that afforded her another way out.

As time passed, James' injuries hurt even more. He didn't think that he broke anything, but he was badly bruised. He had to find a safe location. He needed to rest. He was a member of the local community club as were other doctors who worked at the hospital. It was daytime during working hours, and there was a good chance that none of them would be there. He decided to take his chances. The decision was a good one, and he was able to enter and get situated without any unnecessary attention. He went into one of the private rooms and just laid down. He had to clean up, but for now, he had to rest. He would attend to the other things after a brief respite.

As she immersed herself in the luxury of a warm bubble bath, Andrea decided that if she could not come up with a fool-proof plan, she would take her time and wait until her husband was released from the hospital. She would find another way to terminate his existence, maybe even in a better way. She would, nevertheless, have to control her anxiety level because she wanted him dead as soon as possible; but if she developed a better plan by waiting, she would. The disadvantage to waiting, however, was the risk that the police would find her, and then her goal of exterminating Leonard would be thwarted. The whole thing became a balancing act. It all depended upon what kind of immediate scheme she could conjure up.

James slept for about an hour, then wearily rose to wash off the dirt from his fall. He felt worn and tattered, but he had to rise above those feelings because there was a great deal to do. He had to find Andrea and stop her before she did something that would ultimately dictate her future; and there was no future in a life sentence. He knew that Andrea did not like the motel accommodations where she was recently forced to stay.

The unfortunate fact was that most of the motels in the area were fashioned in the same way. Since she now had some money and a credit card, she just might want to pay for something a bit more to her liking. There was only one such establishment in the immediate area, and he would check it out as soon as he made himself more presentable. He would first go to a car rental location and get new wheels which he desperately needed.

Detectives Krane and Barret had been called to the hospital again to check out a vehicle that looked like Dr. Whitly's car. It was, in fact, his car, but a thorough search of the car only produced a receipt from a motel in a neighboring town. The detectives were sure that Andrea Canella and James Whitly would no longer be anywhere near the place. They checked it out anyway, and their assumption was correct. Both detectives were sure, however, that the two fugitives were still someplace in the area. James still had his wife in the hospital, and Andrea was still determined to kill her husband.

Because of the individual that she was, it was very difficult for Tracy to keep information from her partner; so, in a private moment in their vehicle, Detective Barret felt obliged to get something off her chest: "David, I need to tell you something." She looked quite concerned and serious: "Sure anything, Tracy. What's up?" Tracy hesitantly continued: "When I left the hospital last night and went home, I was greeted with a surprise upon my arrival. Sandra was waiting with bated breath to tell me some important news." David exclaimed: "Don't tell me the two of you are adopting another kid." "No nothing like that, that would be too easy. While I was at work, Sandra had an unexpected visitor, Andrea Canella. You know - one of the two people we are desperately searching for. When the bell rang, and Sandra answered the front door, to her surprise, Andrea, or her aka of Marie Church, was standing there. As Andrea had been previously involved in saving our daughter's life, a story for another time, Sandra felt obliged to at least let her in and hear her story. I know it was a foolish thing to do, and I told her so. Andrea asked to use the phone, and in about twenty minutes, Dr. James Whitly showed up at the house. They left shortly after his arrival. Overall, my wife aided two fugitives who we are pursuing." Tracy took a deep breath and patiently waited for her partner's reaction.

Detective Krane's initial response was not a good one, but one that Tracy expected. He looked at her, and then just looked away shaking his head: "I don't know what you want me to say. I am sure you realize that Sandra violated the law, but more so, she has put you, and now me, in a very compromising position. In my opinion, the right thing to do would be to let our boss know what happened; and after he notifies the district attorney, be guided by what the D.A. tells him. I am sure it will not be to our liking, but that is the right thing to do. However, we do not always do the right thing, do we?"

Tracy Barret looked at her partner quizzically. What was he implying? Keeping the whole scenario from everyone could develop even into a greater problem where losing their jobs could become a real possibility. David Krane looked at her and said: "For now, I think we should continue to run the investigation and bring it to a successful conclusion. That could only serve to help us out. Let's not get bogged down in the 'what ifs' and do our job."

To say the least, Tracy was flabbergasted by her partner's response. She couldn't believe that he would "go-along-to-get-along." It seemed totally out of character for him, but she wholeheartedly welcomed it. Putting things to the side, for now, did not mean that they would disappear. Quite to the contrary, when the time comes to explain the timeline and the facts of the case, everything will come to light. They will then have to describe the actions they took and why those actions were not exposed, why they were hidden and even excluded from the report. That will be the "time-for-reckoning."

Chapter Twenty-One

An Amenity

James took a cab ride to the nearest car rental location and contracted for a very plain looking sedan. He wanted to just blend in with the other vehicles on the road so he could concentrate on the task at hand. Not finding Andrea was not an option. He had to find her and stop her. James drove to the renovated motel in town and hoped that he would find Andrea there. This was a place that was more to her liking and taste. He was feeling very confident that he picked the right place. The hard part was convincing the front desk clerk to divulge information about a guest. That violated the confidentiality that all the guests expected. He would have to be quite creative with his story. He sat in his rented ride and pondered the best approach. James decided that Dr. James Whitly was in search of one of his diabetic patients who was in desperate need of insulin. He was worried that she may have passed out and would be on the verge of drifting into a diabetic coma. It was a matter life and death situation. With his hospital credentials, he could make it work.

Dr. James Whitly entered the motel with his best worried and concerned look. Fortunately for him, the registration clerk was a young female who couldn't have had that much experience. Dr. Whitly produced his medical credentials and, in a most persuasive life and death scenario, convinced the young clerk to allow him to inspect the motel register. He was sure that Andrea would not sign in using her actual name; so, he looked for a possible pseudonym that he thought she might use. Additionally, there weren't that many registered guests he had to review. To his dismay, nothing matched. He was fairly confident that she was not at this motel. Where to now? Was there another location nearby that was an above average hotel or motel? He couldn't think of any location that fit that description. James had to think creatively. With her newly acquired funding, Andrea was not going to settle for inadequate lodging.

James drove around for quite a while just hoping that a new idea would come to mind. Nothing triggered his thinking, and he was about to give up. He would retry again tomorrow. On his way to the nearest motel, he saw a billboard that advertised a new Italian restaurant. In an effort for people to find the new restaurant easily, the advertiser offered a landmark near its location. It said: "We are right across from 'Mom's Bed and Breakfast.'" A bell went off in James' head. Could Andrea have chosen a bed and breakfast? It was better than the local motels. When searching, it wasn't a location that would ordinarily come to mind, and it served good food right on the premises. He had no other options; so, James headed for "Mom's."

As he got closer to the bed and breakfast, he mentally rehearsed the skit that had worked before. The credentials were the selling point, and he had to show that aura of worried concern. James put his best acting face on and entered the bed and breakfast. This time there was a middle-aged man behind the desk. It was not going to be so easy convincing him the way the young woman was so easily persuaded. She didn't even ask what name Dr. Whitly was looking for.

Getting his credentials out and ready for examination, he began: "Hello, sir. I am Dr. James Whitly from Mountain Pacific Hospital. I and others are checking local establishments searching for a patient who may be in imminent danger. She is a diabetic and is in immediate need of insulin. Without it she could very well fall into a diabetic coma and face the prospect of losing her life. She is unaware of the risk, so we are trying to locate her and stop a possible tragedy from occurring. May I look at your register to see if she is here?" The clerk responded: "Because of confidentiality, I can't open the register, but I can check if the person registered."

This is what James feared. He would have to give the clerk a name. The problem was that there were so many possibilities to offer that there was no guarantee that he would pick the right one. He would only get one chance because giving more than one name would surely put doubt in the clerk's mind. Andrea hated her life with Leonard and anything to do with him. She wanted no part of him, and that probably included his last name. Additionally, not too many people would connect her to the name that James was thinking about. He was going to use logic, not that logic always worked in illogical situations, and give the only name that came to mind: "It could be listed under 'A.

McFarland.'" The clerk looked through the brief list and relayed that there was an "Anna McFarland" registered. Andrea was playing it close to the vest; she didn't even use her real first name. In an expression of relief, James acknowledged that she was the individual who was being sought. He thanked the clerk and asked what room "Anna" occupied. Being very careful and cautious, the clerk said that he would take the doctor to her room.

Just as the clerk was about to escort James to Andrea's room, the desk phone rang. Being busy with the caller, the clerk asked one of his helpers to escort the doctor to Andrea's room. Luckily, the helper was a young boy who could care less about what was transpiring. When they got to the room, the young man knocked on the door and said: "Hello, it's the front desk." With that, he just walked away. Thank God for the youth of the day! Andrea took her time coming to the door and very cautiously opened it just a crack. However, it was enough for James to push his way into the room. The escort was already gone, so no one was aware of the forced entry.

Andrea really wasn't surprised. She knew that eventually James would find her, and he did. The initial push-through sent Andrea reeling to the floor. Ordinarily, James would have rushed to help her up. Now, he just stared at her and made no move to assist. She looked up at him and said: "Well, isn't that the grand entrance? It seems that you have recovered from your unfortunate accidental fall. Other than your ego, I hope that I didn't hurt you too badly." If looks could kill, she was a dead woman. James, in a tone that Andrea hadn't heard before, answered: “Who the hell do you think you are? Whatever feelings that I had for you, tumbled with my fall. Originally, I was trying to find a solution to the problems we both faced, and now I will make it my business to see that you never reach your sick goal.”

She didn’t give an inch: “No you won’t. Do you really want to see me sent to jail? Do you want to see me suffer for the rest of my life? I do not think so. And you must understand that I did what I thought I had to, but I didn’t want you to really get hurt. We can still work things out together. Following my final visit to see Leonard, we could disappear together and live happily ever after.” James’ retort was nasty and swift: “If I didn’t know better, I would think you were on drugs. You are living in dreamland. Do you really think that I still want to be with you, someone whose insane goal is to murder her husband? You need help, and I will work to see that you get it, no matter what it takes. If it means that I must tie you up to prevent you from succeeding, I will.”

Andrea realized how serious James was, and she explained that she would not give him any more trouble. She was no fool. She would wait until he let his guard down, and then she would act. James further told her that he was going to call the detectives who were investigating her case and let them know where to come to pick them up. Andrea just listened and calmly said that she understood. She exuded an attitude of defeat and cooperation. James was relieved with what he saw, and those familiar feelings of concern and pity started to rise. However, James was not going to allow those feelings to change his self-dictated mandate. He was going to turn himself and

Andrea over to the police and hope for mercy from the courts. Anything else would just be compounding the problems they had.

Before James made the call, Andrea asked if they could just spend some private time together, since it would probably be the last time that they would get the opportunity. James respected the fact that she was cunning and deceptive, but he could see, what he thought, was a glimmer of sincerity in her request. She was sitting on the bed, and he went to sit beside her on the bed. She smiled and said again how very sorrow she was for what she did to him. She even had tears in her eyes and a quivering lip. James mentioned that things had not turned out as he thought they would, but that the choice to stop running was the right one. In his opinion, there was even a chance that, in her case, her actions could be traced to the almost inhuman treatment that she suffered. That would surely mean something to a sitting judge. He also explained to her that if she had followed through on her threat, there might be very little that could help in reducing a possible sentence.

Andrea just listened and kept nodding her head in confirmation. She grabbed his hand, and he didn't resist. With little or no resistance offered, she then rested her head on his chest. She whispered to him: "I am also disappointed at how things worked out. It is not what I wanted. In fact, it is the opposite of what I really wanted. I am so sorry." James, in a forgiving tone, responded: "It's okay; like I said, it's in the past." Andrea choked a response: "No, you don't understand. I am not saying I am sorry for the past. I am sorry for the present." James tried to make sense of what she was saying when suddenly, as she pulled away, he felt a jabbing severe pain in his neck. Andrea had embedded the bed and breakfast amenity, a pen which was on the night table, into his neck. James immediately gushed blood from the wound and fell onto the bed holding his hand against the puncture wound. Andrea was even more desperate than he thought.

She grabbed his rental car keys and fled out of the room without ever looking back. For all she knew, the once love of her life could be bleeding to death. Without any plan or destination in mind, she just drove away. However, she did not want James to die, so she got to a phone and dialed "9-1-1" for an ambulance. She needed them to respond to the bed and breakfast room where James was bleeding and reeling in pain.

Chapter Twenty-Two

The Pager

With lights and siren employed, the ambulance pulled into the bed and breakfast. The emergency medical technicians had been given the room number; so, they went directly there. They announced themselves and then tried the door which was unlocked. Since the door was open, they quickly entered and searched for the individual who was alleged to have been bleeding profusely. To their dismay, no one was in the room, but there was blood on the bed sheets and in the bathroom sink. Apparently, someone had been hurt and bleeding, but not bad enough to prevent the individual from leaving.

The proprietor of the bed and breakfast told the responding medics that no one left through the front door. If they had, he would have seen them. The only other option was the fire escape exit at the rear of the building. He also mentioned to the first responders and the accompanying police officers that the room had been occupied by a female who apparently was a diabetic. He further related that a doctor from the nearby hospital was searching for her to prevent her from going into a diabetic coma. He was shocked that neither one was still in the room. He began to realize that he had been the victim of a fraud.

When Andrea left the room, she went out the rear exit to the fire escape. She negotiated the stairs and went directly to the car that James had rented. She knew it was the correct vehicle because it matched the description on the yellow tag that was attached to the keys. Andrea was careful not to bring attention to herself by running or racing out of the parking lot. She just went quickly and quietly to the car and drove off as if it was just another ordinary day. Although her actions didn't show it, she was concerned that James might be badly hurt, hence the call to "9-1-1."

Fortunately, the pen that Andrea used against James had penetrated his neck at a point that missed major arteries. However, wounds to the neck and above are prone to bleed heavily. That was the case. The initial attack sent James falling backward onto the bed. The blood stains on the sheets were testament to that. Quickly, James rose from the bed and went into the bathroom where he used a hand towel to apply direct pressure to the wound. Blood had splashed onto the sink and floor before he could use the towel. He was feeling a little dizzy from the shock and loss of blood, but he knew that he could not stay in the room. He zippered his sweater as tightly as he could around his neck and stuffed a clean towel inside the collar. He couldn't very well be walking around with blood oozing from his neck.

He left the room through the same rear exit door that Andrea had used. However, he was a lot shakier going down the fire escape steps than she had been. Staying out of sight, he heard the sirens from approaching emergency vehicles and saw the ambulance. The emergency medical technicians rushed into the room that he had just left. He couldn't wait around much longer because there was a possibility that the responders could follow the trail of blood to the fire escape. He staggered to the street where he caught a cab. He told the driver to take him to the nearest pharmacy and to wait there for him.

Although the blood flow had decreased a bit, James knew that he would need stitches to help close the puncture and protect him from infection. It was obvious that he could not go to an emergency room for help without his identity being disclosed; so, he would have to treat himself. The pharmacy, which was part of a national chain, would more than likely have what he needed. The supplies would not be the exact essentials that he wanted, but without the benefit of emergency room tools and resources, he would have to make do. James purchased gauze, a roll of tape, dental floss, a needle, a bottle of alcohol, and a bottle of peroxide. So far, the towel insert in his zippered collar was holding, but it would not hold for long, and before he knew it, the white towel would turn a certain shade of crimson.

Being in a rush to leave the store, James didn't wait for a bag and struggled back to the taxi with his arms full. Upon seeing him with an assortment of medical supplies, the cab driver commented: "Hey Bud, you're either going to operate on someone, or you're about to enter into a fight that you think you'll probably lose." James just shook his head and said: "You were right the first time. Please take me to the nearest motel.

Thanks." Without saying another word, the driver headed toward a motel that was about a mile from where they were.

After thanking the taxi driver, he exited the cab with a cadre of medical supplies in a bag that the cab driver found in his trunk. James completed the superficial registration process and went to his assigned room. Now the "fun" would begin. James had nothing to numb the area, and it was still sprouting blood. He had to start closing the wound before he got too weak to do an efficient job. He threaded the needle with the dental floss and began to suture. The pain was severe, and, combined with his weakened state, was slowly but surely attacking his consciousness. However, he knew that if he did not complete the procedure, there was a good possibility that someone would find his non-responsive body lying on the bathroom floor. He labored on until the wound was more that ninety percent closed. The flow of blood was reduced to a trickle and would ultimately coagulate stopping more blood loss. Having completed his emergency procedure, James collapsed onto the bed and drifted off to a well-earned sleep. He never heard his pager go off.

Andrea was at a loss to find another location where she could safely hide and relax. She couldn't believe what she had done to James, but he pushed her into a corner and left her little room to escape. She had to do what she did, there was no other option available. Andrea painfully realized that her plan for eliminating her husband and fleeing to a foreign island with James was just a "pie in the sky" dream. Well, at least the last part was. She would still complete one-half of the plan. No one was going to stop her from getting revenge. She had demonstrated that notion twice to James, and if she could show it to him, she could prove it to anyone.

Assuming that James looked at the bed and breakfast as a last best resort for her, Andrea felt that the newly renovated motel now might fit the bill for a layover. She drove to the motel and registered again under a pseudonym. She gave a creditable excuse for having no identification and her "husband's" credit card. She registered this time as "Amy McFarland." She was a creature of habit, or maybe down deep, she wanted to get caught. She didn't mind facing the consequences of capture, but only after Leonard kept his rescheduled meeting with the creator.

Getting settled in her room and giving her mind a chance to wind down, she started thinking about what possibilities she had where she could enter the hospital undetected. The choices were slim. She had to take her time with the plan because now she knew for sure that this attempt would be the last; so, it had to succeed. There were too many people in the hospital who were now alert to her situation. In addition to the security person, the floor nurses would be extra vigilant as they attended to the patients, and especially to Leonard Canella. Andrea knew she needed props and what could be a better prop than one of the portable hospital machines that technicians brought to patients' rooms? That was it! She had to figure out how she could become a radiological technician who utilized a portable x-ray machine. She had the plan, but the implementation was going to be a Herculean task.

After a deep dive into a pain-influenced sleep, James arose still feeling like he collided with a speeding truck. Instead of reducing the debilitating effects of a tumble and stabbing, the rest period brought the pain to the surface. He just wanted to lay back down and let his body repair itself. He couldn't do that. Andrea was still out there, and she was determined to satisfy her contract with the devil. As he got up to go into the bathroom, the hospital pager that he always had with him fell to the floor. As He gingerly bent down and picked it up, he realized that there was a message waiting. He pressed the "go" button and saw the following: "Dr. Whitly, just wanted to let you know that Leonard Canella is showing signs of coming out of the coma." James staff was still loyal to him. They all knew, by this time, what had transpired, and yet they still had his best interests at heart.

The news that Leonard was about to regain consciousness came with good and bad features. It was good that one of James' patients was recovering, and it was also good that, at some point, there was a possibility the James could speak directly to Leonard. James would be able to get a lot of things off his chest. The bad part was that once Andrea knew that her husband had regained consciousness, her plan might become more involved and more difficult to stop. Also, it made Leonard a more vulnerable target if he was not restricted to one spot. James knew that Leonard still was healing from broken bones that he had incurred because of the accident, but his treatment did not restrict the patient's mobility. Regaining consciousness from a comatose state is a slow undertaking, and Leonard would surely need time to allow the normalization process to take hold. For

James, there was a new wrinkle in his pursuit of Andrea. Time had become a double-edged sword.

Chapter Twenty-Three

The Nurse and The Mechanic

The detectives were hitting a stone wall. They needed something to bring either Andrea or Dr. Whitly out of hiding. They approached the administrator of the hospital and laid out the problem before him. The administrator was sympathetic but hesitant to agree to their proposed plan. Detectives Krane and Barret wanted the hospital to page Dr. Whitly with the message that one of his patients was slowly coming out of the coma. Because of Dr. Whitly's commitment to medicine, they imagined that the doctor would try to find a way to see his patient, no matter the risk. They would be ready for him. The administrator did not like the idea of lying about a patient's condition, even though it was explained to him that this ploy might very well save the patient's life. Coincidentally, as the administrator was pondering the detective's proposal, news came that Leonard Canella was actually showing signs of recovering from the coma. With the news now influencing his decision, the administrator gave his permission to allow one of the nurses to page Dr. Whitly with the news.

The detectives were correct in their assumption. Dr. James Whitly needed and wanted to find a way to get into the hospital and visit Leonard Canella. The risk was great, but not doing it, in his mind, produced an even greater risk. He wondered how much he could count on his staff. He would be asking them to violate hospital policy and possibly put their jobs on the line. He didn't want to put any of them in that position, but without their help, he wouldn't be able to succeed. He also had to count on maintaining that existing strong loyalty bond which would also automatically evolve into a confidentiality mandate. James was only sure about the reliability of one of his nurses. He knew that he couldn't rely on his medical colleagues because of the risk that they would be taking. There was no way that he could expect other doctors to put their license to practice medicine in jeopardy. Unfortunately, he also thought that some of them would be elated when the hammer fell because then there would be an opening for the "Chair of Neurology."

James reached out for the nurse who sent the page message. She was surprised to hear from James but was also relieved. Nurse Martha Higgins had been working with James ever since he started at the hospital, and that was a while ago. He was very reliant on her skills but also on her friendship. She had once again proved her loyalty to him. He hoped that this wasn't pushing it a step too far. Nurse Higgins listened carefully to what the doctor was saying and completely understood what her involvement would mean. That having been said, she didn't hesitate for a minute to offer her total cooperation. He was glad to hear that she was willing to help, but hated the fact that he would be putting her at some risk. She didn't care. She knew that Dr. James Whitly was a good man, and he had always treated her with the greatest respect and dignity. That was not the case with many doctors.

It would be Nurse Higgins who would arrange for a certain emergency exit door to remain in the unlocked position. She would also secure the operating room garments and mask that Dr. Whitly would use as he entered Leonard Canella's room. James needed to see how his patient was progressing, but also how aware he was regarding recent events. James would also use the visit to stop by Laura's room. He was concerned about his wife's recovery. He knew that the doctors had performed minor surgery to repair some of the damage to internal organs, and that had turned out better than anticipated. So, she was doing relatively well, whereas Leonard still had bones that needed mending and cuts and bruises that needed to close. It was disappointing that Leonard might be regaining consciousness before Laura, and medicine wasn't always an exact science. What was a foregone conclusion one day could be a calculated theory on another. That was the practice of medicine.

Hey, I can actually feel my fingers slightly moving. I haven't felt that before. I think my toes are moving. My eyes feel different. What's happening? Hey doc, someone, something is happening to me. I need help. I am able to move my head. I can hear an alarm going off. The light is stabbing my eyes. My eyes are open! I can now see people in white outfits around my bed. They're calling my name. They're telling me that everything is okay, and that I am in the hospital coming out of a coma. No kidding. They all seem happier than I am. No, not really. I am glad to be back in the world of the living. I feel stiff and a little disoriented, and I really don't appreciate them jabbing and examining me. I made it, but they are telling me that it will take a while before things actually go back to normal. That's fine with me as long as they do. I nod that I understand because it is still difficult to speak. I guess the initial response has worn off because now there is only one nurse and one doctor who still has his mask on.

"Hello, Leonard. It's Dr. Whitly. How are you doing?" Leonard was able to get out a whisper: "Good." I have been looking after you, and I am the doctor who performed surgery on you. I am sure you know who I am and why, in addition to evaluating your recovery, I am here. Studies have shown that those patients who have suffered head trauma and who are in a comatose state, although not capable of responding, can actually hear and understand what is going on around them. Was that the case with you, Leonard?" Once again, Leonard nodded a "yes."

"Okay, then you know what is happening, and you know that your wife, Andrea, is determined to end your life one way or another. Although you probably deserve her wrath, I am going to do everything I can to prevent her from reaching her goal. Although conscious, you will have to remain in the hospital for a while longer until we are sure about the break and fractures, and until we see no infection at the laceration sites. It won't be long before you will be gone. It is then that I can no longer help you. Once you're out on your own, you're definitely in her ballpark. I will try to convince her to surrender, but thus far, I have failed miserably. I will visit again soon." Without giving Leonard a chance to respond, James headed for his wife's room.

"Hello, Laura. I understand that you are doing well, and that's music to my ears. I have so much to tell you and so little time to do it in. Things have really gotten out of control, and I realize how foolish I have been. Believe it or not, I've had some nasty run-ins with Andrea, and I am trying to locate her so that I can stop her from attempting to kill her husband. By the way, Leonard has regained consciousness but will have to remain in the hospital a while longer. I was hoping that you would recover first, but he is the one who is awake. I am sure that, before long, we will be speaking face-to-face. Leonard said that he could hear and understand while he was in a coma, I am hoping that you can too. If you have heard what is happening, then you know that it is not easy to come to the hospital. If it weren't for Nurse Higgins, I probably would not be here now. Well, I must go for now, but I will keep a close watch on your recovery. Can't wait to speak to you in person. Love you."

Well, thanks for coming by, darling. It's good to see you again. I'm sure it is difficult pulling away from Andrea and her concerns. Boy, it must have been some heavy-duty run-ins for you to finally turn on Andrea, if you really have. You have to understand that I've heard it all before. I hope you really don't believe that you are going to stop that woman from killing her husband. According to you, she seems determined, and there is nothing worse than a woman's scorn. You should remember that for the future. At least her husband will be awake when she attempts to kill him. It's just another obstacle for her to overcome. The way things sound, you are being sought with as much enthusiasm as the police are employing on finding her. You really got yourself into a nasty mess, and I can't believe

that you have dragged that nice Martha Higgins into your chaotic ordeal.

Nurse Higgins led the way, and James exited through the same emergency door he used to enter. He thanked her for her help but mostly for her loyalty. She promised to keep him up to date on what was occurring at the hospital and on his wife's condition. Her sincere understanding and concern brought tears to his eyes. She was like a light in the darkness, and his present world was nothing but dark.

As he negotiated his way through the parking lot, he saw a vehicle that resembled the one that he had rented. But his rental car was nothing out of the ordinary, so it could just be another look-alike. As he got closer, he was certain that it was not his rental, since there was a woman, probably in her sixties, behind the wheel. However, the sighting did bring to mind the task of having to inform the car rental place that the car had been stolen. Just another bump in the road that he would have to negotiate. Unfortunately, relating to the manager that the rental had been stolen, would certainly have a negative effect on renting another vehicle. Additionally, the police would have to get involved, and the way things were going, he would wind up being arrested before the police officer finished his report. It became more prudent for him not to report anything. Just add another charge to the official final court document.

James could not continue his search being on foot. In some way, he needed to get a car. He wandered over to the hospital warehouse that housed all the vehicles associated with the hospital. This was also the location where the hospital mechanics would ply their trade on those vehicles in need of repair and/or maintenance. James had one chance and only one. He needed to speak with the lead mechanic, Jonesy. That's what everyone called him, and most people probably didn't know his full name.

Last year, Jonesy's young daughter needed an operation to correct a nerve problem in her neck that caused the young girl a lot of pain and heavily restricted her head movement. The operation was a very costly one, and Jonesy, even after the application of the insurance funds, didn't have enough money to pay in full. Dr. James Whitly was the operating surgeon who, knowing the circumstances that Jonesy faced, charged one dollar for his services. Jonesy said he would never forget what the doctor had done for him and told Dr. Whitly if he ever needed anything from him to just ask. Well, in James' mind that time was now.

James approached the warehouse hoping that Jonesy was still working. He was in luck. The first person he saw when he entered was Jonesy. The mechanic gave him a huge "hello" and asked how he'd been. Following an exchange of platitudes, Jonesy asked the doctor if he needed anything. It was James' chance to get down to the nitty gritty: "Well Jonesy, I got myself into a little situation." Jonesy interrupted: "Yeah, I heard. What do you need?" "Jonesy, I don't have a car, and I can't rent one. Is there a possibility..." Jonesy stopped James in the middle of his sentence: "Say no more, Doc. I have a black sedan that the associate director usually uses. He's on vacation for two weeks, and no one else will be using the car. If it disappears without my knowing, oh well! By the way, I have to go into the office now. Be careful you do not knock into the table over there where all car keys are kept. Take care, Doc." And Jonesy just walked away.

James could not believe how easily Jonesy would risk all. James looked around to make certain that no one else was watching, and he went over to the table. Each key set was tagged with a license plate number. He looked over at the car that Jonesy had pointed out and stared at the plate number. He then turned his attention to the table and saw the key set that matched the vehicle plate number. He nonchalantly walked to the vehicle. He started it and drove out of the warehouse. Wouldn't life be great if everything were this easy? Life, however, was just one challenge after another to which Dr. James Whitly could easily testify.

Chapter Twenty-Four

Home Sweet Home

Andrea Canella or "Amy McFarland" rested for a long while in her new hideaway. However, she felt uncomfortable. She had been on the run for a number of days now, and it was taking its toll. She was just tired of going from one place to another and sleeping in strange beds. As she pondered her future, an outlandish idea popped into her head. Why can't I be more comfortable? Why can't I be in familiar surroundings? Why can't I enjoy time alone in my own home?

Andrea's thinking, although possibly flawed, was that enough time had passed for the police to no longer stake out her house. That location would probably be one of the safest for her now. She didn't know how long she would have to wait for the perfect opportunity to strike out at Leonard, so she needed a place where she could feel safe and secure, and which didn't cost a ton of money. It would be out of the public eye, and she would bring enough supplies with her so she could stay in the house for an extended period.

Her plan was to enter the house in the middle of the night to avoid the nosey eyes of neighbors. If she could sneak in undetected, that would be ninety percent of the battle. She decided that she would park her "borrowed" car a few blocks away from the house and approach the house on foot. She did realize that a woman walking alone in the middle of the night would be an odd sight, but hopefully there would be very few people out at that time of night. Additionally, she would take every precaution to be as clandestine as possible to avoid bringing attention to herself. As she continued to think about it, she liked the idea more and more.

To implement her new plan, Andrea decided to exercise a "dry run" and see if there were obstacles that she hadn't thought about. If any, and whatever they were, she was determined to negotiate them. No one would ever think that she would have the gall to return to the house of the man she tried to kill. It was a perfect plan. She couldn't wait to drive by and see if anything presented itself as insurmountable. She didn't think so, but better safe than sorry. She didn't want to confront any surprises in the middle of implementing her plan.

When night came, Andrea left the motel and drove to the neighborhood where she once lived with Leonard. She cruised around slowly, but not too slowly because that also could raise attention, and casually just looked at the surroundings. Nothing seemed out of the ordinary, so she finally decided to drive on to the block where Leonard's house was located. It was late so there were just a few people on the street. She knew though as the hours passed; they too would disappear. The house was dark except for one dim light in the rear. The shock came, however, when she got close enough to see more detail. The front door was cris-crossed with yellow police tape that in bold letters said, "Police Line-Do Not Cross."

At first, Andrea was taken aback by the sight. Then it dawned on her that the police barrier would be an advantage to her. She would enter the house through the rear or side door and not disturb the police warning. She assumed that all the entrances would be detailed with the police tape, but it would be much easier to bypass the tape on the rear or side door. Even if she had to "rearrange" the tape on one of the other doors, her handiwork would be out of view from the street and, therefore, bring no attention to the possibility of a breech. Andrea was satisfied with what she saw and had a good feeling about the success of her efforts. She saw no other vehicle around the house and looked carefully to see if the residence was under surveillance. She was satisfied that it wasn't. She knew that there was a possibility that police patrols would periodically pass to make certain that all was okay, but she could handle that. Andrea decided that the quicker the move the better, so she planned to execute her new hide-out scheme the next night.

When James had originally spoken with Martha Higgins about his hospital visit, she inquired about where he was staying. He didn't give her a direct answer for two reasons: one - what she really didn't know the police could not get from her, and two – he really didn't know where he was going to wind up. He didn't have many options, in fact, he hardly had any. It was during that conversation with Martha that she offered to let him temporarily stay in an apartment she had available above her garage. At the time, he thanked her but quickly nixed the idea. Now, however, the offer didn't look so bad. It disturbed him though that by accepting Martha's generous offer, he would be involving her even more in what could amount to legal prosecution. Before he actually agreed to stay in Martha's garage apartment, he would re-emphasize the possible negative ramifications that could affect her future. He was certain, however, that those potential negative comebacks would not influence her decision to have him stay in the apartment.

James didn't want to drive around aimlessly. Just like Andrea, he needed time to plan his next move. Although Andrea knew what her immediate plans were, she had to develop a strategy to counter security measures at the hospital. She was unaware of the fact that Leonard, although weak and still recovering, had regained consciousness. Knowing that fact would surely necessitate her amending any previous murder plan she had. But for now, she was still under the impression that her target was a devil who was lying unconscious in his hospital room. She would plan accordingly.

James drove directly toward Martha Higgins' house. When he arrived, he sat in the car and contemplated, again, if this was the right move. It was definitely the right and safe move for him, but for Martha it could prove to be an awful error in judgement. Once again, it all came down to what choices Dr. James Whitly had. He parked the vehicle, which had identifiable hospital markings on the door, a good distance away from the house. The spot was on a "dead end" block with only three houses on it, one of which looked abandoned. The end of the street abutted a heavily wooded area where James finally parked his vehicle. He walked the extended distance to Higgins' residence and rang the front doorbell. Martha answered quickly, and was both surprised and elated to see Dr. Whitly standing in front of her.

"I hope you are here to accept my meager offer, Doctor." "It is far from meager or insignificant, Martha. You don't know how life-saving this is for me. I don't have to worry about being discovered or interrupted as I plan for my future. I cannot thank you enough for your generosity, but having said that, Martha, I have to reiterate the potential jeopardy associated with this whole debacle." Martha stared at James and said: "Dr. Whitly, I am too old to consider jeopardy, and too tired to really care about it. You are welcome to stay for as long as you wish." James hugged her and thanked her again for what she was doing. Martha escorted James to his new "digs."

Was it the Ritz? No, but it was much better and cleaner than most of the recent rooms in which he stayed. It was airy, bright and most of all, very private. After taking a brief overview of the whole apartment, he exclaimed: "Martha, this is great. It is like staying in a five-star hotel. I cannot thank you enough." Martha left him to get himself situated. She told him to contact her if needed anything at all. He nodded, and she left.

This is what it has come to. The Chair of the Neurology Department and head surgeon at Mountain Pacific Hospital is now residing in an apartment above someone's garage. What a success story! If his wife could only see him now. As he looked around again at his new living quarters, he admitted to himself that he had no one else to blame. He had made his bed, and now he must sleep in it. Even with the depressing situation enveloping him, one disassociated thought screamed in his mind, “Where is Andrea tonight?” He was uncertain, though, if it was a feeling of sincere concern for her that he was questioning, or whether it was a rhetorical question implying as to “what is she up to now?”

Chapter Twenty-Five

Nurse to Nurse

Dr. James Whitly spent the night feeling sorry for himself and thinking about Andrea and her possible next move. His new apartment was relatively comfortable, but it was definitely not what he was used to. When he was speaking with Martha, he noticed that she was staring at his neck. The puncture wound that had been planted there by Andrea was noticeably oozing. It also was beginning to feel as if it was infected. He had everything he needed to retreat and wrap the wound, except antibiotic cream. If the cut was getting infected, he needed something to stop it. He would have to bother Martha to see if she could help.

James went down the staircase and headed to the rear door of Martha's house. Martha lived alone. Her husband had passed a few years ago, and she had no children. Oddly, as James approached the house, he thought he heard her speaking with someone. He peeked through the glass on the back door and saw Martha on the phone. He waited outside the door for Martha to finish her conversation when he thought he heard her say Andrea's name. This caused James to perk up and pay attention. Hearing more of the conversation, he became convinced that Martha was, in fact, speaking with Andera Canella. He thought it strange that Martha and Andrea were in touch with one another. He thought it even more strange that

Martha never mentioned anything about her present relationship with Andrea. As he thought about it, however, he remembered that a long time ago, they had been nurses together at Mountain Pacific. He guessed that their bond was stronger than he realized.

James waited patiently for Martha to finish her phone call. He knocked on the rear door and Martha, who seemed startled and worried, answered with a surprised: "Hi, Doc. What can I do for you?" James, never mentioning the fact that he was privy to her phone conversation, pointed to the bandage on his neck and asked if she had anything to stop an infection. Martha was more than accommodating and quickly fetched an ointment she had in her medicine cabinet. If James didn't know better, he could swear that what was displayed on Martha's face was an expression of both guilt and deceit. It was disappointing, to say the least, that James discovered Martha's involvement with Andrea. It was disappointing but also alarming, and now he had to reconsider how much trust he should place in his relationship with Martha.

James realized that as long as he stayed in Martha's garage apartment, Andrea would know his every move. He could, however, use this to his advantage by utilizing misdirection and ultimately intercept Andrea. James had to consider what the best strategy would be. He really had two choices that would both give him a definite advantage: he could confront Martha now and coerce her into telling him where Andrea was staying, or he could use the misdirection concept and have Martha's relationship with Andrea allow him and the police to surprise Andrea and catch her unaware. He thought hard about both but was leaning more toward his first thought: finding out where Andrea is staying. If he chose the first of his options and discovered Andrea's whereabouts, what would stop Martha from contacting her friend and telling her that he was on the way? Nothing! The only way that he could prevent something like that from happening was to take Martha with him. Did he want to do that? There were so many things that had to be considered he thought his head was going to explode. He had to take a break and give his mind a chance to relax. If he gave it some time, maybe a solution would surface.

It was great for Andrea to have an ally in Martha Higgins. Knowing where James was and being able to find out what he was planning was a great advantage. She didn't have to worry anymore about James surprising her and showing up at the front door. All she now had to evade was the search being conducted by her friendly police detectives and every other police officer on patrol. Even so, with James' search threat no longer an imminent concern, movement and planning would be considerably easier. Not easy, but easier.

The next morning brought no miracle solution to James' options. He was still debating the "pros and cons" of each. His leaning of the night before was weakened by complications that would surely involve Martha. Time was marching on, however, and he needed to decide. James knew that after he failed to show up at the scheduled afternoon meeting with the detectives, that they would pull out all the stops and exercise the same amount of effort in finding him as they did with finding Andrea. So, a decision had to be made.

At noon, James marched down to Martha's back door. He looked again through the glass window on the door and saw Martha with her head in her hands leaning on the kitchen table. She looked pitiful. Not knowing the cause of her state, it bothered him to burden her with even more concerns. He started to turn away, but stopped and turned to face the door, casting aside his immediate emotions. He knocked gently and saw that Martha was apparently deep in thought because she jumped at the sound. Martha dabbed her eyes and proceeded to open the door for James. It was obvious to him that Martha had been crying. Unfortunately, he was going to add to her troubles.

"Hello, Martha. Are you okay?" Martha walked back to the kitchen table and sat down. James followed. Martha pointed to another chair and asked James to sit: "Dr. Whitly, I have something that I need to tell you. I meant no harm by it, but I did something that affects you. I really do want to help you, but I also have a relationship with Andrea. If you remember, Andrea and I were nurses together in Mountain Pacific and were good friends. She contacted me when all this stuff was going on. Andrea was worried that you would find her; so, when I spoke to her the last time, I mentioned that you were staying with me in the garage apartment. I am so sorry if I hurt you in any way."

James was relieved. He didn't have to broach the subject with Martha, she brought it up to him. He let her believe that he was totally surprised by the revelation and offered her some semblance of understanding. He patted her arm and said: "I am sure Andrea told you, from her viewpoint, what has been going on. I am disappointed that you let her know that I am here. It is no longer a haven for me because, in Andrea's state of mind, I really don't know what she would do. I understand that you had and now have a relationship with her, but I need your help to possibly save a man's life and Andrea's future. You stared at my neck yesterday when I was speaking with you. That wound was caused by the impact of a pen that Andrea Canella thrust into my neck. Before that, Andrea pushed me down a flight of stairs. I don't know how much of that she revealed to you, but she is determined to kill her husband, no matter what the cost. Martha, I need your help."

Martha looked astonished. She could not believe what she was hearing. Apparently, Andrea hadn't told her the whole story. "Tell me Doctor, what can I do to help? I want to make up for what I've done." James was very happy to hear her turn-around statement: "Well, firstly, you can tell me where Andrea is staying. I've checked most of the motels. I even re-checked the bed and breakfast that she stayed at. There is no sign of her, and I need to find her. So, please tell me where she is." Martha hesitated just a bit but said: "Andrea went back to Leonard's house. She told me that the police are no longer focusing on it because they think that she will not return. She mentioned that, occasionally, a police patrol car passes but doesn't stop. She also said that the police ribboned the entry doors with yellow police tape, and she mentioned that she will probably sneak into the house tonight."

James looked at her, and now, he could not believe what he was hearing. How could she have the fortitude to go back to Leonard's house? He quietly thought: "She has to have nerves of steel." Martha was cooperating, and hopefully she would no longer openly aid her nursing friend. Martha further mentioned that Andrea was planning to enter Leonard's house at about three o'clock in the morning, using the advantage that mother nature offered – darkness. Martha also stated that Andrea intended to stay in the house for as long as necessary. She would wait there for the opportunity to strike at Leonard.

James had incorrectly assumed that Andrea was unaware that her husband had regained consciousness. With Martha's help, she was well aware of whatever was taking place at the hospital. So, Andrea must have already adjusted her plan of attack. James understood why now she was willing to stay hidden for a time. She wants to wait until Leonard's awakening makes him even more vulnerable to whatever she is planning. Knowing now that Andrea knew all about Leonard, James made the decision that he had to get to her at Leonard's house. Whether he wanted to admit it or not, James' logical decision making was still influenced by his feelings for her. If they were not, why not just notify the police to stake out Leonard's house and make the arrest when she appeared? With everything that had occurred; with everything that she had done to him, both emotionally and physically, he still thought that police intervention, at this time, might be premature. Talk about a glutton for punishment.

James would give Andrea one more chance to right the ship before it sank so deep that it could not be salvaged. He was not giving the idea much hope, but he had to, at least, offer her the opportunity. What could she do, stab him? He comically laughed to himself.

Chapter Twenty-Six

The Surprise

Many things were going through James' mind about how to plan an intercept of Andrea and stop her determined attack. He was weighing a number of options, and all of them would serve the purpose. He could wait for Andrea to arrive at Leonard's home and approach her before she entered the house. He could arrive at the house before she got there and wait inside. The surprise would startle and disarm her. He could notify the police that Andrea and he would be in Leonard's house at a certain time, or finally, he could stay out of it all together and just notify the police about Andrea's plan. One way or the other, Andrea's vengeful plot will soon come to an end. Not only will her murderous attempt come screeching to a halt, but his ability to meet and talk with her will also cease. Probably never seeing her again will be the result of collateral damage if the police are immediately involved. James wanted her stopped, but emotionally, the consequences with the police orchestrating the capture, would be grave. With everything that occurred, with the injuries that he sustained, and the unexpected trauma that he had endured, he still wasn't ready to finalize a permanent separation.

Although James still harbored some distrust regarding Martha Higgins' loyalty, he needed to bounce his options off someone else. Nurse Higgins was the only available prospect. He went to her and explained his dilemma. Because of her former and now her present close relationship with Andrea, Martha frowned when police involvement was mentioned. She thought, as James did, that he either wait in the house for Andrea's arrival or he stop her before she entered. If James opted for the first choice, the police could potentially add another criminal charge to the already existing ones. But the second choice would occur out in the street in public view and where the possibility of escape would be greater. It was decided then. James would enter the house before Andrea arrived and shock her when she stepped into the house. Unfortunately, because of her previous actions, James had to be prepared to restrain her. He wasn't going to use rope, and he didn't have handcuffs, but he did have access to electric wire ties. These would serve the same purpose as handcuffs and would be easy to apply.

Having made his final decision, he thanked Martha and implored her that for Andrea's sake, his mission should remain confidential, Martha agreed but surprised him when she asked to accompany him to the house. To say the least, James was surprised that Martha would put herself in such a compromising position, and his initial reaction was a firm "absolutely not!" Martha went on to explain that she could help with keeping Andrea calm, and if needed, she could assist with restraining her nurse friend. Her pleading influenced him to think more carefully about the whole endeavor. Maybe, Nurse Higgins could help. If nothing else, he would be able to make sure that Martha did not break down and notify Andrea about what was going to happen. That, in itself, was a good enough reason for Martha to come along. He reluctantly gave in and told Martha that he could probably use her help.

Time passed quickly and the mission night was upon James. It was about two o'clock in the morning and James and Martha left in Martha's car for their destination, the home of Mr. Leonard Canella. The streets were almost empty, and moonlight was dimmed by a dense cloud covering. Everything seemed to be in perfect alignment for a successful mission. James parked Martha's car in a dimly lit spot down the block from the Canella residence. They both walked tenuously towards the house. As he walked, James thought about the fact that he and Martha were in the act of committing the crime of criminal trespass. He was already being sought for other crimes, but this would be a first for Martha.

Feeling somewhat guilty for involving her, James whispered to Martha about what he had been thinking. It did not phase Martha in the least. She motioned to James to continue walking. They arrived at the house, and James led the way to the rear door. It was out of the street view and the darkest area around the house. James broke the police tape and moved it to the side. With what he had seen on television, he took out a credit card and inserted it between the locking device and its receptacle. It was a flimsy lock and with little manipulation, the credit card could now be categorized as a burglar tool. If everything went as easily as the entry did, then the night would be a walk in the park.

James was equipped with a flashlight and electric wire ties. He told Martha not to turn on any lights and to stay away from the windows. His small flashlight beam was all the light they needed. Martha sat on a sofa chair, and James sat on the couch. They both anxiously awaited Andrea's arrival, which would probably come in a matter of minutes. Ordinarily, in an atmosphere like this, it would be easy for someone to nod off. However, the adrenaline was pumping so hard and fast that neither James nor Martha felt the urge to even close their eyes.

Although the time passed quickly when they were waiting to leave Martha's house, it seemed to drag on as they awaited Andrea's planned arrival. Three o'clock had come and gone and still no Andrea. It was now three thirty and James wasn't sure that Andrea was coming to the house. Martha reinforced the idea that Andrea was planning the relocation for this morning and was adamant that she heard the details correctly. Just as she finished whispering to James, they both heard rustling at the rear door. They remained perfectly quiet and still, hearing only the loud throbbing sound of their own heart as it beat against their chests.

With just a slight delay, the rear door opened, and Andrea walked up the stairs to the living room where her greeters were waiting. She squinted, not believing what she was seeing. James rose from the couch and whispered an "hello" to the shocked intruder. Andrea looked around to see if anyone else was in the room when she saw Martha sitting in the chair. Martha looked at her and just said: "I'm so sorry." Andrea responded with disdain and a sarcastic: "Yeah, so am I." She then turned to

James and asked: "So, what now? Are you going to tie me up and turn me over to the police? Or are they already here and just waiting for you to signal them to swoop in and capture the fugitive?" James just looked at her sympathetically and answered: "No, I am going to give you a chance to voluntarily surrender to the police. It would be much better for you if you did that." Andrea shook her head: "All this time, and you still don't realize that you cannot tell me what is best for me. I will make these decisions and need no help from anyone, including you." James approached her and said: "I'm sorry you feel that way, but I have no choice." He reached into his pocket and pulled out the electric wire ties.

When Andrea saw the ties, she bolted over to where Martha was sitting and grabbed her around the neck putting a knife to Martha's throat. He shouldn't have been, but he was surprised by the action, and it caught him unaware. He was now compromised. After what Andrea had done to him, there was a possibility that she would harm Martha. Andrea pressed the knife deeply into Martha's skin, and a small droplet of blood appeared. Andrea meant business, and this notion was not lost on James. As Andrea pressed on Martha's neck, she pulled her up into a standing position, looked at James and said: "James, get out of my way. Don't be a fool. You know that I have no further use for Martha since she betrayed me. I will cut her throat if you even take another step toward me. I am going to leave the same way that I came in, so step aside."

Because of the shock of the whole situation, Andrea hadn't been thinking as clearly as she should have been. Slowly but surely, her cunning and planning were, once again, beginning to direct her actions. She motioned to James to step aside. Because of his past experience with her, he wasn't going to test her. With Martha in tow, Andrea gingerly moved past James and told him to empty his pockets and sit back down on the couch. James took the ties and his wallet out of his pockets and placed them on the glass cocktail table in front of the couch. She then said: "I have changed my mind. Since this is a relatively safe place, and apparently the police haven't been notified, or they would have been here by now, I am going to remain here with the two of you. James, give Martha the ties, and Martha fix the ties around James' wrists. As he proceeded to reach for the ties, James leaped from the couch and tried to wrap his arms around Andrea. She panicked and threw Martha at James. The force of colliding into James thrust Martha into the glass table which broke into a dozen different pieces, one of which came to rest in Martha's neck, severing her carotid artery. Before anyone could do anything to help her, she quickly bled out. Nurse Martha Higgins lay dead, and Dr. James Whitly lay stunned on the living room floor. Having lost his balance, he fell down, slamming his head on to the hard tile floor. James was dazed and dizzy and probably suffered a concussion.

Instead of attending to James, Andrea wasted no time in taking advantage of the situation. She rolled the weakened and vulnerable Dr. James Whitly over on his stomach and fastened the electric wire ties to both of his wrists. She now had one live hostage and one dead body. The situation did not change any of her immediate plans; in fact, she felt that it strengthened her position. She knew, however, that she would have to watch

James closely, especially if he suffered a concussion. She didn't want to deal with anymore medical concerns. That's where Nurse Higgins would have come in handy; however, Martha Higgins could help no one now, including herself.

Chapter Twenty-Seven

The Devil Incarnate

A call came into the police dispatcher that there was a car that seemed to be abandoned or stolen. The car had been parked for a while in the same location at the end of a dead-end street. The caller had mentioned that there was writing or some sort of symbol on the front door. The car was described as an official looking black, four door sedan.

When the police arrived, they checked their alarm sheet and discovered that the car had been reported "stolen." It was a car that belonged to the fleet owned by the Mountain Pacific Hospital. Since Detectives Krane and Barret had an active case involving the hospital, they were notified whenever the hospital came up on any call or report. They notified the patrol officers who responded to safeguard the vehicle for possible prints. The officers did just that, and the detectives called for the fingerprint team to respond to the scene. After dusting the vehicle for latent prints, the car was towed back to police headquarters where it underwent a thorough search.

Although nothing of import turned up as a result of the search, the print team was able to lift a number of readable fingerprints. Of course, the team had to go through the process of discarding elimination prints, the prints of those people who had legitimate access to the vehicle, before they could focus on potentially valuable prints. For instance, the fleet mechanics, the associate director, and the director would be part of the elimination print list. These are all people who have a right to utilize or repair the vehicle. Detective Krane knew one of the fingerprint technicians, and he asked if the results could be expedited. The technician assured both Krane and Barret that he would put a "rush" on the process.

David and Tracy had been working the case extra hard but hadn't come up with any good leads as of yet. They were hoping that the fingerprint results would allow them to focus on something specific. While they were waiting for the results, they decided to find out why the car had been parked at the location where it was found. If it was stolen, and Jonesy, the head mechanic reported it stolen, by someone not connected to the hospital, then there would be a good possibility that the thief just abandoned it there. However, if someone connected with the hospital drove the car off the property without the proper authority, then the car was parked where it was because the individual had an interest in the immediate area. It would be tedious work to search the hospital records and compare employee residential addresses to the area where the car was found, but sometimes, methodical, demanding work yielded that one clue which led to solving the case. They had no other leads, so the tedious work began.

Since the detectives were focusing on the Leonard Canella case, they decided to check on anyone who could be even remotely connected to the case. Of course, that would include such people as the victim, Mr. Leonard Canella, Dr. James Whitly, Dr. Charles Strathmore (the other attending neurology specialist), Dr. Richard Cotton (the emergency room doctor), and all the nurses who worked specifically with Dr. Whitly. It was going to take time, but time was something of which they had plenty. They had exhausted all their leads, so grunt work was the next best thing. The detectives split the work. In addition to checking residential address information, the detectives would initiate a second round of interviews. This was standard procedure. It gave the interviewees time to think and possibly recall valuable details. It also created an atmosphere of anxiety that sometimes shook the details tree. Detective Krane was going to interview the doctors, and Detective Barret was interviewing the nurses.

As the detectives were starting their second round of interviews, they came across Dr. Charles Strathmore. The doctor told them that there was no need for Leonard Canella to remain in a recovery room, and that he was going to move the patient to a regular room on the second floor of the hospital. He further explained that there was an immediate need for the recovery rooms to be available for other patients. Although Leonard was being moved, he would still have to remain in the hospital for a while longer. The doctor wanted to continue to observe Mr. Canella's recovery which involved his broken bones and reinflated lung. The detectives made a note of the change and recorded the new room number.

Dr. Strathmore left the detectives and headed for Mr. Canella's room. He notified the patient of the change and told him that it would occur within the next few hours. The doctor explained that Leonard's condition no longer warranted his staying in a recovery room, and that the room was needed for a patient who was presently undergoing an operation. He also explained that Leonard should remain in the hospital for a few more days. The patient agreed.

Charles Strathmore had taken over the responsibilities that James had. So, both Leonard Canella and Laura were his charges. After leaving Leonard's room, as was his routine, he went to Laura's room to check on her. He spoke with her as if she were conscious, all the doctors did, and he checked her vitals, which were normal. He told Laura that she was doing well, and that he expected to be speaking with her face-to-face very soon.

Well, hello doctor. Thanks for coming by. I guess my husband is still among the missing. That's typical. I am really getting tired of everyone telling me that I should be waking up soon, and that everything is okay. It is not okay. I am laying here like a vegetable not being able to communicate how I feel or what I need. Isn't there something that you could do to expedite my recovery? Yeah, I know it's just a rhetorical question. If there was something, I'm sure you would have tried it already. I am sure my husband would have tried. I think! You are a good friend of his. What's happened to him? I can't believe that he let someone come between him and his love for medicine. What's the expression? "A pubic hair could pull a caboose." I am sure that's what's pulling James away from his practice and possibly his future in medicine. No matter

whatever else he messed up, he is a good doctor. I feel bad for him. What's that? What's happening?

As the doctor was leaving Laura's room, the floor nurse came in to change the intravenous bag. She took the old one down, and while she was connecting to the new line, she thought she saw finger movement on Laura's right hand. She stopped and stared. Sure enough, after a few seconds, the nurse was sure that she saw movement. She yelled down the hall for Dr. Strathmore who was still on the floor filling out report work. Hearing the nurse's call, he responded quickly to Laura's room. He started speaking to Laura telling her that she was in the process of regaining consciousness, and that everything she was feeling was normal. Dr. Strathmore again checked her vitals which were well within the normal range. As with all coma recoveries, the process is a slow one. To rush the patient could result in a catastrophe, so everyone just slowly and calmly guided Laura back to the present.

Across the hall, Leonard saw the commotion in Laura Whitly's room, and at first, thought that the staff was responding to an emergency situation. He continued to look and realized, just as they did with him, they were assisting in waking Laura from her extended sleep. Ironic, he thought, she is finally waking, and her husband, who apparently visited quite often, is nowhere in sight. He was sure that Laura was not going to be happy with James' absence. Little did he know that it was not Dr. Whitly's choice not to be there with his wife, especially now that he was being held hostage. The irony is not in James' absence, but in where his attendance was.

Andrea used James' state of confusion and weakness to facilitate immobilizing him. She helped him into a kitchen chair and proceeded to tie him up with an electrical extension cord that she found in a kitchen drawer. He was still groggy from the blow to his head but conscious enough to know that he was in an unenviable position. He was compromised, and there was no way now that he could convince or stop Andrea from completing her task. From his position on the kitchen chair, he could see the lifeless body of Martha Higgins, and it struck his heart to know that he was responsible for putting her in harm's way. He regretted not being stronger when she had asked to come along. Had he held to his decision, Martha would still be alive. The pool of blood around Martha's body was testimony to the vicious determination of the person he once loved, and who he apparently misjudged. Andrea very calmly dragged the body down the stairs and into the basement. Once she wiped up the blood, her heinous deed would be behind her and just exist as an image in her mind. It would be an ever-present acute reminder in James' mind of the presence of evil.

As James pondered his situation, he felt the vibration of the hospital pager as a new message was being transmitted. He couldn't get the pager out of his pocket, and he wasn't sure if he wanted Andrea to see what was being sent. Knowing that Nurse Higgins was the one who kept him informed of hospital happenings, he couldn't figure out who would now be paging him. Erring on the side of caution, the question would have to be answered at a later time.

Following her body disposal and clean-up, Andrea approached James who was slowly coming out of the mental fog that had permeated his conscious thinking. "Well, Dr. Whitly how are we feeling? You look a little better. Your eyes are even able to focus, now."

"What have you done? You have killed a person who only wanted the best for you. She was your friend for a very long time, and you treated her as if she was a mortal enemy. You have total disregard for anyone but yourself. How could I have been such a fool as to not see the real you? You are a murderous devil that should suffer forever in hell."

"Well, Well. Don't hold back, James. Tell me what you really think." She laughed. "With a little bit of luck, you may be able to survive if you follow my directions to the letter."

"You can go to hell." With that, Andrea slapped James across the face and exclaimed: "I am the one holding all the cards, James. I'll admit that without your cooperation, my task becomes a bit more difficult, but don't think for a minute that I won't succeed without your help. Understand though, that if you remain uncooperative, my goal of eliminating one person will be extended to two. Laura is just across the hall from Leonard. Killing her would be quite simple and would not bother me in the least. In fact, I would get some satisfaction out of her death and your suffering. So, before you chastise me and condemn me for my actions, remember that the life of your wife lies in the balance. Your cooperation could mean the difference between her living or dying. It is your choice." Andrea left him to think about her threat and went into the basement to wrap Martha's body.

When Andrea went into the basement, it was James' opportunity to look at his pager. What could have been so important that he was being paged, and who would be sending him a message? Using whatever leverage he had, James wiggled and squirmed until he was able to get the pager from his rear pocket. He twisted his head until he thought it would fall off his neck and pressed the "read" button. Dr. Charles Strathmore was informing him that he was moving Leonard Canella out of the recovery room, and more importantly, that his wife, Laura, was slowly regaining consciousness. James was elated and very thankful that his friend, Charles, would risk paging him. For sure, this message was something that James did not want Andrea to see. He heard her coming up the stairs and hurriedly forced the pager back into his pocket.

With Andrea's bloody hands in his face, she asked if he had thought about her "offer." Knowing about the new situation at the hospital and realizing that Andrea's threat regarding his wife was not an empty one, James reluctantly agreed to cooperate. Although he was the one who was tied to the chair and whose wife's life was being threatened, Dr. James Whitly felt that now, with these new developments, he had the upper hand.

Chapter Twenty-Eight

The Canella Residence

After the doctors and nurses left Laura's room, Leonard saw the opportunity to meet Dr. James Whitly's wife. Favoring his recovery, he gingerly stepped across the hall and entered her room. He introduced himself as a longtime friend of her husband's and asked if she was aware of what had taken place over the last few days. She nodded that she had heard what was occurring, and that through James' visits, she was kept up to date. Following a few more introductory remarks, Leonard got straight to the point: "Mrs. Whitly, are you aware of the relationship between my wife and your husband?"

"Yes, I am aware of a former relationship between the two." Leonard smirked at her response: "No, Mrs. Whitly, one would have to be blind not to see that there is still something very real between the two of them. In fact, I am certain that all this time that your husband has been absent from the hospital, he has been with Andrea. I believe that James has been helping her elude the police and assisting her as she plans my demise."

"I know that my husband has been in Andrea's company, but I also know that there were circumstances that couldn't be avoided. As I lay unconscious, he spoke to me about what was transpiring. I am sure that he cares for Andrea as he would for any other human being who needed help, and I am also sure that his help is all that she will get." Laura was not going to give in to the suggestions and accusations that this stranger was implying. In fact, she was taking offense to the whole conversation, hoping beyond hope, that she was right about James. She knew that Andrea had an enormous influence over James, but deep down she felt that James would see through the emotional appeal, and to what Andrea was all about. Unfortunately, she had no facts to back up her convictions.

Leonard went into more of the specifics regarding his friendship with James. He explained that through no fault of his, Andrea turned from James and desired an intimate and loving relationship with him. He went on to say that James always blamed him for their break-up, and unfortunately, nothing that Leonard said could convince James otherwise. With that false foundation laid down, Leonard went on to explain why he felt very strongly that James would help Andrea in her murderous plot. For James, it would be revenge metered out by a third party but having the desired results as if he had done it himself.

Laura had heard enough: "I am sorry Mr. Canella, but as you know, I am still recovering, and I need my rest. So, if you don't mind, I have to ask you to leave."

"I understand Mrs. Whitly, but don't be surprised when you find out how involved your husband really is with my wife." Leonard had to get his closing shot in before he left. He wished her well and went to his room.

Leonard's visit, although she hated to admit it, caused Laura to have second thoughts about the whole situation. Why was James so involved with Andrea and her circumstances? It seemed that his concern was over-the-top, and Leonard's comments only served to strengthen that thinking. Laura was willing to give her husband the benefit of the doubt, but where was he now? Why hasn't he visited in a while? Why isn't he here now that she had regained consciousness? Laura was getting increasingly upset as she thought about the situation. She forced herself to think about other things, and finally she began falling into the arms of sleep.

Just as Laura was closing her eyes, she heard voices in Leonard's room. They were talking about his moving to a room on the second floor. This would be great news for her. He would not be able to fill her head so easily with so many doubts, though they were lingering there anyway. The move added to the relief she felt as the veil of sleep fell over her. Maybe, when she woke, James would be there to explain everything. Since coming out of the coma, she felt a strong desire to see her husband and work things out. Her feelings, for some reason, were much stronger now than when she was comatose. Maybe, it was the fact that now she was dealing with the reality of the present and not just thinking about it. No matter what it was, Laura wanted James to be there, and she hoped to God that he didn't let her down.

While James languished in the captive environment that Andrea provided, she kept to herself trying to figure out the elements of her next attempt. She now had a surprise positive addition to her plan, and she knew that his forthcoming cooperation would facilitate her activities. She just needed time to pull all the steps together. She was unaware, however, of two very important issues that would negatively affect any scheme she put into place: Leonard Canella was moved to another room in the hospital, and the threat against James' wife was weakened because of the fact that Laura was now conscious. James knew about the new developments, and he would surely use them to his advantage.

As Andrea plotted, as James weighed his advantages, as Leonard moved, and as Laura slept, Detective David Krane and Detective Tracy Barret reviewed the results of the fingerprint analysis. The one item that stood out above all the rest was the fingerprint lifted from the rearview mirror of the vehicle. It belonged to Dr. James Whitly. It wasn't a fact that would break open the case, but it was a lead that they could follow. They had nothing else. The print revealed that James had been in the stolen vehicle, and most likely, had driven it to the location where it was found. They were still puzzled though. Why was the car parked there? To answer that question, they dug deeper into their investigation of employee residential addresses. If it was James Whitly who stole the car, why was he in that neighborhood?

Detective Barret, who was looking at the nurses' information, came upon an address that was about two or three blocks away from the car's location. The address belonged to Nurse Martha Higgins. Further investigation revealed that Nurse Higgins had been working with Dr. Whitly for a long time, and she was one of the nursing staff in whom James had the most confidence. It was a stretch, but worth looking into. After discussing the find with her partner, they decided to take a ride and visit Nurse Higgins, who they discovered hadn't been to work for the second day in a row. They were told that it was quite unusual for Martha to be absent and not to have notified her boss. Her boss had called Martha's home but failed to make contact. Armed with the information that they gleaned from the fingerprint report, the residential address search, and the interview with Martha's boss, the detectives set out to see Nurse Martha Higgins.

It was a quick twenty-five-minute ride to Martha Higgins' house. When they arrived, they looked for Martha's car that had been registered with the hospital for employee parking rights. Her vehicle was nowhere in sight, but there was a garage on the property, and it was a possibility that she garaged her car. As they got out of their vehicle and approached the house, it seemed that Martha Higgins might not be home. The blinds were drawn, there were no lights on, and the morning paper still lay in front of the door. Detective Krane rang the doorbell and waited for a response. He didn't get one, so, he rang it again. That having not succeeded, Tracy used the door knocker to alert Martha of their presence. That also failed.

The detectives decided to go around to the back of the house to knock on the rear door, but also to look into the garage. The garage was empty, and again, there was no answer at the back door. As all detectives do, they continued to look around. Detective Barret noticed that the door on the side of the garage led to what looked like a possible apartment above the garage. There was no bell or knocker, and the door was open. Tracy opened the door a bit and yelled an "hello." She got no response to her salutation. The detectives had no warrant; so, legally they had no right to go up the stairs to the apartment. Not wanting to jeopardize any of their potential evidentiary findings, Detective Krane decided to call the hospital and let Martha's boss know that they were unsuccessful in locating Nurse Higgins. He would also ask the boss if she wanted them to do a wellness check on Martha. Showing his obvious concern for Martha's well-being, the head nurse agreed to a wellness check. This was the tool they needed to further their search.

Since they were at the entrance to the garage door, the detectives decided to search the garage apartment first. There was really nothing much that the detectives found in the apartment; so, they decided to enter Martha's residence. With the use of a credit card, Detective Krane easily jimmied the rear door. They both yelled for Martha but got no return answer. Before looking more carefully downstairs, they went up to the second floor looking into the bedrooms. In some of the cases where a "wellness check" is requested, the individual is found expired in bed, having died in his or her sleep. This was not the case, however, with searching for Martha. Having exhausted their search of the second floor, the detectives concentrated on the entry floor. Nothing caught their immediate attention as they went throughout the floor. The house had no basement, so only the two floors would be able to reveal any clues. They both sat at the kitchen table pondering the situation, when Tracy noticed some writing on a pad attached to the kitchen wall phone. She rose from the table and went to the phone. It was an address, no name, just an address. That was all they had, so they left.

When the detectives returned to their headquarters, Tracy decided to run the address that she had copied from the pad through the reverse directory in their office. It was a long shot, but nothing ventured, nothing gained. Detective Krane was filling out the paperwork for a request of Martha's telephone records. This could help, but the answer from the phone company usually took a while. As Detective Krane labored over the paperwork, Tracy approached him: "I used the reverse directory for the address we saw on the pad in the kitchen. You will not believe who the address comes back to." Before her partner could offer an answer, she emphatically exclaimed: "It is the home of Mr. Leonard Canella. Do you believe that?"

"No, but we are definitely going to visit Mr. Canella's residence. If she were a guy, I would say that Andrea had some set of balls!"

Chapter Twenty-Nine

The Pager

Knowing that his wife was awake and not being able to see her was really bothering James. He not only had to figure out a way to stop Andrea, but he had to find a way to escape and maneuver his way into Mountain Pacific. Right now, the immediate focus had to be on freeing himself from the electric cord that was pressing him to the kitchen chair. Andrea was busy plotting and planning, but she was in plain view. He had to be careful not to alert her to his escape attempt.

Andrea wanted her plan to be perfect so that she would not have to plan again in the future. She knew that she was living on borrowed time, her chances of success were becoming slimmer and slimmer. But Andrea had an ace in the hole, and his name was James. As her plan started to come together, she imagined the good doctor rolling her on a gurney right into the connecting room to Leonard. A doctor with a patient on a gurney would not be questioned about his actions or his destination. The real problem that presented itself was the entry into the hospital by both her and James. Additionally, how was she going to keep the reins on her hostage? By what present threat was she going to convince James to unconditionally cooperate or else?

As Andrea tried to overcome what looked like some insurmountable obstacles, James was busy carefully wiggling and squirming in an effort to loosen his bindings. It was not easy with Andrea sitting in the next room and within a line of sight of James. The electrical wire that Andrea used, although more difficult to loosen than ordinary twine, was old and brittle. It might not withstand the constant stress. His wrists were aching from the pressure, but he was not going to reduce his efforts. Slowly but surely, James felt the wire loosen. It would take more pressure and more squirming, but he was making progress.

In addition to figuring out her new plan, Andrea was worried that Mountain Pacific Hospital would become concerned when Martha Higgins did not show up for work. According to people who knew her, Nurse Higgins was a dependable employee with an excellent attendance record. So, when something like unusual absences occur, her boss would reach out for her. If the hospital staff couldn't contact her, they might even visit her residence or have the police take a look. There was even a possibility that the police might enter the house. If they did that, would there be anything in the house that might jeopardize Andrea's safety? She wondered if Martha had written anything down, for instance, a name, phone number or address. If the police found something like that, Andrea was sure that they would follow up on the information. So now, what she originally felt to be a pretty safe place, might turn out to be the very location where she is captured and arrested.

Even though Detectives Krane and Barret were on their way to the Canella residence, David Krane had his doubts that

Andrea would be so bold as to return to Leonard's home. After all, according to her, this was where she went through her own private "hell." Why would she want to return to the torture chamber? He guessed for the very same reason he was thinking that she wouldn't. No one would believe that she would go back there, and she was counting on that for her safety.

As Andrea thought about it, she became more and more concerned that Martha might have left some information that would lead the police to Leonard's home. She wasn't sure, but she couldn't take the risk of being caught, not now, when she was so close to achieving her goal. Andrea decided that, at least for tonight, she would take James with her and park Leonard's car down the street from the house to see if any unusual police activity would take place. Andrea grabbed James by the arm and directed him through the connecting door to the garage where Leonard's car was parked. She opened the rear door and roughly pushed him into the seat. She told him to stay face down as she closed the car door. Andrea knew that as the automatic garage opener pulled up the garage door, there would be more noise than she wanted to have. So, she disabled the automation and manually lifted the garage door. Not to bring any unnecessary attention to her activities, she did it as carefully and quietly as she possibly could. She was satisfied so far.

Andrea did not start the car. She was so paranoid regarding unnecessary attention that she decided to push the vehicle out of the garage and into the driveway. When she got the car on the driveway, she would go back to the garage door and close it as carefully and quietly as she did when she opened it. The driveway was gently sloped down toward the street, so pushing the car out into the street was no difficult task. The dark night was giving her cover, and she was confident that she had succeeded with her plan. She got in the car and drove it to the next block and parked it within sight of Leonard's house. She told James to stay down, and she just waited.

It was not long before a car pulled up in front of the Canella residence. Andrea saw two figures exit the car. Two people she knew were detectives. Apparently, her assumption that Martha might have left some useful information at her house was correct. Detectives Krane and Barret walked carefully around the perimeter of the house to see if there were any obvious entrance breeches. The only thing they saw was that some of the police tape that was affixed to the rear door had been torn away. However, that was not a definitive indicator that someone was inside. The tape separation could have been the result of the weather. In fact, at this point, there really was no reason for the police tape barrier. The house was not a crime scene location, and the owner of the house would soon be leaving the hospital to come home. However, since the residence was somewhat still under the control of the police, the detectives decided to go inside. They did not need a credit card for entry, they had the key.

From her vantage point, Andrea saw the detectives go to the rear of the house. She waited and did not see them come back out. She had to assume that they entered the house through the back entrance. That meant that the body of Martha Higgins would be discovered. It also meant that Andrea had to find another safe location where she could hide out, and that was no easy task. She didn't wait around to see what happened. She knew she had to get out of the area, and when the police realized that Leonard's car was gone, they would put out an alarm for a stolen vehicle. So, even the car wasn't a safe option. She had run out of hide-out options, and she didn't want to just drive aimlessly. She started to panic so she headed away from the area and drove to a remote area of a state park. At least there, she could calm herself for a while and collect her thoughts.

David and Tracy cautiously entered the house taking nothing for granted. There was nothing in the entranceway that caught their eye. However, when they went up the stairs to the living area, they noticed glass on the floor and a broken cocktail table. More than that, they saw what they assumed to be dried blood on the floor next to the table. Now, there investigative juices began to flow. They split up and searched the rest of the house.

"Dave, I am in the basement. You'd better come down and see this." From the tone of Tracy's voice, Detective Krane wasted no time getting to the basement. There, he was greeted with the grizzly sight of a body wrapped up in an old carpet. They had found Nurse Martha Higgins. If the location had not been a crime scene before, it definitely was now. The detectives called for the crime scene unit to respond and secured the area until the unit arrived. While Tracy remained in the house, her partner went to search the garage. It was then that he realized that Leonard Canella's car was gone. He went back to the house and told Tracy what he found. She took the bull by the horns and called in the alarm and description of the stolen car. If all this was the possible handiwork of Andrea Canella, she was now a potential suspect in a homicide case.

In the corner of the living room on a small area rug, Tracy noticed a square black item lying right beside one of the legs of the sofa chair. As she bent down to investigate, she realized that it was a pager. It had the Mountain Pacific Hospital symbol engraved on it, and Dr. James Whitly's name printed below it. Tracy had found James' hospital pager. With a little help from one of the police technicians who had arrived on the scene, she was able to open the messages. The last message that Dr. Whitly received was from Dr. Charles Strathmore, who apparently notified James that Leonard Canella had a room change, and that Laura Whitly had finally come out of her coma. When Tracy showed the message to her partner, he knew that, if possible, Dr. James Whitly would want to see his wife. The strategy now would focus on surveilling the hospital with special attention to Laura Whitly's room. Things were finally beginning to come together.

Chapter Thirty

The Park House

Andrea Canella was so engrossed in the replanning of her plot that she didn't immediately notice the small State Park building just about 50 yards away that looked abandoned. Andrea had no place to go. She was out of options for a secure location, but there right in front of her was a possible safe haven. When Andrea finally noticed the cottage-looking building (called a park house), she decided to take a closer look. She checked on James who was still bound and lying on the back seat. Satisfied that James was not going anywhere, Andrea left the car and walked toward the building. She saw that there was a lock on the front door, but the lock seemed to be attached to wood that had rotted through a long time ago. Detaching the lock from its hold on the door would be a relatively easy task. She didn't know if there was heat or electricity inside the building, but she had to hope for the best. She had no other choice, and she considered this find like discovering a pond in the desert.

Andrea looked around and thought it safe to move James into the building. She went back to the car and helped James out of the back seat. She escorted him to the entrance of the building, and, with the tire iron she took from the trunk of the car, she disengaged the locking device from the wooden door.

The inside of the building smelled of dampness and mold. Andrea reached for the light switch and crossed her fingers with the hope that electricity was still flowing through the lines. Her prayers were answered when a dim flicker of light was produced from the one fixture hanging in the middle of the two-room haven. She pushed James over to an old wooden chair in the corner of the room and went to the old radiator to see if there was any heat filtering through steel pipes. The device was not stone cold, but it was obvious that neither she nor James would be sweating while they stayed there. The purpose of the little heat that was emanating from the radiator was to ensure that the pipes in the building would not freeze.

Andrea was far from comfortable, but she found a place that was off the beaten path, and therefore, out of the public and police eye. She needed time to think. She had to find a way to exterminate Leonard, and now because of her part in the death of Nurse Martha Higgins, she had to make certain her escape was guaranteed. There was a possibility of facing life imprisonment and ultimately even a death sentence. She was not up for either one of those.

James continued his attempt to free himself from the electric wire straight jacket, but he was feeling the effects of the possible concussion. He was feeling dizzy and was on the verge of passing out. He called out to Andrea who saw that James was not feeling well. He was slurring his speech, complained of nausea and a headache, had dilated pupils and was somewhat incoherent in his comments. He needed rest and sleep. Andrea did not need this new complication and thought that maybe this new obstacle should be eliminated. However, she did need James' participation in her overall plan. She decided to help James back to good health. This was not a decision based on what would be best for James, but what would be best for the success of her scheme.

Seeing that James was struggling to maintain his balance on the chair, Andrea decided that since he was apparently reeling from the effects of the concussion, he would not present an escape threat. She loosened his bindings and helped him over to what looked like a Red Cross army cot from World War II. He stumbled onto the cot and moaned with the uneasiness he was feeling. Although an objective observer would sympathize with how badly James was feeling, James was exaggerating his condition in hope that he would find the opportunity to surprise his captor and finally take control of a dangerous situation. He feigned sleep but laid there with one eye open. His attempt had to be well-timed so that he would face a minimum of resistance. Although he wasn't as bad as he portrayed, he didn't feel one hundred percent. With Andrea's adrenaline running at well above average levels, she wouldn't be easy to take down. If he failed, things would definitely take a turn for the worse, and he worried, not only for himself, but more so for his wife.

Andrea was worried that the police would be on the alert for Leonard's car; so, while James was tied to the chair and somewhat "out-of-it", Andrea went out to the car and drove it to a desolate area of the park where the woods were bounded by a man-made lake. She put the car in "neutral," and looked around to make sure that there was no one else in the area. Then, with a stick she found on the ground, she jammed the gas pedal. Andrea thrust the gear shift into "drive," jumped out of the way, and the car drove itself deep into the murky water. She no longer had to worry about someone seeing the car, nor a diligent cop noticing a stolen vehicle. That problem was solved, but sometimes the solution to one problem introduces you to another. Andrea now had no means of transportation at her disposal. However, she thought like everything else, when it came to the time that she needed wheels, she would think of something. But for now, Andrea rushed back to the park house to check on James and to relax in the safety of its confines.

Laura Whitly was feeling better as each hour passed, but she was very much concerned about James and where he was. When Dr. Strathmore came into her room to, once again, check on her, she asked him if he would do her a really big favor: "Dr. Strathmore, I know that you and James are close, and I am really worried about him. Would it be possible for you to contact him or page him and let him know that I miss him and am waiting for him to see me? It is not like James to stay away and not contact me at all."

"Just so you know, Laura. I have already paged James. I left a message that Leonard moved to another room, and more importantly, that you had regained consciousness. So far, I have not received anything in return, but I am sure that as soon as James is able, he will get in touch."

Laura was somewhat relieved but still concerned that James had not yet reached out for Dr. Strathmore or her. She was glad that James couldn't hear or see her thoughts as she lay unconscious in the hospital room. She regretted her sarcastic attitude and nasty thoughts. Now, she only wanted James to be at her side, and usher her back to total health and comfort. It would be horrible if she didn't get the chance to tell James how much he meant to her, and that she definitely wanted to bring back the luster and feelings that their marriage once had. Tears welled up in Laura's eyes as the prospect of not seeing him again was front and center.

Charles Strathmore, hearing Laura's desperate pleas, decided to send another message to his colleague and friend, James. He emphasized again that his wife, Laura, was doing well and getting better by the day, and that she was patiently but anxiously awaiting his visit or call. Dr. Strathmore also mentioned that he would help in any way that he could, and that it was important to contact him.

When James' pager went off, it was in the possession of Detective Tracy Barret. The police technician enabled the pager so that Tracy could view any messages that were on the pager or newly coming to the pager. When the pager vibrated, Detective Barret saw the message from Charles Strathmore. She discussed it with her partner, and they decided to visit both Laura and Dr. Charles Strathmore. Apparently, Dr. Whitly had not answered the first page, so Dr. Strathmore was trying again. The detectives wanted to emphasize to both his wife and his friend that James was being sought for a number of reasons involving the commission of particular crimes. They also wanted to put both of them on notice that their total cooperation was needed if they did not want to possibly be charged with obstructing an official investigation. This might work with Dr. Strathmore, but they doubted that Laura would, in any way, betray her husband.

James Whitly was moaning so loudly that not only could Andrea not think straight, but she was becoming worried about his condition. As he lay there, she stared at him, and she felt some of those old feelings pulling at her heartstrings. The feelings had never really disappeared, they just laid dormant. However, as she stood there, the feelings came back stronger than she imagined. Andrea tried to fight them off because she knew that emotions would only weaken her resolve to continue with her crusade. If James were now to apply his argument for surrender, she might be hard fought to oppose his suggestion. Andrea knew her vulnerabilities; so, she quickly turned away and began thinking about her next move. It wasn't easy, however, to just cast away the thoughts of the past and her early years with James. If she worked on it, she imagined that she could still convince James to give their relationship another chance. As she thought of the possibilities of life with James, involuntary feelings of hate toward Laura Whitly flooded into her mind. Laura had done nothing to her, but she was just holding James' heart captive. Andrea had to free him from that captivity. Laura Whitly's time had come!

Chapter Thirty-One

The Bait

Early the next morning, Detectives Krane and Barret drove to Mountain Pacific Hospital. They had to inform Mr. Leonard Canella that his house was now a crime scene. They were informed that Mr. Canella had a room change and was now located on the second floor of the hospital. Having been given his room number, the detectives went to the second floor and located Leonard.

“Hello Mr. Canella, we hope you are feeling well. We have some current information that we want to share with you, if you have a minute.”

“Well, I’m not going anywhere fast, so you have my attention.”

Detective Krane took the lead: “Yesterday, we acted on some information that we found at the house of one of the nurses. It led us to believe that your wife, Andrea, might be heading back to your home.”

“That is crazy. She is smarter than that. That would be the last place that she would go.”

"Well, that's what we thought too. But we followed the lead and went to your house. Since the house was no longer really involved in the present investigation, we did one last check, and removed all of the police tape. We checked the entire house, and when we went to the basement, we were greeted with a disturbing sight. The body of Nurse Martha Higgins was wrapped in an old rug and laying on the basement floor. Nurse Higgins had a close working relationship with Dr. James Whitly, and we discovered that she also had a former relationship with your wife. In fact, Andrea is now our prime suspect in the homicide, but we are not excluding the possibility that Dr. Whitly had some involvement in Nurse Higgins' death. Unfortunately, your home is now classified as a 'crime scene,' and even if you were released from the hospital today, you wouldn't be able to go back to your house."

To say that the expression on Leonard Canella's face was shock and surprise would be an understatement. For the first time in a very long while, Leonard was at a loss for words. He just kept shaking his head and staring at the detectives.

"Mr. Canella, do you understand what I am saying? You cannot go back to your house until the forensic crime team finishes their investigation of the house. In addition to blood stains, there are a number of other items that the team is looking at. We are not sure how long it will take, but we will let you know as soon as your home is cleared. With homicides, however, it can be a while."

The detectives gave Leonard a chance to mentally digest all the information that they gave him. He seemed to be deep in thought when he asked: "Do you know if anything was taken from the house? Was the house in disarray? Was anything destroyed?" The detectives were somewhat surprised at this line of questioning. These would be the normal questions that a homeowner would ask if he or she was just notified that there was "break-in." It was not what they expected from someone who was just told that a female was apparently murdered in his or her home. They assumed that it was the shock of the announcement that impacted Leonard's questions.

"As far as we could tell, Mr. Canella, there was only one item that was damaged. We found the living room glass cocktail table in pieces on the living room floor. Other than that, we found nothing else damaged or destroyed, but you will have time to inspect the house when we release it. There were some blood stains on the living room and basement floors, but other than that we haven't detected anything else. We will keep you informed. Our advice to you is to stay here for as long as you can and until we finish inspecting the house."

Leonard, apparently still in a state of shock, just nodded his head. What was streaming through Leonard's mind was the fact that if Andrea could kill someone whom she liked, and who had done nothing to cause rage in Andrea's heart, then killing him would be a no-brainer for her. It would be a walk in the park. He was concerned and looking for some reassurance from the detectives that Andrea's possible attempt would be thwarted, and that her arrest was imminent.

"You do know that Andrea has threatened to kill me, and if she is responsible for the death of someone who never did anything to her, then I think there is a strong possibility that she will use anything at her disposal to carry out her threat against me. What I want to know is how are you going to protect me?" Detective Tracy Barret addressed Leonard's concern: "First of all, Mr. Canella, we are not even certain that Andrea actually committed the murder, and secondly, if our boss deems it necessary to offer you official protection, you can be sure you will get it. We will bring your concerns to the boss and discuss the possible actions available to us."

"What do you mean if he deems it necessary. It is well known that Andrea wants me dead, and as you said, she is the prime suspect in the Higgins' murder. If she could kill Nurse Higgins, rest assured, she can easily kill me. I need protection."

"As I said, Mr. Canella, we will bring back your concerns and address them accordingly. Just so you know, everyone, including security, is well aware of what is taking place. It will be very difficult for Andrea or James Whitly to enter the hospital without someone knowing. That, plus potential additional police coverage, should be more than ample to secure your safety. We will be in touch." With that, the detectives left a bewildered Leonard to ponder his fate.

"Between you and I, Dave, Andrea Canella has been more than resourceful in eluding us and finding her way into the hospital."

"Yeah, that's true, Tracy, but we are not going to remind Mr. Canella of that fact. We do not want to make it so secure that Andrea decides not to attempt to complete her goal."

"What do you mean? Are we actually going to use Leonard Canella as bait?"

"The longer this goes on, Tracy, the more difficult it is going to be to catch her. We must bring her out on our terms. If she comes to the hospital on our terms, we will be more than ready to snatch her up. Who knows? We might get both James and Andrea at the same time, and I do not need to remind you that we have to bring this case to a close as quickly as possible. There are still certain clouds hanging over our heads. It is in our best interest to force Andrea's hand."

Detective Barret looked at her partner as if she could not believe what he was saying, but in her heart, she knew that he was probably right. It went against everything she was taught, but so have some the actions that she had taken thus far. Why not one more that might bring the nightmare to an end?

While the detectives were figuring out their strategy, Andrea was searching for ways to penetrate hospital security. But even before that, she now had to find a way to transport her and James to the hospital. This time she was coming up empty with possible solutions. Unfortunately, at this point, James could not help. He had a rough night, and she was awake for much of the time. She rationalized that it was fatigue that was the culprit denying her a clear route to potential solutions. She had to get some rest, and then, she was sure she would be able to work things out. Since James still seemed to be out of it, she hesitated tying him up. But what happens if he wakes up while she is resting? He would then have the advantage, and who knew what would happen. She erred on the side of caution and bound

James again with electric wire cord. She sat in the wooden chair to which she originally tied James and dozed off to sleep.

James was not asleep. He was aware of what Andrea was doing, and that she was exhausted from the night before. As she bound him this time, he was able to spread his arms a bit so the binding, once he relaxed, would not be so tight. However, he really didn't have a good night, and he wasn't feeling good enough to attempt to take control of the situation. When he was feeling just a little bit better, he would surprise Andrea and put an end to her conquest once and for all, but he had to choose the right time. Even though he would be able to surprise her now, he did not have confidence in his ability to overtake her in his weakened position, and he would only have one chance to be victorious, and that wasn't now.

Chapter Thirty-Two

The Maintenance Worker

Although Andrea had fallen into the grips of sleep, James knew that it was not the time to exercise his take-over. So, he laid back and just rested trying to regain as much strength and stamina as he could. He was going to need all of it to stop Andrea. As he laid back, he thought of his wife and how disappointed she must be that he's not there with her as she regained her consciousness. He hoped that, because of his absence, that she didn't give up hope on him, on them. He would make it up to her for the rest of his life. James knew that the minor operations that Laura underwent were successfully healing, and he had been informed that the pressure on her brain was all but gone. The physical complications worked out very well for her, it was the emotional trauma that James was worried about. Not just the emotional stress of physical recovery, but the emotional pressure of saving a marriage. He needed to get to her so he could reinforce his focused desire to begin again and bolster the feelings that might have laid dormant for a while.

Being engrossed in heavy thought, James didn't realize how much time had passed. Before he knew it, Andrea was slowly awakening from her much needed rest. She opened her eyes and saw that James was not breathing the recognized rhythm of sleep, so she went over to him and gently nudged him awake. James opened his eyes and smiled at her. He had to make Andrea feel comfortable with him so she would ultimately let her guard down. Easier said than done.

"How are you feeling, James. You had me worried there for a while. Apparently, you suffered a nasty concussion. You look a lot better now. Not exactly one hundred percent but better than you were."

"Thanks, Andrea. I am still feeling a little off, but I am a lot better after getting some sleep. In fact, I could go for some food, but looking around, this is not the Ritz."

Andrea laughed at his comment and agreed that she had stayed in better locations than the one they were presently in, but any port in a storm. As she was speaking to James, she heard a weird sound coming from outside the park house. She went to the door and opened it just enough to see a state park maintenance van parked about twenty yards from the house. She looked carefully to where she thought the sound was originating. It was coming from a spot directly on the other side of the van, an area that was not within her view. Andrea wanted to know what was going on, and if, of course, she could use the noise instrument and the van to her advantage. Before she left the park house, she turned to check on James and was met with a sharp blow to the head. Contrary to his earlier thinking, James had decided that this was the time to act.

Andrea reeled through the front door of the park house and landed on the grassy area in front of the entrance. As a result of the blow, she was dazed and not in full control of her faculties. This enabled James to roll her over and tie her up with the same cord that Andrea had used on him. Due to all the commotion that the struggle between James and Andrea was causing, the State Park maintenance man, a man in his early sixties, came around the van and witnessed a fight between a man and a woman, where the male attacker was desperately trying to subdue the female and tie her up.

Although not in the best of health, it was a natural reaction for the park employee to jump into the fray and help free the female victim. He landed squarely on James' back and was able to push him from Andrea. James attempted to explain what was happening, but he was met with a barrage of punches and kicks that sent him rolling onto the ground. Andrea, taking total advantage of the situation, kept screaming "help me, help me." This encouraged the worker to follow James and jump on him, once again. This time James was able to fend off many of the punches and get the man's attack under control. In fact, all of sudden, James hardly felt any resistance at all from the man. The man went limp in James' clutch. The sixty-year-old apparently had heart problems and suffered a fatal heart attack as a result of his heroic but misinformed efforts. James was holding a dead man.

Andrea regained her wits and immediately went to immobilize James. She came up behind James and elbowed him in the neck, being careful not to hit his head that was already hosting his present concussion. Another blow to the head could potentially produce fatal results. She was well aware of that fact.

Even though James had abused her trust, she still needed him, and she still had hopes of convincing him on the merits of a romantic relationship with her. She quickly thought to herself “it might just be wishful thinking, but what if it isn’t?”

Following the impact from Andrea’s blow, James released his grasp on the body of the worker and fell to the ground on one knee. Andrea quickly pushed him the rest of the way, and he landed face down. She was able to utilize the same electric wire cord that she had originally used, and which was bouncing back and forth between the two of them like a ping pong ball, to bind James’ wrists, once again. The park house was in a remote area of the park; so fortunately, there was no one in sight.

The first thing that Andrea did was to help James back to the park house, half dragging him there. She pushed him into the chair where she had slept and bound him to it. She now had to deal with the body of the man who saved her. She actually felt bad that the man had died trying to save her, but his body was a definite problem for her. She checked the van for tools and other items that might be of use and found the keys on the sun visor. She now had tools and transportation, and one dead man. Although feeling melancholy about it, she decided that a watery grave was her best option. She struggled to get the man into the van, and then drove the park vehicle to the same location where she hid Leonard’s car. She weighed down the body with some large stones she found, said a prayer, and committed him to the depths of the lake. She headed back to deal with James, and her transportation problem had been solved. She also had a hedge trimmer that the man was using, some rope, various landscaping instruments and assorted other items that a maintenance and landscaping individual might use. She hit the lottery!

The park supervisors would probably not be looking for their worker until much later on in the day. This gave Andrea plenty of time to plan. No one would ever expect Andrea to be driving an official state vehicle. She could get close to the hospital without ever raising any suspicion. That wasn't the problem any longer. It was how to get into the hospital and what to do once in there. Again, she had to think of a pending threat to James' wife for James to really cooperate. After his last move, Andrea had very little confidence in James' loyalty. She thought and thought until she came up with an even more diabolical plan. It wasn't so much that she had to do the killing, it was more that she just wanted her husband dead. Did it matter who killed him as long as he died and knew, in his last moments, that his demise was perpetrated on her behalf? No, it did not matter, not at all.

Andrea's plan was coming together even better than she thought it would. Of course, James' role in its successful execution was critical. She now had the imminent threat for which she was searching, and she also had the executioner, albeit an uncooperative and reluctant one. She looked at James as he adjusted himself to the new bindings. Her feelings ranged from love to hate, from pity to envy, and from doubt to confidence. For her, he encompassed all of them. She would include James in knowing her plan only when she was sure that it was at a level that ensured success. She knew that he would balk vigorously at first and refuse to be involved in any part of it. But James wasn't just going to be a part of it, he was going to be the main operative part in bringing her crusade to a successful conclusion. His integral part in the operation not only furthered her goal, but it left him with no one to turn to but her. If she pulled this off, she would get two for the price of one, one death - Leonard's, and one life – James'. The more she thought about it, she might even be rewarded with two deaths – Leonard's and Laura's. With Laura gone, the obvious competition would be eliminated. That wouldn't be so bad.

Andrea was busy planning, but so were Detectives Krane and Barret. They knew that, at some point, Dr. Whitly would risk coming to the hospital to see his wife. They also assumed that Andrea Canella would not be far behind. It was a plan that involved bait, deception, risk, and patience.

In addition to the two detectives and other police personnel being involved, many of the hospital staff would also have to participate. The hospital was going to be secured, but not to the point that it would be impossible to breach. It would be okay if Andrea and James were able to enter the hospital because the flashpoint would not be at the hospital entrance but in either Laura Whitly's or Leonard Canella's room. It would be there that the capture and arrest of one or both of the fugitives would most likely take place. The police would be in control of both rooms, and escape would be nearly impossible. The only problem that the police had to overcome was that they had to be ready at any time from here on in. The execution of the plan, however, was totally dependent on a major unknown,

Andrea's schedule. Time was to Andrea Canella's advantage, but in the eyes of the relenting detectives, it was her only advantage.

Chapter Thirty-Three

The Executioner

Andrea had to be both creative and threatening when she presented her plan to James. He was still hurting from the fight and the ultimate blow to the neck that Andrea had administered, but he was conscious enough for Andrea to start laying out her strategy, and the integral part that James played in it.

"How are we doing James? You put up a good fight, but it's a shame that you don't have eyes behind your head, you could have warded off my blow. You do realize that I could have directed my shot to your head, and you know that a blow like that could have killed you. I didn't because of two reasons: one, I still care about you, and two, I need you to help me finalize my contract with the devil. Before you start shaking your head and saying something like 'absolutely not,' hear me out."

James weakly interrupted: "I don't care what you have to say, I am not going to help you kill someone." "No, James. You have it wrong. I do not want you to help me kill someone. I want you to kill someone all by yourself." James smirked and looked at her with a stare that said: "You have to be out of your mind."

"James, you're staring at me with a look that says I'm crazy. If you hear me out, you'll understand how logical and well-orchestrated my plan can be. I have even included an escape strategy that allows us to flee to freedom together. I know down deep you still care for me. You just need some fuel to ignite the embers that are still glowing in your heart."

"Andrea, in addition to all of your other problems, it sounds like you're on drugs. After all that you have done and plan on doing, do you really think that I want to be anywhere near you, let alone run away with you? Yes, you're right, I still have embers glowing, but I want to use them to ignite and destroy you as I send you to hell."

"James, you are not thinking clearly. If nothing else, you have to know that I am determined, one way or the other, to end Leonard's life. So, if you value your life and the life of your lovely and unknowing wife, Laura, you will listen carefully to what I have to say."

"You leave my wife out of this!"

"Oh no, James. She is already a part of it, and how she fares when all is done, is totally up to you. Unfortunately, I have to ask you to violate a tenet of the Hippocratic Oath that you took where it says, 'and do no harm.' James, you will definitely be doing harm. In fact, you will be administering deadly harm. If you don't, the administrator of that deadly harm will transfer from you to me, and I will meter out that harm on your wife who you will never see alive again. Do we understand each other, James?"

"What are you talking about. I don't understand."

"If you listen carefully to me and do not interrupt, I will explain the whole thing and how you can save your wife from harm. Now, shut up and pay attention."

Andrea went on to explain her intricate plan to James. She told him that she was going to wear the uniform that she took from the park maintenance worker before she dumped him in the lake. In uniform, she would boldly enter the hospital right through the main entrance. Andrea also told James that he would have to find a way to get into the hospital. She was going to drop him off about a half mile from the hospital, which would give her time to get to her location in Mountain Pacific without him being able to notify anyone. By the time he got there, she would be in the planned position to inflict a lot of harm on his wife, if necessary. Andrea further explained that once she witnessed Leonard's death, James' wife would be out of harm's way. Andrea also elaborated on the escape plan which included him - the doctor, rolling her - a patient, on a gurney to the elevator. She told him that she would be more specific about everything as the time got closer.

Dr. James Whitly listened carefully, and when Andrea finished with her presentation he said: "So, let me get this straight. You want me to march into Mountain Pacific Hospital, go to Leonard Canella's room, kill him, and then aid in your escape. It sounds like a walk in the park!" Sarcastically, he continued: "Oh, by the way, is there a specific method that you want me to use for the murder?"

"I'm glad you asked that, James. I was thinking that a garrote would be the most expeditious method. It would be silent, tortuous, and efficient. With the tools I have just acquired, I am going to attempt to make one. If it can't be done, then you will have to resort to the tried-and-true method of just choking him with your bare hands gripping his neck. One way or the other, he will take his last breath at your hands."

James knew that Andrea would not hesitate to hurt or even kill his wife if he didn't cooperate. He also knew that he was not capable of killing another human being in cold blood. There had to be a way to stop her. There had to be a way that he could notify the police without putting his wife in jeopardy, but that notification had to come well before Andrea's designated time of execution. That notification also had to guarantee that not only would her attack be stopped, but that Andrea's capture was assured. It was obvious to James that if Andrea's plan were thwarted, but she wasn't captured, she would make it her business, out of revenge, to direct her attentions to the extermination of James' wife. She would have to hurt him the same way, by his actions, he had hurt her.

The time for James to make his move was now. He couldn't risk waiting and then being involved in the slaughter of another human being. By waiting and not succeeding in stopping Andrea, he would also put his wife in potential deadly jeopardy. He never felt so helpless. He was still hurting and felt that overpowering Andrea was a difficult task even when he was at full strength. Now, he was in need of additional help, maybe in the form of a weapon. He had already tried playing on Andrea's emotions; so, he knew she would no longer be susceptible to that tactic. How else could he persuade her to drop her guard? He came up with only one course of action. He would have to disable himself to the point where his participation would no longer be attractive to Andrea. Ironically, he was a doctor thinking of hurting or even maiming himself, but it was all for the greater good. That was when he spotted a rusty nail sticking out of the wooden chair that was slowly falling apart. A rusty nail would do the trick. He had to work up the courage to use it on himself, though at heart, he was a coward.

Chapter Thirty-Four

The Rusty Nail

Detectives Krane and Barret met with their boss and explained the plans they had for capturing Andea Canella and possibly Dr. James Whitly. Their supervisor wasn't exactly keen on using a patient and the potential victim as bait in the operation. Detective David Krane went on to explain how the coverage would be employed and that, in his opinion, there was very little chance of anyone getting hurt. The detective supervisor reiterated that he did not like the possibility of the potential victim becoming the actual victim, and he advised Detective Krane to review his strategy so that the potential for risk would be reduced to near nothing. He further explained that he had confidence in both David and Tracy implementing a plan that would produce the desired results, and one in which no one was at risk. Both detectives agreed to the review, but they both knew that there was nothing that they could change to make it risk free.

After leaving their boss's office, the detectives went to the office conference room to work out how they were going to present their plan to the hospital staff, who would play an integral role in the successful outcome. They were certain that there would be some reluctance and possibly even refusals, and they were going to have to use all of their persuasive powers to emphasize that this was the best chance to keep everyone safe. The detectives spent a good hour discussing all the pros and cons and ultimately decided that they had belabored the issue enough. Their next step was to present their strategy to the hospital administration, and then to the specific players who would have an active role in implementing the plan.

As the detectives were strategizing over their next move, Andrea and James were still in discussion over what they were going to do. James had many questions about his participation, and he wasn't getting the definitive answers that he was expecting: "After all that has happened, and everyone at the hospital probably knowing what has occurred, you want me to sneak into the hospital and get to the third floor. Then, I should slither into Leonard's room and choke him to death. Finally, and very professionally, you want me to wheel you out of the hospital on a gurney. First of all, how do you expect me to easily get into the hospital?"

"James, I didn't say that it was going to be easy, but you have to find a way to get into the hospital because I will be waiting with your wife for your arrival."

"Not that I don't trust you, Andrea, but what guarantee do I have that you will not hurt my wife after I complete my task?"

"You don't have any guarantee, but you also do not have any choice. Do you want to risk her life on a doubt that you may have? I wouldn't think so."

James knew that Andrea would not give him a straight answer, but actually hearing it, unnerved him. As far as he was concerned, time had run out. If he was going to do something to throw a monkey wrench into Andrea's operation, it had to be now. Throwing all caution to the wind and not really thinking about his next action, he thrust his body to one side and was able to tilt the old wooden chair. It fell to the ground and splintered into pieces. On the way down to the floor, James intentionally scrapped his wrist against the rusty nail that he previously saw protruding from the chair. James got the desired result as blood started oozing freely from the cut. He groaned as the pain mixed with the emotional trauma of what he had just done. He realized that if Andrea didn't react and tend to his wound, he could possibly bleed out and die. He had successfully complicated the implementation of Andrea's plan, but he didn't really want his actions to result in the loss of life – his.

Andrea turned quickly as she heard the noise and saw James lying on the floor. As she got closer, she saw the stream of blood emanating from James' wrist. She voiced a number of expletives that came from seeing the seriousness of James' wound, but also from the realization that he may not be able to participate in her masterplan. He was an important part of her strategy, and she felt that without him, her success was in jeopardy.

As she thought about it, it was even more than that. There wasn't enough time to develop another plan. She needed James for this plan. There was no other. She was going to take care of James so that he would mend, at least to the point that he could still perform as instructed. She looked at some of the resources that she had gleaned from the maintenance truck and spotted a roll of tape that she could use to wrap James' wrist. It was the stickiest tape that she had ever seen. It was even better than that for which she had hoped.

Since she had nothing to use to stitch his wrist, she decided to squeeze his wrist as tightly together as she could and apply this extra strong tape to the laceration. Hopefully, like a butterfly bandage, the tape would hold the skin together and curtail the bleeding. She had to act quickly since James was losing blood. It was a rusty nail that did the dirty work; so, she needed something to disinfect the cut before she wrapped it. She searched the park house and found an old can of paint remover. While not the best remedy for disinfecting, it did contain a certain amount of alcohol. She had no choice but to use it.

"James, stay with me. I am going to pour some alcohol on your wrist, and then wrap it the best that I can. It is going to hurt, but I have to do it, so you don't bleed to death. Do you understand?" Andrea had to shake James to keep him alert and in the moment. His eyes fluttered as he nodded weakly that he understood. When Andrea saw that James acknowledged her, she began pouring the paint thinner onto the open wound. James howled in pain. His scream could have wakened the dead, but Andrea continued to pour the painful disinfectant on the open wound. If it did anything, it brought James back from fading into oblivion. When Andrea finished pouring, she explained to James that she was going to apply the tape that she found. She noticed that the artery was not severed, but, in her opinion just "nicked." He probably could have used a stitch, but there was no way to accomplish that. She told James that she was going to squeeze his wrist very tightly in the hope that the tape would keep the wound closed. Once again, He just nodded to her. She grabbed his wrist and with a strong squeeze brought the skin of the open wound together. Again, James yelled out in pain. This time, however, the duration was much shorter. She then applied the super sticky tape to the closure and watched to see if the flow of blood decreased. She saw the flow reduced to small droplets. She hoped that coagulation would begin and stem the flow of blood altogether. Whether it did or not, she felt that she did as much as she possibly could, under the circumstances. She did it for him, but, in reality, she also did it for her. As she looked at her handiwork, she realized that she did not want to be around when that super sticky tape had to be removed. She was certain that the removal would also take with it some skin. It might even cause the wound to reopen, but that concern was for another day. James laid his head down and passed out, but Andrea was relieved that, at this point, it was not from the continuous loss of blood. She was letting James temporarily recuperate from her make-shift medical procedure, but she would only let him rest, however, until such time as she needed him to fulfill his obligation to join her in her quest. Unbeknownst to James, that time was upon him.

Chapter Thirty-Five

The Administrator's Issue

Detectives Krane and Barret called and made an appointment to meet with the Mountain Pacific Hospital administrator. He was curious as to why the detectives wanted an appointment, but David and Tracy were able to skirt around a specific answer. They wanted to explain their position face-to-face. By the body language of the administrator, Mr. Theodore Washington, they would be able to tell whether to continue on the track they chose or to switch tactics and approach the situation from another angle. They would be meeting with him later on this afternoon; so, it gave them even more time to smooth out the wrinkles and avoid possible problem areas.

By reputation, Mr. Washington was a hard-nosed individual who had no strong liking for police officers. His brother had been in a crowd that became disorderly in front of a local bar, and to which police officers responded. It turned nasty and got out of control. The officers effected a number of arrests, and Calvin Washington, Theodore's younger brother, was one of them. In addition to Ted, Theodore, not agreeing with the arrest, it was how the police officers utilized "necessary force" to effect the arrests that really bothered him. According to Ted, the police were relentless in swinging their nightsticks and hitting whoever got in their way. It was Ted's opinion that the officers panicked because of the size of the crowd and were out of control. Although many of the arrestees, including Calvin, signed civilian complaints, nothing had, thus far, been adjudicated. All the complainants had to show were the bruises that they suffered at the hands of the overzealous cops. So, one can understand that convincing Theodore Washington to fully cooperate with the police was no easy task. Although he was civil most of the time, you could tell that he still carried a chip on his shoulder.

Tracy and David approached Mr. Washington's secretary and announced that they were there for the scheduled appointment with the administrator. She acknowledged the appointment and told the detectives that Mr. Washington was on the phone. She directed them to have a seat as they waited for Ted to become available. The detectives knew that the administrator was a busy man, but time was not on their side. They needed to meet with Ted as soon as they could. Ten minutes evolved into twenty minutes, and twenty minutes slowly moved to one-half hour. Detective Krane had enough. Just as he rose to show his angst, Theodore Washington's door opened, and the administrator greeted the detectives ushering them into his office.

"Sorry for the wait, but I had to deal with some pressing matters that had to be settled right away. What can I do for you?"

There is no way that either detective thought that Theodore Washington was, in any way, sorry for having them wait. In fact, it was the consensus of opinion between the two of them that the delay was intentional. Just another way for the administrator to show his dislike for what happened to his brother at the hands of the police.

The meeting had already started on a negative tone, as far as the detectives were concerned. They had to choose their words carefully and emphasize that their strategy plan benefitted both the police department and the hospital, his hospital.

"Mr. Washington, we're sure that you are aware of what has been taking place here at the hospital. Just to clarify some of our concerns, one of the patients here at Mountain Pacific is potentially in danger of bodily harm escalating to what could be his life. The wife of Leonard Canella has vowed to end his life. We're sure that you are aware that your security department has been giving Mr. Canella special attention. We and the hospital security department have been providing specific security for Mr. Canella. It is difficult for us to continue with that service. We want to end the threat to Mr. Canella by implementing a plan that would include some of your staff."

"Detective Krane, are you telling me that you want me to approve my hospital staff taking part in a police operation where they could be put at risk? That's not to what these medical professionals have dedicated their time, education, and life. Is it not in the purview of police officers, even at risk to their own well-being, to ensure the safety and security of individuals? I do not see any reason why hospital staff should take on that responsibility."

Both detectives knew that convincing Theodore Washington to adopt their risky plan was not going to be a walk in the park, but they did not think he would be as insulting, demeaning and adamant as he was. They went into plan "B," and Tracy addressed the administrator: "Mr. Washington, the participation that we would be asking of the hospital staff would be minor and relatively risk free."

"Detective Barret, let me interrupt and ask you what the term 'relatively risk free' really means. If I understand you correctly, you want me to sign off on a plan that most likely will be risk free. Detective, that's not good enough. Since this is not something that the hospital staff originally signed up for, their participation should involve absolutely no risk."

It seemed like the detectives hit a stone wall. Detective Krane gave it a last-ditch effort: "Mr. Washington, you are worried about your staff, and we understand that. This plan that you have not yet even looked at, will potentially save one of your doctors, Dr. James Whitly, from further potential harm. If the plan works as we know it will, Dr. Whitly will also be on the scene. As you are probably aware, the doctor has been involved with Mrs. Andrea Canella. His involvement more than likely has entailed violations of the law. In addition, it is our strong contention that Mrs. Canella is a desperate person who will do anything and hurt anyone to accomplish her goal of killing her husband. If Dr. Whitly has not totally cooperated with Andrea Canella, there is a good possibility that he may have already suffered some harm. This plan, if you care to listen to it, may save him from additional damage, both physical and mental. You are worried about your staff, and this is a way that you can help at least one of them. Why don't you take a moment and listen to what we have in mind?"

Detective Krane apparently struck a note with Theodore Washington. Ted's refusal now not to cooperate could possibly put one of his staff members in further jeopardy of physical harm. The administrator took a few minutes to digest what he had just heard and then nodded to Detective Krane to continue. The detective went on to explain, in detail, what they were planning to do. David told Washington that they had Dr. Whitly's hospital pager in their possession. He also mentioned that they saw a message from another doctor to James Whitly letting him know that his wife had come out of her coma, and that his patient, Leonard Canella, had been moved from the third-floor recovery room.

"Mr. Washington, we are sure that Andrea Canella will attempt to get to her husband, and we are equally confident that Dr. Whitly will want to see his wife. We do not think that Andrea knows that her husband has been moved, and that is a great advantage for us. His being on a different floor almost ensures his safety. Andrea will be concentrating on the third floor while her husband is in a room on the second floor. Mr. Canella will be out of the line of fire, so to speak. Additionally, we will place police officers in the areas where Andrea Canella would believe her husband or Mrs. Whitly might be. So, both Mr. Canella and Mrs. Whitly will be safe. We just need your staff to be cognizant about what is going on and to act routinely as the operation continues. We would also like to meet with the doctors and staff who will be working on the third floor to answer any questions they may have."

"Detective Krane, when will this whole thing go into effect, and when would you want to meet with the staff?"

"Mr. Washington, the answer to both of those questions is 'as soon as possible.' I believe that Mrs. Canella wants to get things done quickly. The more time it takes, the more obstacles that can come her way, and she knows that. So, I would like to have everything in place as soon as tonight. We also believe that Andrea will attempt to enter the hospital during the evening hours when darkness will be to her advantage."

"Well detectives, you have given me a lot to think about. But even if I agree to cooperate with you and your plan, I do not know if we can put it into effect by this evening. Let me work on it, and I will get back to you as soon as I can."

"Mr. Washington, I don't have to emphasize that time is our enemy. I would hate to miss the opportunity to stop Andrea because we couldn't set up in time. Please work as quickly as you can. We will all be better off if we start this evening."

"Understood Detective, but I can only do what I can to contact everyone and get them together. Rest assured that I will try."

The detectives understood that the conversation was over, and that they would have to wait for Mr. Washington's phone call to start the ball rolling. There was a lot on the line, and they had to answer to both their boss and the administrator of the hospital. If things went off track, their reputations and their jobs would be in jeopardy. If it went the way they hoped it would, many issues would disappear, and they would be lauded for a successful but risky strategic piece of police work. What they needed now was Andrea Canella's cooperation. She was methodical and creative. They had to be prepared for anything. This was somewhat worrisome, but the two detectives would only admit that to each other.

Chapter Thirty-Six

The Blare of a Siren

Mrs. Laura Whitly was getting stronger with every passing hour. Physically she was getting better, but emotionally she was worried about her husband. He had not visited or called, and she was beginning to worry if he was okay. Dr. Strathmore had not mentioned anything else about James, which probably meant that Charles had not heard anything from him. She had so many questions that could not be answered. Why was James not contacting her? Was he still with Andrea Canella? Where is he staying? Are the police still searching for him? Are Andrea and James involved with each other? Did she lose her husband to somebody else's wife?

Thankfully, her question bombardment was interrupted by a familiar voice: "Hello Mrs. Whitly. We heard you are getting well. We're glad to see that you are up and about. That is a real good sign. Before you know it, you will be heading back home."

"Hello Detective Krane, Detective Barret. What brings you to this neck of the woods? Are you going to tell me that you have found James and that he is, okay?"

"No Mrs. Whitly. We were hoping that you were going to tell us that your husband contacted you. We are still looking for both your husband and Mrs. Andrea Canella. We aren't sure if they are together or not. Apparently, you haven't heard anything from Dr. Whitly."

"That's right, Detective. There have been no phone calls and obviously no visits. Also, it is my understanding that James hasn't even contacted his friend, Dr. Charles Strathmore. Frankly, I am beginning to worry that something might have happened to him. Unfortunately, there is a good possibility that if you find Andrea Canella, you will probably find my husband. As you know, she has a powerful influence over him, but I am not giving up on him."

Tracy entered the conversation: "Laura, may I call you, Laura?"

"Of course, by all means. We are not going to stand on formalities. We are working on the same team to find James. Aren't we?"

"Absolutely, Laura. Just to reassure you. There is a strong possibility that the more time Dr. Whitly spends with Mrs. Canella the more he will see through her façade and realize the type of person she is. We are here to ask for your help with a plan that we have developed in the hope that we will finally catch up with both Andrea Canella and your husband. So, for now we are asking if Dr. Whitly reaches out to you that you do not reveal anything we are telling you today. Are you okay with that?"

"I guess I am, but I would like to hear what you have in mind before I make any commitments. Will James be in any danger? Will I be in any danger? I need to know the whole thing. I want to help if it will get James back home safely."

It seemed that Mrs. Whitly reacted better to Tracy's comments than Detective Krane's. So, he let her continue with the conversation. He just added some specifics where he thought they should be emphasized.

"Laura, I'm sure by now you know that there is no love lost between Andrea Canella and her husband, Leonard. In fact, Andrea, in no uncertain terms, has reiterated that she wants her husband 'dead.' We are of the mind that she will stop at nothing to reach her goal. That includes using everything and everyone, including your husband, James, to terminate Leonard's existence. Here is where the difficult part comes in. We want to move you to another room so that you are removed from any possible danger. However, no one can know that we are moving you, especially your husband. We think that Andrea will want to use James in fostering her plan, but we also think that James will not cooperate freely. In our opinion, he will not react to any personal threats against himself, but he might react positively to threats against someone else, someone else who he still loves and cares about. We think that Andrea may be getting James' cooperation by leveling threats against you. Therefore, if we move you to another location in the hospital, one that neither James nor Andrea knows about, then we will be ensuring your safety."

Detective Krane jumped in: "Once again, we have to emphasize that you tell no one about the move, especially James."

"So, let me get this straight. If James were to contact me and find a way to enter the hospital without being stopped, he would come to this room and find no one or someone else where I should be. What would he do then?"

Tracy started again: "That's the point, Laura. Once James gets to your room, we will be there to greet him. Yes, he will be in our custody, but both you and he will be out of immediate danger. Laura, we are asking for your cooperation in maintaining the secrecy of our plan. If Dr. Whitly were to find out that you have been moved, there would be a strong possibility that Andrea would also find out. Then, we would have nothing. We would have to start from square one again, and unfortunately, the longer the case goes, the more difficult it is to bring it to a successful conclusion. We do not want that, and we're sure you don't want that. Understand Laura, that a successful conclusion means that the fugitives are in custody, and that no one has been injured. Knowing how hard it will be to keep information from James, if he contacts you, we are asking that you keep in mind his safety as you speak with him."

Mrs. Laura Whitly stared into space as she mentally digested what was being asked of her. There were a number of things she didn't like: one, she didn't like deceiving her husband; two, she didn't like that James could be in danger; three, she didn't like that she could be in danger; and fourth, she didn't like being used as a pawn by Andrea. As she weighed all these factors, she wondered if the detectives could be wrong about the relationship between Andrea and her husband. Suppose James had, once again, fallen for Andrea's persuasive methods and was not acting under any threats whatsoever. Just suppose, James was helping Andrea so that she could end her crusade, and they could run off together and live happily ever after. She was driving herself crazy! She was letting her imagination get the better part of her. Suddenly, she put up a mental barrier, turned to the detectives, and said that she would cooperate. If James was conspiring with Leonard's wife, then the only danger that he would face would come from Laura herself. She would kill him for the angst and anguish that he had put her through.

Both Detectives thanked Laura Whitly for her cooperation. She had agreed and she inquired as to when the plan was going into effect. "Immediately," was the joint response from both David and Tracy. Although they told Laura that the strategy was imminent, they knew that they had to wait for Theodore Washington to gather the staff members and get a positive consensus. They had emphasized to Ted that time was of the essence, and he said that he would do what he could. However, the longer they had to wait, the more difficult it would be to put the plan into motion.

They wanted to start immediately; so, they began to ask their boss for some additional personnel. These would be the plain clothes officers who would substitute for both Leonard Canella and Laura Whitly. In addition to these officers, there was a need for uniformed officers to secure the hospital, once the two fugitives were confirmed to be there. The need for additional personnel was never greeted with open arms. All the units were short of personnel and the additional need, many times, meant the incurring of overtime expenses. So, when

Detectives Krane and Barret requested additional officers for the operation from their boss, he wanted to make certain that the hospital, its administrator, and staff, were totally on board. When queried by their boss, both detectives, without hesitation, strongly confirmed the hospital's cooperation. Dave and Tracy were putting a lot on the line.

As the detectives were putting things in order for their sure-fire operation, Mrs. Andrea Canella was doing the same. She had worked out most of the specifics regarding her part in the plan and was now helping the reluctant Dr. Whitly to put his mind to the task at hand. The cut on his wrist was still oozing blood, but according to Andrea, he was going to live, which meant that he was able to assist Andrea with the operation. As the two of them discussed the strategies, James thought to himself that he had failed again. He failed so many times with his attempts at stopping Andrea, and even now he couldn't inflict enough damage to himself to delay her plans. In despair, he thought to himself that he was a good doctor but seemed to fail at everything else. He was wallowing in self-pity which did not help the situation in which he found himself.

Andrea saw that James was not concentrating on the present problems; so, she gently reminded him of the jeopardy in which he was placing his wife: "James need I remind you that your wife's health is at stake here. I think you should clear your mind and work on a plan to get into the hospital, do the deed, and escape with everyone being safe and secure, including your wife. We do not have much time, so I urge you to put your thinking cap on."

When James heard the expression: "put your thinking cap on," it reminded him of his wife who, when she needed help and asked it of him, would preface her request with that very expression. It jolted him out of his malaise, and he returned to the problem at hand. How was he going to get into the hospital avoiding the scrutiny of those who were on the alert, searching for him? As he mentally tossed the problem around, he heard the distant blaring of an emergency vehicle. It brought a potential solution to the forefront. He got Andrea's attention and discussed it with her. He did this with the intention of showing her how determined he was in his cooperative effort.

"Andrea, do you hear that siren in the distance? That is my ticket for entry into Mountain Pacific."

"I don't understand, James. Please explain how a distant siren is going to help you gain entry, unnoticed, into the hospital. I guess I am missing something."

"Yeah Andrea, you are. When an emergency vehicle, not any emergency vehicle, but an ambulance, pulls into the emergency receiving area of the hospital with a dire case, whoever is on duty in the emergency room runs to the ambulance to assist the emergency medical technicians. There could be three or four staff members plus the EMT's at the rear of the ambulance to help with the removal and immediate treatment of the patient. At that time, the emergency medical technicians are giving vital information to the attending staff. I will not be entering the hospital through the main entrance but via the ambulance emergency entrance. I will be just one of the many who will be helping with the emergency. I will be hiding in plain sight, as the expression goes. I will be noticed, but not to the point where anyone will connect me to the fugitive for whom the police are searching."

Andrea was amazed. James might have actually come up with an option that could work. He definitely knew his way around an emergency room. He spoke their language and knew what the procedures were. He would be involved but not be in the way. The others would see him and assume that he should be there. While others were busy treating the emergency patient, he would make his unobserved exit and head directly for Leonard's room. It could turn out to be a lot less stressful than previously anticipated. Andrea joined in with James and agreed that his plan might just work. He had extra medical equipment and white uniforms at home; so, they would make a brief stop there before proceeding to Mountain Pacific. Mrs. Andrea Canella was feeling better and better about a successful conclusion to her quest. She decided that tonight, before James had a chance to think about it and change his mind, would be the best time to strike. She was devilishly and privately celebrating that justice would finally prevail, her justice – revenge.

James felt that he had convinced Andrea about his cooperation. In fact, his strategy about the emergency room was based on solid ground. He probably would be able to enter through the ambulance emergency doors, and his quiet, stealth exit would surely go unnoticed. While he had Andrea's attention and obvious praise for his efforts, his thoughts went to the pager message that he had received from his friend, Dr. Charles

Strathmore. Leonard Canella's room had been changed, and he was now on the second floor of the hospital. All James had to do now was, as Andrea was observing his every move, work out how he was going to deal with an empty room on the third floor, or a room on the third floor occupied by a total stranger. He would probably enter the room from the adjoining bathroom door, but what then? How do you explain to whomever is lying in that bed that the intruder is there to strangle him to death, or more succinctly to make it look like he is being strangled to death. James had overcome some other hurdles already. This was just another bump in the road, a bump that if not negotiated properly, however, could result in a fatality – his wife's.

Chapter Thirty-Seven

The Assignments

Theodore Washington was keeping his promise and was in the process of contacting as many of the staff members as he could, doctors and nurses, who would be actively involved with the police operation. Since most of them worked closely with Dr. James Whitly, they were aware of what had been taking place. They were all concerned for James, but their initial response was similar to Ted's. Why do they have to get involved with a police plan? It took some time, but the administrator was able to convince them that their cooperation was in the best interests of a fellow employee as well as the hospital's. He also emphasized that they had lost a staff member who was loved by all, and whose death affected everyone. Recalling the untimely death of Nurse Martha Higgins became the turning point for the group. If there was outright resistance, the memory of Nurse Higgins destroyed the barrier.

The staff who worked closely with Dr. Whitly was a close-knit group. Once you convinced many of them to agree, the others just fell into line. So, it was at this meeting. Administrator Theodore Washington had convinced even the most leery colleagues that it was the right thing to do, even their obligation to do it. As soon as Ted got the unanimous agreement of the concerned staff, he contacted the detectives and advised them that he had garnered the staff's full cooperation. He suggested that the detectives meet with the staff as soon as possible to alleviate some of their fears, but more importantly, to offer instructions regarding their role in the plan, which for some was very minor.

The detectives agreed and scheduled a brief meeting for early afternoon. They were still waiting for solid confirmation from their boss about the additional police personnel. However, they were proceeding as if they had already received it. Time was of the essence, and they could not waste it. Although the boss was thorough and questioning their need for additional resources, they were sure, by his body language, that their request would be granted. They were also sure that it would be granted at their own peril. If their operation failed, they did not want to think of the consequences.

In addition to meeting with the concerned hospital staff, the detectives had to meet with the police officers and other detectives who would be participating in the operation. In order to save time, the detectives decided to split their responsibilities. David Krane would meet with the police personnel and Tracy Barret would meet with the hospital staff. It was intentionally divided in this manner because they both knew that the police personnel, especially in an operation like this one, would be more responsive to a male leader than a female one. Was it right that this attitude permeated police operations? Absolutely not! But did it actually exist? Absolutely! So, both David and Tracy were smart enough to realize that this prejudice existed, and they did not fight it. The most important thing was getting the implementation of the plan started as soon as possible.

Detective Tracy Barret met with the hospital staff who were anxious to understand what role they were being asked to play. Her addressing the staff was also a calculated move since her approach was a softer one than David's. They didn't want to scare the staff, they wanted to downplay the operation so that no one would have any qualms about participating. Tracy's soft approach was a welcomed format to diminishing whatever fears might have been festering. She told them that, for the most part, they would continue with their regular routines. However, their patients might be different. They were also told that if any of them recognized either Mrs. Andrea Canella or Dr. James Whitly that they were to take no action but to notify the nearest police officer. She listed the locations where police officers would be clandestinely located on the floor. She further explained that the police wanted both fugitives to be able to enter their targeted rooms where officers would be waiting for them. The idea was to confine Andrea and James to an area that is workable for capture and arrest with the minimum risk of injury to both the subjects and the police officers. So, although the anxiety levels would rise for sure, everyone had to act as if it was just another day at Mountain Pacific Hospital.

Detective David Krane, who was recognized by most of the people in the room, began his instructional session with the phrase: "We will only have one chance to succeed." These words mandated the attention of all the officers present. He first addressed his comments to the uniformed officers who were in attendance. He explained to them that they were the stop gap measure if all else failed. Once the operation began, and it was confirmed that both Mrs. Andrea Canella and Dr. James Whitly were in the hospital, the uniformed officers would come out of their sequestered locations and secure the exits from the hospital. Therefore, if something went wrong with the original plan for capture, and the subjects were not captured, they would still have to remain in the hospital because there would be no means of escape through the exit doors. The notification for execution of exit security would come over the police radio. He emphasized that their attention to detail, even if the third-floor operation failed, ensured the potential success of capture and arrest.

Because of his successful career and his time in the Detective Division, David Krane commanded the respect of everyone involved in the planning. Following his instructions to the uniformed officers, Detective Krane turned his attention to the plain-clothes officers and detectives in the room. While thanking them for their attendance, he reiterated that the assignment was a voluntary one, and that their withdrawal from participation would not be looked upon as anything but a personal choice. No one left; no one even moved. David expected that this would be the case, but it was his obligation to repeat the voluntary status of the operation. He again thanked everyone for their enthusiasm and loyalty. Krane further stated: "I don't want anyone to think that there is any excessive pressure on either Detective Barret or myself. There is absolutely no pressure on successfully completing this operation, but if it fails, Tracy and I will be selling hotdogs around the corner from the station house." This unexpected comedic line evoked reserved laughter and served to reduce the angst in the room, but it also put the officers on notice that it was essential to the futures of both detectives that the conclusion of the present investigation be a successful one.

Following his opening remarks to the plain-clothes officers, he went into the specifics. He needed volunteers to dress as nurses and/or doctors who would be on both the second and third floors of the hospital. They would go into action as soon as the subjects entered the targeted rooms. They were a necessary back-up for the officers who would be in the actual rooms. Without immediately accepting anyone for these positions, he went on to explain the roles of the officers in the rooms.

"The officers assigned to the target rooms will be substituting for both Mr. Leonard Canella and Mrs. Laura Whitly. We are not exactly sure when Andrea or James will visit the rooms, but they will believe that Andrea's husband is in his assigned room and that James' wife is in hers. Understand that Andrea has stated, in no uncertain terms, that she wants her husband dead. What does that mean? It means that the officer substituting for Leonard Canella has to be alert at all times. His life may depend on it. Additionally, it is our belief that Andrea Canella will use James' wife, Laura, as leverage for James's cooperation. In fact, there is a strong possibility that because of a potentially fatal threat to Laura that James might wind up being the subject in Leonard's room. According to the hospital staff and James' colleagues, we do not think that James would actually commit murder, but he would be laboring under a possible threat to his wife's life. This could drastically change one's mindset. If this is Andrea's plan, we have no idea how James Whitly would escape its implementation."

Detective Krane took a break and motioned for Tracy to come up to the podium to join him. This solidified the fact that they were in this together, and it showed a unity of thought between the two. Detective Barret addressed the group and told them to take a few minutes to digest what they had just heard. Just as she finished her statement, a voice rang out from the back of the room: "We are all here because we want to be. We do not need time to think about anything. Just tell us where and when you want us, and we're there." The room exploded into repeated "Yeahs." So typical of police camaraderie. Tracy and David were grateful for the spontaneous response, but now they had to decide who was going where. It is never easy to make a decision where an officer is put into a risky situation. However, it had to be done. There were about the same number of female officers as male officers in the group.

The first decision that the detectives had to make involved the choosing of substitutes for both Leonard Canella and Laura Whitly. Their parameters were restricted to officers who, in some way, resembled the person for whom they were substituting. They looked for general body stature, skin complexion, hair style and color. In addition to meeting the general description criteria, the detectives were looking for officers who had some time on the job. Waiting for someone to come into a room where you are lying, knowing that he or she wants to kill you, could be a harrowing experience even for the well-seasoned officer. It was really no place for a newcomer to plain clothes. An attack of nerves could blow the whole operation and put that officer and others in danger of being hurt.

Finding a good body double for Leonard Canella was not too difficult. The officer that they chose was a close match to Leonard's overall look. However, picking the substitute for Laura Whitly was more difficult than they expected. It came down to two female officers who had both disadvantages and advantages to their being chosen. One of the females, who was on the job for quite a while and who had plain-clothes experience, really didn't match Laura's overall description as well as they wanted her too. However, she seemed to be hard as nails and would not flinch when the intruder entered her room. There would be no attack of nerves with her. But if Andrea entered Laura's room, as they thought she would, would she realize that it was not Laura who was lying there? If that were the case, then the successful case conclusion would be in jeopardy.

The second female volunteer was a much better match for Laura Whitly's overall look. She was a good match right down to the hair color and style. It would be difficult for someone like Andrea to determine, in a dimly lit hospital room, that the patient was not Mrs. Laura Whitly. That part was great, but what about her experience, or lack of it, and her reaction to the potential of a life-threatening situation? There was a lot to consider. The officer was "gung-ho" with wanting to be a part of the plan, but did her desire to be a part of a real police action balance out her lack of time on the job and plain-clothes experience? Detective Krane and Detective Barret both knew that it did not. Even though indecision on their part now would not make for an easier decision later on, they both decided to think about it before a final assignment was made. The detectives, in an effort to save time, decided once again to split their responsibilities. Tracy was assigning the uniformed posts and locations while David made the plain-clothes appointments. These included assignments as doctors and nurses, but also included sequestered locations in the target rooms.

The detectives finished their individual tasks, but now had to face the daunting decision of whom would substitute for Laura. Whoever they chose to be the body double would be protected by the other female officer who would be hidden in the room. So, they both had an important role to play. The detectives couldn't put it off any longer. They made the decision to have the better match play the role of Laura Whitly. It was necessary that, if Andrea entered the room, she would believe that Laura was lying in that bed. The decision was based on effectiveness not on the "what ifs" of inexperience.

When they announced the decision, the female officer who was not chosen approached Tracy and David. They were prepared for some pointed remarks but were surprisingly gratified when the officer stated: "I believe that you have made the right choice. If she more closely resembles the patient, then that's who should be in the hospital bed. But don't you worry, I will take on my role with as much determination as possible, and I will make certain that nothing happens to our substitute Laura."

The detectives could not have been happier with the officer's response. They just hoped that the officer's comment: "...that nothing happens to our substitute Laura" went from her lips to God's ears.

Chapter Thirty-Eight

Dr. Whitly's Wife

Mrs. Laura Whitly was concerned that the police plan involved the capture of her husband as well as Andrea Canella. She was worried that as the plan developed, James would be caught in the turmoil of the arrest and could possibly be hurt. She often thought that he was a good man and unfortunately got involved with someone who really didn't have his best interests at heart. As time passed, she realized that Andrea was a piranha who would attack anyone to gain an advantage. Unfortunately, at the time, James was too emotionally involved to see through her veil of deceit. She hoped, by now, James realized with whom he was dealing and the type of person who would want to kill another human being. Laura wanted to speak with the detectives again to get some reassurance about her husband's safety. Unfortunately, both Detective Krane and Detective Barret were too busy with coordinating the police operation to visit with Laura Whitly.

Laura had already been moved to a second-floor room, out of harm's way. She had an officer assigned to her, but her bodyguard couldn't answer many of the questions that Laura posed. Her anxiety was on the rise, and she was having trouble breathing. Her nerves were bringing on a panic attack and she needed help. The officer saw Laura reacting to an apparent anxiety attack and tried to calm her down. Her efforts failed and the female officer tried unsuccessfully to calm her down. The officer needed help, and she ran to the nurse's station for assistance.

As soon as the officer left her room, Laura ran to the stairway and went to the third floor to find the detectives. She needed her questions answered. She was running with reckless abandon trying to find either Tracy or David. Neither detective was on the third floor. They were still in the conference room speaking with the cadre of officers who were assigned to the special operation. Seeing no one who could address her immediate concerns, Laura Whitly actually started panicking. Now, her breathing was coming in short gasps, her heart was pounding, her vision was blurred, and she was feeling dizzy. She felt that she was out of control. Laura ran, lost her balance and crashed into one of the Xray machines that was parked in the corridor. Her collision sent her reeling to the floor, and the resulting whip lash smashed her weakened head squarely into the tile floor. The impact was severe, and she was still not fully recovered from the damage she had previously suffered. Once again, Mrs. Laura Whitly lay unconscious. When the hospital staff got to her, she was bleeding profusely from her head and ears. Laura Whitly lay bleeding and unresponsive in the corridor of the third floor at Mountain Pacific Hospital.

"Can I speak with Detective Barret, please? This is Dr. Strathmore at Mountain Pacific Hospital. Sure, hold on a minute."

“Detective Barret speaking, can I help you?”

“Detective, this Dr. Strathmore at Mountain Pacific. I have some sad news for you. Mrs. Laura Whitly had an accident at the hospital, and she has expired.”

“Dr. Strathmore are you telling me that Laura Whitly is dead?”

“Yes Detective, she reinjured her head and her brain suffered irreparable damage. Laura lost a lot of blood and was bleeding from her head and ears. We worked on her for a time but could not save her. I am sorry to bring you the terrible news.”

“Thank you, Doctor. I will notify our team.”

Detective Barret was beside herself. She had to tell her partner that things may have changed, and their plan may have to be altered. She could just imagine David’s reaction. It would not be a good one. That notwithstanding, the quicker he knew, the better the chances to regroup and rethink the next steps. Tracy found her partner speaking with a couple of the officers who were a part of the volunteer group. She approached him and interrupted him mid-sentence: “David, I have to speak with you.”

“In a minute, Tracy. As soon as I am finished speaking with these officers.”

“No, not in a minute. Right now!”

David Krane was shocked at Tracy’s rudeness. He had never seen her so direct and demanding. Something must be up for her to be so crude. He excused himself from his present conversation and turned to Tracy: "Wow, that was out of character for you. Besides being rude and discourteous, you probably turned off the officers with whom I was speaking. Now, what could be so important for you to be so ill-mannered as to abruptly interrupt our conversation."

"Get off your high horse and stop the lecture, David. You would have done the same thing in delivering the news I have. Dr. Charles Strathmore from Mountain Pacific Hospital contacted me a little while ago. He informed me that Mrs. Laura Whitly had an accidental fall on the third floor of the hospital. She was apparently looking for one of us to answer some questions that she had. Laura went into panic attack mode and dizzily crashed into one of the hospital machines parked in the corridor. Her collision caused her to fall to the floor." Tracy paused, and David saw the opportunity to jump in and bring the conversation to a quick close: "Okay, so she fell. It doesn't really matter if she is treated on the third floor or the second, does it? It really doesn't change anything."

"Dave, she fell to the floor and reinjured her head. Dr. Strathmore said they worked on her for a time but couldn't bring her back. Dave, Mrs. Laura Whitly is dead."

"What! Laura Whitly is dead? How can that be? I cannot believe it!"

There was silence between the two of them. Krane just looked off into space trying to piece things together, and Tracy stayed within herself rethinking the information that she had just shared with her partner.

"Do you have any idea what we do now, Dave? I don't think we could have received worse news. I feel terrible that Laura died, but we are left having to deal with the ramifications. What do you suggest we do?

"Tracy, let's think about this. As long as the news of Laura's death doesn't reach Andrea or James, I don't think anything changes. We just have to make sure that neither one of our fugitives finds out. That means we have to get to Dr. Charles Strathmore and swear him to secrecy. Understand that if Andrea finds out about Laura, she loses her threat hold on James. If James finds out, we really don't know what he will do. We have got to get to Strathmore now."

James and Andrea were still discussing the details of their hospital attack. As Andrea listened to James, she was more and more convinced that he would follow through with his task. As long as she held the threat of bodily injury or death to his wife, he would toe the line. In the middle of their meticulous discussion, James stopped cold. He became quite pensive and directed a strong comment to Andrea: "Before we go on, I want to know that my wife is well and recovering from her injuries. I have not been in touch with her for quite a while now, and I am sure she is worried. I think it would be good for her to know that I am okay, and that I am asking about her. Our planning stops here if I don't contact her and find out how she is doing."

Andrea saw how determined and focused James was about the inquiry into his wife's health. She decided to let him find out about Laura, but not directly from her. Andrea figured that Laura's phones, both hospital and mobile, would be tapped by the police. He could find out from someone else how Laura is doing.

"James, I have no problem with you finding out about your wife, but you cannot speak to her directly. I am sure that the police will have her phones tapped; so, you will have to contact someone else."

James thought about it and told Andrea that he understood. He went through a list of possible contacts and settled on a call to his friend, Dr. Charles Strathmore. The question arose, however, as to how he was going to make the call. He explained that after picking up his uniform and medical gear at the house that he would call from the house phone. Andrea did not even like the fact that they had to stop at his residence, let alone use the house phone. She told James that she would take care of getting a phone. He looked at her in disbelief and reemphasized that he wanted to find out "now" how his wife was doing. There was no working phone in sight; so, he was confused by Andrea's response. Where was the phone? Andrea saw the questioning look on James' face and responded: "James, when I was conveniently given ownership of the state vehicle, I looked around for items that I could possibly use. I saw a cell phone lying on the floor in front of the passenger seat. I assumed it was the state employee's phone that had fallen to the floor. I didn't bring it to the park house because I didn't want to give you the possibility of using it and getting help. I took the temptation off the table. So, I will now retrieve the phone, which will probably still have battery life, and you can use it to find out about your poor wife."

James ignored the intended sarcasm and waited for Andrea to return with the cell phone. She was only gone for a minute or two when she came through the door with the employee's cell phone. She handed it to him with the warning: "James, I will be listening to every word that you say. If I feel that, in any way, you are trying to let your friend know what is going on, I will grab the phone and end the conversation. You will not know anything about your wife. Be smart."

When James took the phone and pressed the "on" button, the battery life showed only a red indicator on the screen. The call had to be a quick one before the battery died.

"Hello, Dr Strathmore's office, can I help you?"

"Yes, this is Dr. Whitly. Can I speak with him? It is urgent!"

"I am sorry, Dr. Whitly. Dr. Strathmore is not here right now. He went to the third floor. I can tell him to call you at this number when he comes back which should be momentarily."

"Thank you, and please tell him that it's important that I speak with him."

"I'll let him know, Doctor."

James hung up, and his face showed disappointment at not having spoken to his friend, Charles. With the little battery life that was left, he wasn't sure that he would be able to answer the call and spend any time speaking with his colleague. He looked at Andrea who was listening on speaker and just shook his head. Holding the phone, he waited patiently for the return call, the red indicator light staring at him. Before long, the cell phone rang, and James hurriedly answered without giving any thought to the speaker button. All James heard was: "James, I am so sorry." The phone shut down.

Chapter Thirty-Nine

The Surprise Gift

"James, are you all right? It looks like you just saw a ghost. Is everything okay at the hospital? What did Dr. Strathmore have to say?"

James wasn't sure if everything was okay at the hospital, but he wasn't going to let Andrea know, one way or the other. He thought about what Charles had said in the few short moments that they were connected. He could have been saying how sorry he was that James was in a compromising position. He could have been saying how sorry he was that James' future with practicing medicine was in jeopardy; or he could have been telling James that something catastrophic had occurred, and that his wife was gravely injured or even dead. He did not want to think the worst, but by the sound of Dr. Strathmore's tone, things weren't good.

"No Andrea, I am fine. As you can see, we didn't have much time to speak, so I really didn't get to ask any questions. I still don't know how my wife is doing, and I wanted her to know that I am concerned about her. I guess I will just have to tell her when I see her."

Andrea thought to herself, “that’s if she is alive when you get to see her.” Although James had answered that he was okay, he sure didn’t look like he was okay. He looked concerned and even worried. However, in the very short time that James was on the phone with his friend, Charles, not much could have been said. So, Andrea was just going to chalk it up to his general malaise. She couldn’t worry about that now. There were more important things to think about. The time was getting near when they would have to leave for the hospital. She needed the present focus to make sure that she and James were on the same page. So, she wanted to go over the whole plan, once again, especially the part involving James’ entrance into the hospital, and his clandestine entry into Leonard’s room.

James went over his role in the scheme, and when it came to the part where he had to strangle Leonard, Andrea interrupted: “James, hold on for a minute. I have a surprise for you. I know that you are squeamish about actually putting your hands around Leonard’s neck and squeezing the life out of him; so, I have a surprise for you. I am going to make it as easy as possible for you.”

James watched as Andrea reached behind her back and presented James with a gift. It was a surprise, and one that James could have done without. Andrea put out her hands and presented James with the gift. She had been able to put together a rough garrote so that James would be able to choke Leonard without ever touching his neck. The wire on the garrote would do that. Andrea was one thoughtful soul! James looked in shocking surprise at the hand-made implement of death. He had seen one before in a museum, but now, Andrea was pushing it into his hands. He didn't voluntarily open his fingers; so, Andrea took his hand and forcibly opened his fingers. She placed the garrote in his spread open palm and said: "I know you are flabbergasted by my generosity and creativity. No need to say, 'thank you'." She left him to ponder how he was going to utilize his newly acquired tool.

As James held the surprise gift in his hands and contrary to what Andrea wanted him to work out, he thought about how it would look around Andrea's neck. He imagined her squirming and gasping for breath as she slowly left this world. In shock as to what he was thinking, he quickly shook his head to get the vision out of his mind. What is he doing? He felt himself sinking into the same delirium as his demented captor. He had heard of the Stockholm Syndrome and wondered if he was falling prey to its effects as an unknowing victim. He knew Andrea was unrelenting in her goal to end her husband's life, and he knew that she would eliminate any and all obstacles in her way. However, did Andrea Canella deserve to die? Well, if she did, he'd absolutely decided that it would not be by his hand.

The seriousness of the situation, once again, flooding his consciousness, he decided to try talking some sense into Andrea's thinking. Though it might have been in vain, he had to apply a last-ditch effort. When he attempted to address her, it seemed like Andrea was deep in thought. He called out her name a couple of times before she acknowledged him.

"What is it, James? Do you still want to thank me for my thoughtfulness?"

Andrea was still as determined as ever. Her non-wavering focus on the dastardly deed almost convinced James to veer from any attempt at sanity. In fact, she was acting as if her whole reason for being existed in the solitary world of revenge. He was almost positive that his attempt would fall on deaf ears, but something inside pushed him to try anyway.

"Andrea, let's stop and think about what is occurring, and the aftermath that both you and I will have to face. I realize how badly Leonard treated you, and no one should have to endure the suffering and demeaning existence that was forced upon you. But if you think about it, as a result of the accident, Leonard has already suffered at your hands. He will always walk with a limp and have some never-ending nagging health issues. They would serve as a constant reminder of the revenge you brought upon him, and you would know that each time he ached, you would come to his mind. In my opinion, that is an even stronger remedy for revenge than death. Also, you could revel in the fact that he is suffering while you could have the possibility of escaping to a foreign land where you could live out your life in the warmth and freedom that he once stopped you from having. Think about it. You could leave now and no one, including me, would know where you went or when you decided to go. You would be free as a bird with your whole life ahead of you."

Surprisingly, Andrea didn't interrupt and listened quite attentively. James thought that, by her attentiveness and body language, he might have penetrated that wall of hate and revenge that was stopping Andrea from thinking logically and sensibly. She just stared at him with sort of an eerie gaze. She remained silent for what seemed like an hour, then without commenting, turned away from James and bowed her head, putting it in her hands. To James, this was another positive sign. It was an indication that she was having second thoughts about the whole idea. Also, he felt that his last-ditch effort might have been a successful one, and that his words had the desired impact. For the first time in a long while, he was on the verge of feeling happy and relieved. He did not want to interrupt what looked like some very heavy thinking on Andrea's part; so, he waited patiently for a response.

Before long, Andrea turned to face James. She looked directly into his eyes and said: "James, you mentioned 'in my opinion.' What makes you think that I give one hoot about your opinion? In fact, I could care less about your opinion or what you are thinking. Did you see me in deep thought? Do you know what I was thinking about? I was debating whether I should kill you now and not have to worry about you failing me when the time came, or whether I should take the chance with you since you value your wife's life more than your own. Don't talk to me about how well off I would be if I stopped my pursuit and just left now. Show me where the guarantee exists that my leaving now wouldn't result in my imminent capture and arrest. Let me answer. There is no guarantee. So, I could get caught and spend the rest of my life in jail without ever exacting the punishment I had planned. No thanks, James. Let's say that you tried and failed! And James, more than ever, I will be watching your every move. If I am not satisfied with what I see, I promise you that, right before your very eyes, I will kill your wife. And at that point,

I won't even care if I don't escape, but unfortunately for you, there is a good possibility that I will."

James stared in disbelief. His attempt at sensibility and logic had miserably failed. It resulted in the totally opposite effect. Andrea seemed more determined now than she had been before. Her eyes looked sinister, and her overall demeaner reflected the image of a witch standing above a cauldron of fiery boiling gases rubbing her hands together thinking about the satisfaction gained by a successfully deceitful and damaging act of violence. James was looking at the personification of evil. His thoughts centered around the possibility that he may have to sacrifice his life to save his wife's. Without hesitation, when it came to that, he was more than willing to do so.

Andrea seemed to revel in James' astonishment and mental anxiety. She wanted to make sure that James knew where she stood. and that she would not accept anything but success. She was sure that she had erased any thought of her doing an about face. She was committed and she needed James' commitment to ensure a smooth, effective, and efficient operation. Her success depended on it.

Andrea was unsure about letting Laura live or not. Now, she wasn't even sure that she wanted James to continue living. He is the one who seemed to turn one-hundred and eighty degrees. At one point, it was she who James had wanted. He risked everything to be with her and, so many times, it seemed that he had saved her from impending doom. Now, his attention seemed to be focused solely on his wife and her good health. Andrea's revenge was taking precedence over her feelings about

James. She was not even sure if those long-ago feelings still existed anymore. Would it be such a great loss if James met his demise? With one fell swoop, she would eliminate Leonard, Laura, and possibly James. She would eliminate a past that had plagued her. She would weigh all her possibilities as the time for execution came near. In her mind, however, no one was safe!

Chapter Forty

The Call to Charles

Mountain Pacific Hospital had lost an employee, Nurse Martha Higgins, and a patient, Mrs. Laura Whitly. The administration and staff were reeling from the recent unfortunate circumstances. They were now involved in a police operation which could possibly put some of their members in additional jeopardy. Administrator Theodore Washington was definitely having second thoughts regarding his commitment to have his staff actively cooperate in the operation. His son, Calvin, was visiting his father and could not believe that his dad would do anything with the police. In fact, he was shocked that his father even met with the police. After some very intense discussion, Ted told his son that he was not going to change his mind because the hospital would benefit from the successful completion of the police plan. He emphasized that it was a way to further ensure the safety and security of the hospital staff.

Calvin Washington was still not convinced that cooperation with the police was what his father should be promoting. He was livid that, in his opinion, his father had such a short memory. Calvin had suffered at the hands of the police, and his father seemed to be ignoring that fact. Calvin left in a huff uttering the comments that, as far as he was concerned, if there was any way to "screw up" the operation and "fuck with" the police, he would. Ted called after his son, but Calvin didn't even turn around. Calvin knew some of what was going on, and he realized that the possibility of interfering with any plans was quite remote. But he wanted to stick it to his father for what he deemed to be a betrayal. He also knew that his last comments would bother his father. Calvin knew his father well. Theodore was bothered when there was just a slight disagreement between the two of them, and now Ted had seen his son walk out on him and voice total disgust.

Just as Calvin and his father were ending their meeting, Detectives Krane and Barret got off the elevator and headed toward the administrator's office. They caught the last part of the conversation and saw that Theodore Washington was visibly upset. Detective Krane queried: "Hello, Mr. Washington. Is everything okay? Is this a bad time?"

"No Detective. Just another day in the life of the Washington's. Sometimes, as you may know, fathers and sons don't always wind up on the same page. How are things going? What can I do for you?"

"I'm sorry to hear about your family problems, Mr. Washington. Is there anything that we can do?"

"No thanks. It is ironic, though, that you are offering to help when the cause of the initial disagreement involved the police. However, that is a story for another day."

The detectives, having done their homework and research, were well aware of the incident and ultimate arrest of

Ted's son, Calvin. This was not the time, however, to open a discussion on the pros and cons of police procedures. They used their better judgement and just let it lie.

"We just wanted to touch base with you and let you know that we will be all set for this evening and onward. Detective Barret and I will be on the scene for as long as it takes. Is there anything that is bothering you, or is there anything else that you need to know?"

"No Detectives, but there is something that you need to know. A short while ago, I had a visit from Dr. Charles Strathmore, a close friend and colleague of Dr. James Whitly. He told me that he had spoken to James but was cut off quickly."

Detective Krane was concerned: "Did Dr. Strathmore mention anything about Dr. Whitly's wife?"

"Charles said that he only told James that he was 'sorry' before the call disconnected."

"Did Dr. Strathmore tell Dr. Whitly why he was sorry or indicate that anything had happened to Laura?"

"Detective Krane, according to Dr. Strathmore, he only got out the words, 'I'm so sorry,' before the call abruptly ended. Those words do not necessarily imply that anything at all happened to James' wife. Charles could have been sorry for a number of reasons concerning his friend. I would not assume that James knows anything new about his wife's condition and her untimely death."

"Mr. Washington, Let's hope that's the case. Because if James knows or assumes that his wife has died, there exists a good possibility that he would not be able to hide that news from Andrea. And if Andrea knows, then the potential threat that she was holding over James would disappear. That would cause Andrea to rethink her strategy and possibly change her plans. We would not be able to adjust as quickly as we should, and we would be more in doubt as to the success of our operation. Are you certain that Dr. Strathmore only had time for that short comment?"

Administrator Washington was becoming a little perturbed with the grilling that was taken place. He answered in an aggravated tone: "I told the two of you that Dr. Strathmore told me what he said. I have no reason to doubt Charles' veracity. If you still are not comfortable with what I have told you, maybe you should speak directly to him. Now, I have to attend to some important business."

With that last statement, Theodore Washington pointedly dismissed the detectives and definitely implied that, to him, there was more important business than the apprehension of two fugitives. Without uttering a word, Detective Krane and Detective Barret left the administrator's office. Once they were well out of sight and sound of Washington's office, they turned to each other, and both began to speak at the same time. Their comments to each other were similar in nature, and they reinforced the thinking that something was really bothering Theodore Washington. Conversing as they walked, Tracy mentioned the visit by Ted's son, Calvin. Both detectives had heard and seen what was definitely a disagreement between the father and son. She wondered if this might have set Washington's mood.

"Tracy, let's remember that we had a hard time convincing Washington to cooperate with us. I am sure that the incident with his son and the police influenced his attitude toward us. And if we are to judge his true feelings, you can be sure that his son challenged his father's decision. I am sure that Ted discussed some of the plans with his son, and I wouldn't be surprised that if Calvin could, he would try to derail our operation. I think we should alert our team members and let the uniformed officers know that Calvin Washington presents a risk to our plans."

Tracy agreed and started the alert process. Just what the detectives needed, although remote, another possible fly in the ointment. Laura Whitly's death, Ted Washington's challenging attitude, and now a potential threat from Calvin, things were just going along without a hitch and as smooth as silk!

Chapter Forty-One

Calvin's Plot

Following a final review of the plan, Andrea told James that it was time to leave for the hospital. James reluctantly agreed, and as they both walked toward the door, they heard the sound of a car engine. When Andrea peeked through the door, she saw another state vehicle pulling close to the park house. The driver exited the vehicle and started looking around. He apparently was searching for the other state worker. After a preliminary and superficial examination of the area, the driver approached the park house. He stopped when he saw the broken door lock. Not knowing who or what could be inside, he went back to his vehicle and picked up a tire iron. He opened the door very carefully and yelled an "hello, is anybody there?"

Standing behind the door and ready for the worker's entry, Andrea held her newly made weapon in the ready position. As soon as the worker cleared the doorway, Andrea applied the garrote around his neck and employed the necessary pressure. While gasping for air, he struggled to get free. However, his efforts were in vain. He slowly slumped to the ground and died. Andrea dragged the body into the back of the park house and covered it with some old rags that had been lying in the corner.

James just stared in shock and could not move. He couldn't believe how cavalier Andrea was about taking another human life. She just continued on as if the murder of another human being was in the natural course of events. Andrea realized that James was having a hard time dealing with what had just occurred; so, she ushered him out of the park house and into the state park vehicle. She thought about utilizing both vehicles but was concerned that James would not wait until she was in position in Laura's room before he entered the hospital. With James in the passenger seat, she headed toward Mountain Pacific Hospital.

David and Tracy were doing their last-minute checks, and everything seemed to be okay. If things worked out the way they planned, both Andrea and James could be in custody as early as the evening. For some reason, maybe just a gut feeling, they both believed that Andrea would attempt to get to her husband this night. That was why they were in a rush to get everything set as soon as possible. They were only going to get one chance at capturing Andrea and stopping her from killing her husband. They had to be ready.

After his heated discussion with his father, Calvin just wandered around the hospital. Because of his dad, he knew quite a few people. He was in no rush to leave, and he had time to kill; so, he just wandered around the hospital saying "hello" to whomever he knew. He came upon one of the nurses who worked on the third floor and who apparently was late for her shift. They had gone for coffee a few times and remained a little more than just friends. Nurse Shanice Connor couldn't stop to talk and just commented that she didn't want to be late especially if it went down tonight. Calvin wasn't sure what Shanice meant, so he asked: "What do you mean it?" She spoke in sort of a whispered tone and said: "You know, the police thing." Calvin just nodded as he realized what she was saying – the police plan.

Calvin saw this chance meeting as an opportunity to throw a monkey wrench into the whole police operation in which his father was so involved. He started thinking of ways in which he could muddy the waters and still remain anonymous. There had to be something he could do. He racked his brain in an effort to come up with a potentially damaging stunt. No matter what it was, he had to be as careful as possible not to give any reason for someone to think that his father might be involved. He disagreed with his father, but he didn't want to damage his reputation. Calvin just kept walking aimlessly around the hospital trying to think of an obstacle to the success of the planned operation.

As he walked, he came upon an old "No Smoking" sign. It mentioned the health dangers to smoking but also emphasized the danger of fire. Calvin just stared at the sign, and it hit him. He had the perfect option. He imagined the chaos that would ensue if there was a fire alarm in the building. Nothing would be able to go as planned. Pulling the alarm was simple, and it also offered the strong possibility that he would never be connected to setting it off. His father had mentioned that what the police were waiting for could occur at any time, but most likely at night, and possibly even this very night. The only thing left for Calvin to do was to decide the time and the specific location of the target alarm.

The police personnel were all alerted to the possibility that Calvin might do something to complicate matters. So, as Calvin walked, the police officers who observed him, let Detectives Krane and Barret know his changing location. It was the opinion of both David and Tracy that Calvin's negative attitude toward the police just might influence him into doing something stupid. There had been too much effort put into the whole operation to let an angry young man screw up the works. As far as the detectives were concerned, that was never going to happen.

Because of the effects that her actions had on James, as Andrea drove, she repeated her plans with him again. She reinforced the fact that she was going to drop him off at the far end of the parking lot which would give her time to set up before he entered the hospital. After each statement, she asked if he understood. All she got in return was a nod of his head. She began to worry about how dependable he was going to be. Andrea had to get him back to the present and shock him into the reality of the moment. She pulled the maintenance vehicle off the road and parked. She grabbed James' face and turned it toward her so she could look directly into his eyes that seemed glazed. She loudly called out his name and then with all her strength, she slapped him across the face. His head spun in the opposite direction, and he looked startled. It was just the jolt he needed to shock him back to the "here-and-now."

“Hey, what was that for? You almost knocked my head off. Are you nuts.”

“No James, I’m not nuts, but you were fading, and I had to get you back. You have to understand that I do what I have to do to succeed. I didn’t enjoy taking that man’s life, but it was something I had to do. Now, if you don’t want your wife’s life to be taken, you’d better get with the program!”

James was back on track. Her actions were successful, and she continued on her way to Mountain Pacific Hospital. As she drove, she imagined some pitfalls that might arise. Mentally, she was able to overcome all the “maybes,” and this made her more comfortable with the plan. Although Andrea was still a little worried about James’ participation, she was certain that he would not jeopardize his wife’s safety. James knew that if he did not act according to Andrea’s instructions, he might very well forfeit his wife’s life, and Andrea relied on James’ knowledge of her determined threat to force him into her murderous world.

Chapter Forty-Two

The Surprise and The Leap

As Andrea pulled up to the entrance to the main hospital parking lot, she instructed the very nervous Dr. James Whitly to wait for her to park the state vehicle before he walked to the emergency ambulance entrance. James was going to wait for the arrival of an ambulance before he attempted to enter the hospital. Hopefully, he would just blend in with the rest of the emergency room hospital staff as they attended to the transported patient. He carefully maneuvered through and around the parked cars as he waited for an ambulance's arrival.

James observed Andrea park the state vehicle and enter as a uniformed state worker through the main entrance of the hospital. She entered the hospital without incident and even nodded to the uniformed police officer who was assigned to the area. As soon as she entered, James proceeded, as instructed, to the emergency entrance. He waited for just a brief time when an ambulance arrived at the entrance. The ambulance, with its emergency lights glaring, was accompanied by a police vehicle also in emergency mode. Many times, this was an indication that the patient was a person who was in the custody of the police, a prisoner. As the patient was carried from the ambulance, the police officers remained close to the gurney. This was another indication that the ambulance had transported an injured prisoner. In fact, the patient, who had been armed and who attempted to rob a merchant at gunpoint, had been shot in the shoulder by the police.

Just before the ambulance emergency medical technicians entered the hospital with their patient, large numbers of people started exiting the hospital. It seemed that those exiting were leaving in a rush. It became difficult for the escorting EMT's and police officers to maneuver around the group of evacuees and enter the hospital. As they finally gained entry, they realized why groups of people were rushing toward the exits. The fire alarm bells were sounding throughout the hospital. There were regulated general procedures that the staff had to follow. One of these and probably the most important was to get the patients to safe locations. This process was well under way as the staff hurriedly moved into patients' rooms. To a neutral observer, it seemed like organized chaos. The fire alarm affected everyone but more so the police officers and detectives, Mrs. Andrea Canella, Mr. Leonard Canella, and Dr. James Whitly. It would have also affected Mrs. Laura Whitly, but unfortunately, nothing affected her now.

When the fire alarm sounded, Andrea Canella was on her way to Laura Canella's third floor room, and to her advantage there were many people reacting to the alarm bells. As she approached Laura's room, she heard voices coming from the room. She stopped and listened. What she heard turned her blood cold. She was incensed. Apparently, the lack of experience of the police officer substituting for Mrs. Laura Canella became obvious. Andrea heard the young police officer asking her partner if they should react to the fire alarm. Of course, the answer was "no," but the damage had been done. Laura Canella was not in her room! The threat that Andrea held over James had been dissolved. Her only hope was that James didn't know. Unfortunately for Andrea, James would notice that she was not in Laura's room, and that the threat to Laura's life was no longer imminent. Andrea had to decide what her next move was going to be. She had analyzed some pitfalls that she might face but didn't expect to encounter this.

Because of Charles Strathmore's page message, James knew that Leonard Canella had been moved from his third-floor room. The problem remaining for James, however, was faking the strangulation of whomever was now occupying the bed that Leonard once slept in. Unfortunately, James did not know that a police officer was the substitute patient. James was also wondering how the alarm of fire was affecting Andrea's plan. Amid all the confusion, how was Andrea going to get into Laura's room without being noticed. Maybe the fire alarm was a blessing in disguise, and maybe he would be able to escape his assigned task without putting his wife, Laura, in any jeopardy. He would only know when he arrived at the former third floor room occupied by Leonard Canella.

On the first floor in the emergency room, the injured prisoner was being escorted by one police officer while the other officer remained in the car notifying the dispatcher that they had arrived at the hospital. The prisoner saw the fire alarm and the one-officer escort as an opportunity to attempt an escape. He figured that this would be his best chance. Moaning and rolling to one side, he pushed the attending nurse into the officer who collided with a staff member trying to evacuate. The prisoner bolted from the emergency room and joined the groups of people who were running to evacuate or who were assisting with patient relocation. He melted into the confusion, and there was a prisoner on the run in Mountain Pacific Hospital.

Things couldn't get more convoluted for Detectives Krane and Barret. Their well-planned operation was deteriorating before their very eyes. They were sure that Andrea's plans had also changed. She would have to adjust just as they would. In addition, the detectives were not even one hundred percent sure that Andrea would attempt her scheme tonight. To say that they were beside themselves would be an understatement. However, they adjusted and alerted all the detailed officers to stay in position and remain vigilant. Tracy and David realized that with all the chaos and confusion, recognizing Andrea and James' would be more difficult.

As soon as Andrea heard the police officers in Laura's room, she set out to find answers. She moved with the staff members and singled out a specific nurse who was going into the supply room for more resources. When Nurse Shanice Connor entered the room, Andrea closely followed her. Shanice felt the strong pressure of an arm around her neck as in a choke hold. She tried to get free, but Andrea had the advantage.

"I do not want to hurt you. I just want some answers. But If I find that you are lying to me, I will kill you. Do you understand?"

The frightened nurse could only nod her head. She was very frightened and felt that whoever was behind her was desperate. She did not want to provoke her assailant. Shanice ceased trying to escape Andrea's strong hold and hoped that by her action, the woman behind her would relax the choke hold. Shanice felt the pressure diminish just a bit.

"First, I want to know where Laura Whitly is. To what room has she been moved?" Andrea lessened her hold a bit more so that the nurse could answer.

"She doesn't have a room. Mrs. Whitly died a short time ago."

The choke hold increased in pressure: "Don't lie to me. I will kill you. As sure as I am standing here, I will kill you. I will ask you just one more time. Where is Mrs. Laura Whitly?"

"I am telling the truth. She had an accident and it killed her. I am not lying. She's lying in the morgue."

Nurse Shanice Connor was crying as she was speaking, and it convinced Andrea that the nurse was telling the truth.

"Question number two. Where is Mr. Leonard Canella's room? What is the room number?

"I don't know the room number, but he was moved to the second floor."

"Why was he moved? Did it have to do with threats against him."

"No, as far as I know, the hospital needed recovery rooms for other patients. We needed his room for someone recovering from a recent operation. I didn't hear anything about threats."

"Okay. That's all I have for you. Sleep tight." Andrea applied pressure until Nurse Connor passed out. She took the knife from her pocket and turned to exit the supply room. Just as she turned, the door burst open, and Calvin was standing in front of her. He hesitated, looked at Shanice's limp figure and then leaped onto Andrea. The brief moment of Calvin's hesitation allowed Andrea to defend herself with knife in hand. Calvin landed on Andrea and the blade cut deeply into his side. The cut forced him to discontinue his assault, and he laid in pain on the floor next to Shanice.

It was Andrea's opportunity to run; so, she headed for the door and with reckless abandon raced into the corridor where she collided with the escaping prisoner. They both fell to the ground, but the escapee retrieved Andrea's knife. He put it to her throat and forced her up. He saw the uniformed police officer halfway down the corridor and started running to the back stairway with Andrea as his hostage. Detective Barret came out of her hidden position when she heard the commotion. She quickly evaluated the situation and was the closest officer to the prisoner and his hostage. Without hesitation Tracy joined the pursuit.

Smoke, the hardened prisoner's street name, ran through the back door into the rear stairway. He headed up toward the roof but was threatened with how close Tracy and the uniformed officer were getting. When Tracy burst through the stairwell door, Smoke, on the stairs, cut Andrea's throat and cast her bleeding body at the detective. His action to stop the close pursuit was successful. As Detective Barret stopped and caught a bleeding Andrea, she told the uniformed officer to stay, apply pressure to Andrea's wound and call for an ambulance. Smoke had a bigger lead now, but Tracy was determined to catch up with him. She heard the roof door slam and cautiously proceeded to the roof. She got there just in time to see Smoke jump from one roof to the rooftop of the adjoining wing of the hospital.

Smoke had been wounded by a police officer's bullet that passed through his shoulder. His leap to the adjoining roof was just short of a successful landing. He was weak and was now hanging onto the ledge with one good arm and one injured shoulder. Tracy looked at the distance between the two rooftops. She was in decent shape and felt confident that she could successfully complete the jump. She ran at full speed, leaped, and landed on the target rooftop. Detective Barret quickly reached over the edge and told Smoke to grab onto her hand. He couldn't hold on much longer, so he grabbed Tracy's extended hand. With his injury diminishing his strength, he realized that he was not going to be able to get back on the roof. However, he held on as tight as he could to Tracy. As he grasped her hand, an obvious sneer appeared on his face. With all the strength he had left, he pulled the unsuspecting detective off balance and over the edge. Detective Tracy Barret, with Smoke in tow, fell six stories. They both lay dead and joined Andrea Canella who bled out in the hospital stairwell.

Chapter Forty-Three

He Knew

Calvin Washington was able to crawl out of the supply room and yell for help. His father was notified and responded to where his son was being treated for a severe but not life-threatening wound. In the bed next to Calvin was Shanice Connor. She had suffered blunt force to her neck and lost consciousness but suffered only a minor injury. She was there mostly for observation. She looked at Calvin and Theodore with an expression that could only be viewed as a "thank you." Calvin smiled in return and had probably secured a much stronger foundation on the "more-than-just-friends" scale.

Detective Krane tried to work through the loss of his partner. Dr. James Whitly had surrendered to the police, so David Krane had time to devote to the fire alarm scenario that ultimately caused his partner's death. There were cameras throughout the hospital, and he needed to review the footage associated with the location of the device that was initiated. The fire panel had given the exact location of the pull stop that had been triggered. So, it was not difficult to locate the cameras that would yield the information that he needed to complete the investigation and make an arrest. In addition to setting a false alarm, the perpetrator could possibly be charged with other crimes like manslaughter. Detective Krane wanted to throw the book at the perpetrator. He would not rest until he found the perp and put him behind bars.

As Theordore Washington spoke with his son, Calvin interrupted and just uttered: "I am so sorry for what I did. I was just so angry at you and the police that I didn't think straight. I guess that I will be arrested for pulling a false alarm. I didn't want any of this to happen. I just wanted to 'mess with' the police. Dad, I am so sorry."

"Don't you worry son. I will take care of everything. Just don't talk to anyone about what happened without my being there. Things will work out."

Calvin didn't understand what his father meant, but he had full confidence in his father, and if his father said that things would work out, he had to believe it, no matter how improbable it seemed. The administrator knew that the police would want to view camera footage associated with the false alarm. It would be the starting point of the investigation. Without that footage, it would be next to impossible to determine who pulled the false alarm. He was waiting for a visit from Detective Krane who he knew would want to head up the investigation. Theodore Washington did not have to wait long before the detective's visit materialized.

"Hello Mr. Washington. I am sure you know why I am here. I would like to view the camera footage in the area around the triggered fire device. Not only will there be charges of initiating a false alarm, but I will make it my business to charge the perpetrator with anything that will stick. He or she deserves to be behind bars for a long time, and I owe it to my partner, Tracy."

"Firstly detective, let me say how sorry I am to hear about your partner. Detective Barret was very dedicated, and I'm sure she will be dearly missed. David, I have no problem with your viewing the footage, and I hope it will help you in catching the individual who caused so much pain and havoc."

Detective David Krane expected Theodore Washington's cooperation, but he wasn't expecting it to be over the top. It almost seemed that he was making it too easy for the detective to solve the case. However, Krane took whatever he could get and went to the camera room. The security officer who was assigned to the camera room helped Detective Krane locate the camera and the footage that he needed. David sat down to concentrate on what he was about to see. When the security officer brought up the camera and the anticipated footage, all that appeared was a black screen. The officer apologized and tried again. But again, the black screen appeared.

"Detective, it seems that the footage you are looking for may have been accidentally erased or possibly the camera at the location was not working properly at the time." Detective David Krane did not believe in coincidences, so, he went straight back to the administrator's office. He passed by the receptionist and burst right into Washington's office. Theodore Washington was startled and looked at David Krane in feigned surprise.

"Who are you covering for? It has to be someone real close for you to risk so much. Tell me. Who deserves that kind of loyalty? You know who did it, and you know what the individual did; yet you still sit there with an 'I-don't-know-what- you're-talking-about' look on your face. I have been in this business much too long for me to accept that incriminating footage was accidentally erased, or that just as the alarm was being pulled, the camera malfunctioned. By the look on your face, I know that you will give me nothing, but the time will come when I have the advantage, and then you will regret your actions."

"Detective Krane, that sounds like a threat."

"It doesn't sound like a threat. It is a threat!" With that Detective David Krane barged out of the administrator's office, slamming the door behind him.

Dr. James Whitly was being held in a security room in the hospital. He was in handcuffs and was being read his rights as the police prepared him for the ride to the station house. James pleaded with the police officers to let him see his wife one last time. He asked them to take him to the hospital morgue so he could see her before they left for the precinct. The officer looked to his supervisor who gave a cursory nod. The police officer escorted James down into the bowels of the hospital and into the morgue. There on a stretcher laid his wife's body. As James approached, he burst into tears. He sobbed so hard that he needed help from the police officer to remain standing.

"James, I am so glad that you came. I am alive, just barely, but I am alive. Charles was the first to get to me after my accident, and without treating me, he pronounced me "dead." No one bothered to examine me after he made his pronouncement. My pulse was very weak, and my breathing was shallow. To the naked eye, I am sure that I looked like I had

died, but Charles knew that I was still alive. He immediately covered me with a sheet and told the orderlies to take me down to the morgue. I was once again unconscious, so I couldn't move. I couldn't let anyone know that I was still alive. I didn't realize how cold it is down here. James, you never realized that I was seeing Charles, and that he was making love to your wife. That's the reason he wants me dead. This way you'll never find out.

After James spoke to Laura in whispered tones, the police officer motioned that they had to leave. As they approached the exit door, Dr. Charles Strathmore appeared in front of them. Upon seeing his good friend, James just bent his head into his handcuffed hands and feigned debilitating grief. With the police officer's guard being down, James reached for the officer's gun. He drew it from the holster and within seconds discharged two rounds directly into Charles' chest. The mere sight of Charles had initiated an insane rage in James. The officer wrestled the gun away from James, but the damage was done. Dr. Charles Strathmore would never treat another patient, nor would he betray another friend. Dr. Charles Strathmore was dead.

"What's that sound? It sounds like gunshots. I can hear the police officer speaking to someone. It sounds like James shot and killed Charles. I can't believe it. James knew what was going on all along. Good for you, James. You deserved better. You killed Charles, and I am about to take my last breath. Both of the people who betrayed you will be gone. I am glad that I lasted long enough to know that, for your sake, you made

things right. Oh no, the pain! I can’t catch my breath! I can’t breathe! Goodbye, James.

Chapter Forty-Four

Accidents will Happen

It was finally time for Leonard Canella to leave the hospital. Things had turned out relatively well for him. The friend that he had betrayed a long time ago was in police custody, the woman who he had turned into a slave, tortured and sexually demeaned was dead, and he was free as a bird to start all over again. His recovery was going well, and although he had some lasting effects from the accident, they were nothing that he couldn't deal with. He was patiently waiting for his discharge papers and the nurse escort who would wheel him out of the hospital to the waiting taxi that he had scheduled.

As Leonard reviewed the recent events, he couldn't believe how lucky he was. He must be doing something right to come out relatively unscathed. He laughed to himself as called to mind how the others who were involved in this confusing and convoluted life story ended up. Even Laura Whitly, who he believed was just an innocent bystander to the unraveling events, ended up in a bad way. His recollection was interrupted as the escort nurse and a student nurse, a candy striper - so called because of the red stripes on certain parts of the uniform - arrived with the discharge paperwork and the wheelchair to transport him out of the hospital. He instantly signed the papers, and the nurse helped him into the wheelchair.

The attending nurse left Leonard with the student nurse who wheeled him to the elevator. They waited in silence as the elevator bell finally rang. It was a short distance to the exit area so there was no need for extended conversation, but Leonard saw it as another opportunity to ingratiate himself to a pretty young woman. Why not? He had nothing to lose, and it served him well in the past.

As the automatic exit doors opened, Leonard addressed his escort: "Thank you for helping me, I don't even know your name. As he turned to look at her name tag and before he could fully mentally associate the name, the wheelchair "accidentally" became lodged in a hole in the sidewalk, propelling Mr. Leonard Canella into the street and into the direct path of an arriving emergency vehicle. The ambulance was transporting a severely injured child and was rushing to get the boy treated. The ambulance driver had no chance to avoid Leonard. Mr. Leonard Canella was pronounced "dead" at the scene. His good luck ended in tragic fashion.

The student nurse, Miss Allison McFarland, recovered quite quickly from the unfortunate situation involving the death of Mr. Canella. She decided that the medical field was really not for her. Her sister, Andrea, had suggested that she look into medicine, but she was more focused, especially now, on her first true love, a murder mystery writer.

Epilogue

One Year Later

A full year had passed since he had been involved in all the chaos surrounding Mountain Pacific Hospital. He was in his room and staring out of the window which overlooked a beautiful spring-blooming garden. It was a calming scene, and it allowed him to discard the bad memories and reflect on only the good. And yes, there have been plenty of good times to remember. He also smiled with satisfaction as he recalled how things finally played out. The most significant of those, without a doubt, was the fact that those individuals who had done him wrong, one way or the other, were no longer around to bring him down. His pleasant memories, unfortunately, were marred by one overpowering desire. He missed not being able to practice medicine.

James Whitly was a particularly good doctor, and he had saved many patients from pain and suffering. He thought about some of the surgeries that he had performed and unconsciously nodded his head in approval. Yes, he bathed in the thoughts of the successes he had initiated. If he could only get back to the operating table, then all would be right with the world again. His sanity was anchored to that possibility. It was something that he would hold on to as if his life depended on it, and for all intents and purposes, it did. Among the smiles emanating from the happy memories, if one looked closely, a tear of regret was also present.

James' trip down memory lane was abruptly interrupted when he heard the sound of his room door being unlocked and opened: "Hello James. You have a visitor." His institutional caretaker left, and his visitor walked into the room. She had visited before, so James was not surprised to see her again.

"Hi James. How are you doing today? I missed you so I decided to come and visit. I hope that's okay."

"Allison, you know that it is always okay to visit. I enjoy our time together, and I look forward to your visits."

Allison McFarland was a frequent visitor, and James depended on her to keep him up to date on current events, especially if it had to do with medicine and his potential for release. She had been concentrating on influencing the sitting judge in James' case, whom she knew quite well, to rehear some of the arguments that were offered by James' defense lawyers.

"James, I have been meeting and speaking with the judge, if you know what I mean. As you know, I can be quite persuasive when I have to be, and I'm not afraid to use all the tools in my arsenal."

"Yes, I know, Allison. You don't have to convince me."

"I do think that after a couple more meetings, Judge Jenkins will be more than happy to consider my request. He just loves to meet with me!"

James did not want to hear what persuasive methods Allison was employing, so he turned to look out of the window again. Allison continued speaking, trying to reinforce how persuasive she could be.

"After all James, look how persuasive I was with Calvin. He was very hesitant until I convinced him that by one quick pull, he could enjoy the sweet satisfaction of revenge." Hearing Allison, James wished for the time when he would once again be able to look out of the hospital window where he was not the patient, but the practitioner. Allison McFarland would continue to work her "magic," and James Whitly would continue to dream.

Author's Bio

Martin J. Roddini is a twenty-three-year veteran of the New York City Police Department who served as a Police Officer, Detective and Deputy Chief on loan to the Traffic Department. His expertise led him to the position of Chief of Police with various departments in both New York and New Jersey. He is still active in the law enforcement arena by utilizing his time to conduct survival training for Active Shooter events and creating vulnerability studies for schools and businesses. He has been the Director of Security at a number of Higher Education Facilities and served as a Security Consultant. Martin lives with his family in Nassau County, Long Island and is now devoting his time to his new passion of writing novels.

Acknowledgements

I want to thank my wife, Lisa, who employed her creative juices and came up with the original idea for the book. Additionally, she has been my sounding board for suggestions, ideas, and certain quotations. Without her active participation and support, the book would have been a much more difficult endeavor. I also want to thank my son, Marty, who took the original idea and added his unique twist to the story. He has also been a great help in finding and eliminating errors that might have made the book more difficult to read. Thank you to Boulevard Books and my publisher, Avi Gvili, who never gives up on producing the best product possible. Thanks also goes to my editor, Aliyah Manuel, who has the difficult job and patience to constantly interact with me. Her expertise allows for an efficient and expedient delivery of the final reading. I also want to mention Mr. Dave Manzolillo who spent his time perfecting a cover that definitely depicts the theme of the book. He has the ability to make the book come alive through his obvious talent as a graphic artist. Thank you David.

www.ingramcontent.com/pod-product-compliance
Lightning Source LLC
LaVergne TN
LVHW051101231224
799770LV00016B/389

9781942500919